Myrna Mackenzie

"Ms. Mackenzie has an outstanding style,
and the lively characters bring joy to the reader."
—*Rendezvous*

"Readers will enjoy Ms. Mackenzie's polished writing style
and emotional intensity."
—*Romantic Times BOOKclub*

"Mackenzie delivers a gripping tale—
one packed with romantic conflict,
electrifying sexual tension and unexpected twists."
—*Romantic Times BOOKclub*

"Myrna Mackenzie pens a romance that's sure to
please romance readers of all ages."
—*Writers Unlimited Reviews*

Dear Reader,

Spring is on the way, and the Signature Select program offers lots of variety in the reading treats you've come to expect from some of your favorite Harlequin and Silhouette authors.

The second quarter of the year continues the excitement we began in January with a can't-miss drama from Vicki Hinze: *Her Perfect Life*. In it, a female military prisoner regains her freedom only to find that the life she left behind no longer exists. Myrna Mackenzie's *Angel Eyes* gives us the tale of a woman with an unnatural ability to find lost objects and people, and *Confessions of a Party Crasher*, by Holly Jacobs, is a humorous novel about finding happiness—even as an uninvited guest!

Our collections for April, May and June are themed around Mother's Day, matchmaking and time travel. Mothers and daughters are a focus in *From Here to Maternity*, by Tara Taylor Quinn, Karen Rose Smith and Inglath Cooper. You're in for a trio of imaginative time-travel stories by Julie Kenner, Nancy Warren and Jo Leigh in *Perfect Timing*. And a matchmaking New York cabbie is a delightful catalyst to romance in the three stories in *A Fare To Remember*, by Vicki Lewis Thompson, Julie Elizabeth Leto and Kate Hoffmann.

Spring also brings three more original sagas to the Signature Select program. *Hot Chocolate on a Cold Day* tells the story of a Coast Guard worker in Michigan who finds herself intrigued by her new downstairs neighbor. Jenna Mills's *Killing Me Softly* features a heroine who returns to the scene of her own death, and *You Made Me Love You*, by C.J. Carmichael, explores the shattering effects of the death of a charismatic woman on the friends who adored her.

And don't forget, there is original bonus material in every single Signature Select book to give you the inside scoop on the creative process of your favorite authors! Happy reading!

Marsha Zinberg

Marsha Zinberg
Executive Editor
The Signature Select Program

SAGA

ANGEL EYES

Myrna Mackenzie

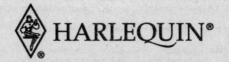

TORONTO • NEW YORK • LONDON
AMSTERDAM • PARIS • SYDNEY • HAMBURG
STOCKHOLM • ATHENS • TOKYO • MILAN • MADRID
PRAGUE • WARSAW • BUDAPEST • AUCKLAND

ISBN 0-373-83697-X

ANGEL EYES

Copyright © 2006 by Myrna Topol

This edition published by arrangement with Harlequin Books S.A.

® and TM are trademarks of the publisher. Trademarks indicated with ® are registered in the United States Patent and Trademark Office, the Canadian Trade Marks Office and in other countries.

www.eHarlequin.com

Printed in U.S.A.

Dear Reader,

Every house has its hopelessly lost items, things that disappear seemingly into thin air. Where do they go and how does one track them down?

It's a topic that has fascinated me since I was a child and read *The Borrowers* by Mary Norton. When, as an adult, my own children would lose beloved objects, I remembered those stories, especially since, with practice, I've developed almost a sixth sense about the hiding places of lost things.

The idea that someone might have an innate ability to find things others could not began to grow. What would life be like for a person who had the psychic ability to find missing objects? What if those missing objects were people? How might a person's life be changed if people knew of her skill? And what if the person in question was a child whose father saw her as a potential money machine?

That's how Sarah Tucker was born. Grown up now, she can find many things, but she's also missing essential elements in her life and not all of them can be easily found. She's a person I wanted to get to know. This is her story....

Best wishes,

Myrna Mackenzie

CHAPTER ONE

"THIS WAS A BAD MOVE, a major mistake. I can't believe I'm doing this." Sarah Tucker's head pounded. She turned the steering wheel, rounding a curve. Most women who were nearing thirty were leaving home, but not her. No, she was returning to her hometown after nearly twelve years away, and she didn't want to think about the reasons why.

Pulling up at the stop sign just before one of the last few turns leading to the town of Gold Tree, Wisconsin, Sarah popped the clutch and wrestled the aging beige rustmobile through the gears, negotiating the snaking road. In the winter the road would be slippery with snow that threatened to send a car skidding into the trees, but in the July heat the tires clung to the asphalt and held tight into the turns.

Ever since she'd made the decision to come home a headache had been threatening, and now the pain blossomed. The steering wheel thrummed beneath her fingers. The licorice road with its yellow center stripes was like a rope pulling her back into the past.

Her younger years had been ordinary, even happy... right up until that day when she had been ten and had had her first vision. After that her world had changed, and nothing had ever been ordinary or right again, especially where her father was concerned. He had tried to use her gift to make money. He'd become a verbal abuser, and he had continued his using and abusing until she'd finally bolted just after her eighteenth birthday.

She hadn't been back since. When she'd lost the baby she'd been carrying by a boy who had promised her everything and then left her with nothing, she had swallowed the grief that threatened to consume her and continued to run, knowing that her father and the boy weren't unique. There were others who would use her or any offspring she might have. A normal life wasn't in the stars for someone like her.

She passed the road leading to Lake Apple. She was getting close now. The pain in her head seemed to increase. "Nonsense," she told herself. "It's just nerves."

Probably because her communication with home these past twelve years had been sporadic and stilted. There were days early on when she would have liked to have had the chance to see her mother and little sister, but her father had made it clear that he would not provide the funds for anyone to visit her and if she came home, she did so on his terms. That meant using her special talents to find missing objects or people who sometimes turned out to be dead. All for money. It meant living with nightmares, so she'd kept her distance until the distance no longer seemed to matter and her past seemed like something she'd once watched in a movie. A movie she didn't want to sit through twice.

And yet, here she was, headed toward Gold Tree.

"Not quite the conquering heroine marching into

town wearing jewels and a tiara, either," she said, rubbing one aching temple. "I can see the headlines of the *Gold Tree Weekly* now. Sarah Tucker Returns Home Almost Broke, Completely Homeless, Jobless and in the Company of a Questionable Companion," she said, turning toward the passenger seat, wrinkling her nose. "What do you think?"

Her companion wagged his tail.

Sarah smiled wearily. "Yeah, pretty unlikely. I'm yesterday's news now. I doubt anyone here cares about my former quirks. And yes, I'm sorry for the insulting comment, Smooch. You're the best companion a woman could have."

She looked at the big dog strapped in to the low, torn bucket seat. Smooch, a gold-and-brown mutt of indeterminate ancestry, was a mass of wayward, fuzzy fur. His right ear looked as if it had been chewed on many times by other dog bullies, and it probably had. He had the words "street tough" written all over his wiry, scarred body, and he had undoubtedly lived a violent and abused life before Sarah had pulled him from the animal shelter, brought him home and finally coaxed him to tolerate her company. Still, despite his checkered past and the fact that he had every reason to distrust humans, his big brown eyes held no accusation and plenty of unabashed loyalty and devotion, his body wriggling just at the sound of her voice. He was the only male she had ever known who had not passed judgment on her or tried to use her. And he didn't care about her particular talents or even if she had any talents at all. For that alone she loved him.

"Stick with me, pal, and sooner or later I'll find us a good home," she promised, throwing out a hand. "For now, we've got to stop here for a few weeks."

And she wasn't just stopping because her boss in California had closed his antique shop to retire, leaving her out of work, or because her landlord had raised the rent and instituted a no-pets policy, even though those were both good reasons for coming home.

If that had been the case, she would have been here six months ago for her father's funeral. She hadn't been able to bring herself to do it, not even when she found out that he had left her the shop, Tucker's Lost & Found Emporium, where her father, R. J. Tucker, had tried to harness her powers and turn her into a golden goose, punishing her whenever she refused. It was the last place she ever wanted to go. He had probably known that and left it to her as a final punishment.

Instead, she had ignored the bequest. She hadn't even wanted to think about that place, but then the taxes had come due, and with almost no money in her pockets, it was obvious she would have to do something about it.

She'd tried to think positively. Her life these past few years hunting down antiques for hungry dealers had been mostly good. The fact that she'd met with a few setbacks lately was just life. She'd reasoned that she could sell the shop, handling the transaction from afar.

Then yesterday her mother had called. Madeline Tucker never called. She had to be the world's most retiring woman and had never made any demands of Sarah in her life.

"I think your sister, Cass, is in trouble. I think she might be…becoming like you. I wish…I wish you would please come home," was all her mother had said.

It was the first time in all these years that her mother had said the words "come home" or implied that Sarah might be needed. Her request, her worries about Cass hung in the air, and this time Sarah couldn't stay away. Despite the fact that she didn't even know her younger sister. Cass had only been six when Sarah had left home.

Becoming like you. Sarah knew what her mother meant. If what she said was true, then Sarah had to help Cass, because no one else could truly understand. Cass must be frightened. Sarah knew every bad thing that went along with her gift. She knew the fear of seeing things not meant to be seen…and the horrified looks of the townspeople when they learned about her gift. Maybe she could protect Cass in some way or at least teach her how to handle a situation the way she wished there had been someone to help her.

Sarah rounded the last curve, the big pine trees bending low over the car. She breathed in the heady scent of woods, of green, of earth, of long-lost little-girl memories. The good ones, the only ones she planned to allow herself.

"We're home, Smooch," she said. "I might not want to be here, but it can't be helped, so we'll do the best we can. We'll settle here for a few weeks, see if we can help Cass if that's possible. We'll use this as our base until we regroup and find a new place to stay."

In the meantime, she was going to do her best to make lemonade out of the lemons she had been given and come to terms with her past, maybe even rid herself of the nightmares at last. She would take that shop her father had left her and rip it apart, shred it, sell it.

And this time when she left, it would be because she had chosen to leave town, not because she had no choice.

This time things would be different. When she had

lived here before she had been known as an oddity, but that had probably been because of the way her father presented her. He had wanted people to be in awe, to be a bit frightened. This time things were bound to be different, better.

Sarah stopped and got out of the car a half mile outside of town. She looked up, up, way up into the crests of the tall pines that swayed with the wind and brushed at the town with their branches.

"I'm back," she declared to no one in particular. Yes, the witch of Gold Tree was back, but with one major difference. She had submerged the clairsentient powers that had cursed her all her life. In doing so, she had finally, finally lost them.

She could touch something nowadays and not feel a thing out of the ordinary other than a slight pain behind her eyes, no worse than a mild sinus headache.

She was glad. At last she was free. And no man would ever chain her up, tie her down or try to use her again. No man would ever have a hold on her or any say over her life.

In fact, if she played her cards right, men would only play a marginal role in her life.

OFFICER LUKE PACKARD surveyed the scene before him and immediately swung into action, grabbing for his radio.

"Ben, get an ambulance over to the Tucker place pronto," he said, dropping to his knees beside Madeline Tucker. She was lying at a crooked angle at the bottom of the stairs. Her ankle was swelling, she had a lump on her head and she was blinking as if she didn't know who he was. He didn't like any of this.

"Luke?" she asked, her voice weak.

He managed a small smile. "Well, welcome back to the world of the living, neighbor," he said. "When I heard that you were hurt, I was pretty worried." He decided not to mention the fact that Madeline's eighteen-year-old daughter, Cass, had delivered the news that her mother had fallen and then Cass had immediately disappeared. As a concerned friend, he definitely needed to know what that was about, but now was not the time to ask.

Madeline tried to sit up.

"Mad, no," he told her. "You were unconscious when I came in, and there's definitely something wrong with your ankle. No sitting up until the doctor says it's all right, and that's not going to happen until the ambulance arrives."

A look of distress came over Madeline's face. Normally she didn't look her age, which was probably fifty-something, but right now her pallor and the worry lines on her forehead made her look much older.

"Where's Cass? Where's Danny?" she asked, referring to her daughter and Luke's son, whom she'd been babysitting. Her voice broke.

"Not here, but Cass is the one who called me to the scene. She dropped Danny off at the police station, and Jemma is adding looking after him to her clerking duties. He's fine." He didn't tell her that Cass was fine, because he didn't know. Again he wondered what had happened here and why Cass hadn't come home.

Madeline gave a tight nod of her head. Her hands clenched. She looked as if she might cry. He almost closed his eyes. He'd seen so many women in pain. His mother, every time his abusive father had beaten her, his wife when she'd realized he didn't love her. He didn't want to ever see another woman hurting, but of course he would. He was a cop. He didn't get to turn away. In fact, part of the reason he'd gone into law enforcement was to be able to protect women who were in danger, to try to prevent some of the tragedies he had seen.

"Want to tell me what happened here?" he asked quietly.

He saw a slight flicker in her eyes and knew what that meant. He'd seen it too many times. She was going to either lie or give him an edited version of the facts.

"Nothing. Cass and I argued a little and I wasn't paying attention and slipped on the stairs. But I can't go to the hospital, Luke. Sarah is coming. I have to be here."

"I'll leave a note on the door."

"No, you don't understand—"

He did, at least a little. Sarah was Madeline's other daughter, the one who had apparently run away at eighteen and been gone for a dozen years. The prodigal daughter was finally returning home.

"If she comes and I'm not here…if no one's here…"

Luke withheld a sigh. He really needed to get Madeline to a doctor, to find out if she was all right. He'd had too many experiences with people who thought they were fine and then weren't. His wife had died while insisting that she didn't need or want to go to the hospital. Besides, Madeline wasn't just another person he was sworn to serve and protect. She was his neighbor, his friend. "I'll stay and wait here for your daughter," he promised.

Madeline didn't stop frowning. "I don't know exactly when she'll be here."

"Don't worry about it. I'll stay."

"Don't you have work?"

Tons. Today he'd been in the office catching up on paperwork. "Someone will bring it to me, Madeline. That won't be a problem."

She bit her lip. "I wanted to be here when Sarah showed up." She turned her head, and Luke's heart ripped a bit. He didn't have a clue how she felt. He'd only been a father for two years, and he'd never faced the prospect of his son growing up, walking out the door one day and not coming back for twelve years, but Madeline was clearly in pain, both physical and mental.

"I'll ask the medics if they can move things along and get you back here quickly," he promised. "If I have to I'll bring your daughter to the hospital."

Suddenly her eyes were shocked and stricken. "Oh, no, I don't want to bother her like that. Or you," she amended.

And what the hell did that mean? She was hurt, and she didn't want to be a bother to her adult daughter? What kind of a daughter was this Sarah anyway?

But he had no business asking that kind of a question of his neighbor, and anyway, within seconds the ambulance appeared, sirens blazing.

"I'll wait for her," he promised as the paramedics wheeled Madeline away and the ambulance headed for the hospital.

An hour later a battered beige sedan appeared as a dot on the horizon. Might be the daughter. By then Madeline's announcement to the paramedics, nurses and aides that her eldest daughter was coming home at last had had its effect. The telephone lines had started to buzz with whatever memories people could dredge up from twelve years ago or more.

His cell phone had already rung more times than he cared to think about, townspeople wanting to know if Sarah had shown up yet. Some of them seemed eager to drop hints about her past.

Apparently Sarah Tucker was more than just your run-of-the-mill prodigal daughter. She was a vulnerable woman with a colorful and questionable past. There was also some nonsense about her being a psychic.

Luke frowned. He had a personal aversion to the word *psychic*. His wife had been friends with a so-called psychic. Maybe if he'd given her the love she needed, she wouldn't have turned to other people for comfort. Maybe she wouldn't have taken up with her psychic friend, and she wouldn't have refused to go to the doctor when he'd thought she was ill but the friend had insisted she was fine. If he'd loved Iris enough, maybe she wouldn't have died of a blood clot two days after coming home from giving birth to Danny.

The psychic friend wasn't the only one to blame for Iris's death. He'd made his share of mistakes during his marriage, but that still didn't absolve people who bandied about that load-of-crap psychic title and pretended to know things no human could possibly know.

"Turn it off, Packard," he said to himself. *Get it together. Remember who you are and what your duties are and where your loyalties lie. Remember what's important.*

It was a mantra he'd been repeating to himself ever since he'd assumed sole responsibility for his son and ever since he'd taken this job in Gold Tree a year ago. He was the law in this town, a community representative. No matter what his personal feelings were, he had a duty to every member of this town and to every visitor.

What's more, Madeline was his friend who babysat his son, and the woman causing the buzz, the woman he was dreading to meet, was her daughter.

Sarah Tucker would be arriving soon and he was going to have to be the official welcoming committee.

He intended to do it right, even if it meant battling the beasts that lived within him.

CHAPTER TWO

SARAH PULLED INTO her mother's pebbled driveway, immediately noted the police officer sitting on the front steps, and her heart started to do that nervous thud that she hated.

This was so silly. There was no reason for her nervousness. It wasn't as if she had a problem with authority figures.

"I don't," she said, pretending to say the words to Smooch but knowing that it was herself she was trying to convince. Hey, she could deal with authority figures. She did it all the time where her boss and her landlord were concerned. It was just that the uniform made her nervous. Sarah had had only one experience with the police, but it had been a vivid one. That long-ago day when she had first had a vision of Pattie Dubeaux, the little girl who had been missing and whose body Sarah had found at the lake's edge. The police officer in charge had questioned her mercilessly, even going so far as to insinuate that she might have known too much to be completely innocent. The memory had stuck.

"This guy isn't him," she reminded herself. Which was absolutely true, but then why was he here?

Turning to Smooch, she freed him, then climbed from the car and let him out to sniff his new surroundings. She wanted nothing better than to take some time to acclimate herself, too, but the police officer was waiting, unfolding his long, lanky frame from the steps and moving toward her. His dark uniform, his height and dark hair all served to make him look very official and forbidding. Sarah nixed that thought.

He's just a man. As if she'd had any better experiences with men than she'd had with police officers.

Still, she managed to conjure up a smile from somewhere. She moved forward, trying to quiet the butterflies fluttering around inside her. What had happened to bring this guy to her mother's house? And where was her mother?

"Officer, allow me to introduce myself. I'm—"

"Sarah Tucker," he supplied. "Luke Packard."

She blinked. "You were expecting me. Is something wrong? Okay, that was a ridiculous question. Obviously, something is wrong. What is it?"

He held up one hand as if to stop her questions. "Your mother had a fall, but she's fine. I've spoken to her and to her doctors and she has a bump on her head and a badly sprained ankle, but other than that she's all right. Right now one of her friends is driving her home." He didn't smile reassuringly the way some people might have, as if speaking to a child. Sarah gave him credit for that.

"You haven't heard anything from your sister, have you?" he asked.

Something too careful in his tone made Sarah's breath catch. She had no clue why he was being so careful or why his tone affected her. "No. I've just arrived home after having been away for many years."

"I'm aware of that."

She raised one brow. "My mother told you?"

He shook his head. "Madeline told me you were coming—that was all, but this is a small town, Ms. Tucker. You've been gone a long time. People take an interest in the comings and goings of its residents. Your name may have been mentioned once or twice."

From the way he said that, Sarah understood that once or twice was an understatement.

"In what context?" she asked, although a part of her didn't want to know.

He shrugged. "Probably nothing that bears much resemblance to reality. You know how it is. Stories grow and change over time."

Or maybe the stories didn't change at all, Sarah thought, a sick feeling of dread growing inside. There had been plenty of things said about Sarah when she was living here, plenty of people who distrusted her or thought she was some kind of freak. But this man hadn't been here then. He hadn't been around to witness that time.

"I told your mother I would wait here to tell you what had happened to her so that you wouldn't worry," he said, "but I would have gotten around to introducing myself sooner or later. I'm your mother's next-door neighbor. Madeline watches my two-year-old son when I'm at work. She really wanted to be here to greet you, but I'm afraid I'll have to do as a welcoming party until she arrives. Welcome back to Gold Tree, Ms. Tucker."

He was holding out his hand. Not an unusual circumstance. People shook hands all the time, but Sarah had stopped doing that years ago, ever since the day she made a conscious decision to exert total

control over her so-called gift and refuse to acknowledge her clairsentience. The day she had fled Gold
Tree she had promised herself a normal life. No
longer would she touch someone and feel the
shadows of their thoughts. She would cease to be the
odd duck in every group, a woman who couldn't
control her own mind and reactions to situations. It
had been the hardest thing she'd ever done in her life,
harder even than leaving home.

But her persistence had worked. She hadn't had a
vision in years, and usually her reluctance to touch
people wasn't a problem. She anticipated the situations
where hand-to-hand contact or hugs might insinuate
themselves and was prepared for them, tactfully sidestepping the issue. Today, however, she had been
caught off guard by her own tension at returning to
Gold Tree, her mother's unexpected absence and the
very presence of Lucas Packard.

Her head throbbed, and her hand felt as if it weighed
ten thousand pounds. She should just bring it forward,
steel her mind and give the man the briefest of hand-
shakes. But she looked up at him then, into dark amber
eyes that were studying her intently.

For half a second she wondered if he had special
talents, too, if those piercing eyes saw things that others
didn't see. A woman's soul, her needs, her desires or
her deepest regrets and secrets. It would be a very useful
talent for a police officer…or for a man, for that matter.

But, no. There was suspicion in those eyes, maybe
even sympathy. He had heard things about her. He
probably knew a fair amount of her personal history.
He would know that touching people was a much
bigger deal for her than for other human beings.

"My apologies, Ms. Tucker. I'm not testing you," he said suddenly, withdrawing his hand. But his jaw was like a blade.

She felt warmth suffuse her cheeks. "I'm sorry, Officer Packard. I didn't mean to be so rude." But she didn't offer him her hand, either. There was something unusually vital in those eyes. She had this terrible sense that if she touched him, she would feel things that went beyond the simple act of fingertips and palms sliding against each other in a casual greeting.

"Thank you for giving me the news about my mother," she continued. "Coming home after being away for so long is disorienting. Showing up and finding the house empty would have made the situation even more difficult. I appreciate your time."

It was a dismissal of sorts. She felt a bit guilty about that. It had been nice of him to stay and greet her. He was still in uniform. Unless he slept in the thing, he probably had been working or had just gotten off from work. He would want to be getting back to his work or his life. And he'd said he had a son, one her mother watched while he worked.

"Who's watching your son if my mother isn't here?" she asked.

That amber gaze intensified. A frown line appeared beneath heavy dark brows. "Your sister dropped him off at the station."

"So Cass went to the hospital with Mom?" But hadn't he asked where her sister was? What was that about?

He shook his head. "She wasn't here when I arrived. Your mother was unconscious, on the floor alone." He studied her as if gauging her reaction, assessing her to see if she knew anything.

"Cass left Mom on the floor, injured, and didn't come back? Has anyone heard from her?" A slight sense of panic crept in. Her mother had intimated that something was wrong with Cass. What was going on?

"No one at the station has spoken to her since she brought my son in to drop him off and told the desk clerk that your mother was hurt. Someone would have called me if they'd seen her. I'd like to ask her some questions."

Sarah felt sick at the thought, sicker still at the suggestion that Cass might have been the cause of her mother's accident.

"Do you think Cass is to blame for my mother's fall?"

"I think your mother would say that she wasn't. I'm not saying otherwise. I just want to know what happened and why Cass ran. And for the record, I'm not planning on dragging Cass into the station in handcuffs. My questions are purely those of a concerned neighbor and friend. No crime has been committed unless your mother says otherwise."

This was apparently all Luke intended to say on the subject. "It was nice meeting you, Ms. Tucker," he said. "Let me know when you hear from your sister."

"What if I don't hear from her?"

He blew out a breath. "She's eighteen and she hasn't broken any laws that I know of."

His radio buzzed at that moment and he answered the page. A low curse slipped from between his lips. He signed out and turned and looked at Sarah.

"My sister?"

"You." The word was like a bullet—cold, metallic and biting.

"I just got here."

"Yes, well a fight just broke out at the bar. You were the topic."

Sarah closed her eyes. "Tell me why."

"Half the room claimed you had special powers. The other half thought that was a load of crap." Already he was turning to leave.

"Officer Packard?"

He looked back over his shoulder. "Ms. Tucker?"

"Tell the load-of-crap people they're right. I don't do that stuff anymore."

His eyes met hers and he studied her as if she had just claimed she could turn grass into gold. The word *anymore* hung in the air.

Instinctively Sarah wrapped her arms around herself in a protective gesture. So people hadn't forgotten. Already she was being judged.

"I'll do that, Ms. Tucker. I like to keep things as quiet and peaceful as possible in Gold Tree."

She raised her chin. "I came home to see my mother, to take care of some business and to—" she hesitated, then plunged on "—to see if I could help my sister."

"Good. I suspect that she's been hanging around with the wrong people, but she's young. An older sister might be able to help head her off, Ms. Tucker."

"Sarah."

Luke nodded. "Sarah."

His radio buzzed again. "I'm coming," he said to the air, ignoring the radio, although his frown grew.

"Thanks for staying here to greet me, Officer Packard. I appreciate it. I'd come with you to clear the air, but I'd better wait here to help my mother if she's on the way home."

"Do not go to The Crazy Pig when a fight is going on. I don't care how reasonable you are, you're likely to get a chair broken over your head."

"In your peaceful, quiet town?"

"Even here," he said with a grimace. "I'm working on it."

"Then let me reassure you once again. I haven't had a vision in years. There's nothing for anyone to fight over. Or for you to worry or frown about."

Those amber eyes swept over her. "My apologies, Sarah. Sometimes I'm an ass." And with that he walked away.

And sometimes I'm a liar, she thought, because while it was true that she hadn't had a vision in years, there was still cause for worry. Because while she no longer had visions, she did still have dreams just as any normal person did. And as Luke Packard walked away from her, she knew for a certainty that she had seen him in a dream.

He had been walking away from her then, too, and she had been…disappointed and scared and heartbroken, which was all wrong because she definitely didn't want to ever get so close to a man that he could make her feel those kinds of things, especially not a man with eyes that saw too much and whose commanding presence made her wary. She'd had enough of men, especially commanding men with power. What on earth did a dream like that mean?

But…she didn't really want to know the answer to that question, after all, and thankfully she didn't have time to think about it, because at that moment, a car swept around the curve.

Her mother was home. Sarah tried to ready herself for the reunion.

CHAPTER THREE

IT HAD BEEN TWELVE years since Sarah had seen her mother, and had she been able to anticipate the circumstances of their next meeting, it would have been nothing like this.

A big black Lincoln Town Car pulled up. The man at the wheel looked vaguely familiar. Like Luke, he was dressed in police blue but Sarah didn't know who he was. He climbed from the car, tugged at his hat in greeting to Sarah and circled around to help her mother from the car.

The door opened and Sarah peered inside to see Madeline Tucker, still pretty after all these years, even though she was twelve years older with gray hair that swept her shoulders in a modest cut. She looked small and fragile given the size and opulence of the car. Her heavily wrapped ankle and the crutches the man was holding for her combined to emphasize how delicate she was.

The man held one arm out to help her from the car, but Madeline looked to her daughter. "Sarah." The word was almost a question, a sigh. "It's…good to see you."

"Mom. It's good to see you, too." Despite the formality and stark simplicity of the exchange Sarah felt her throat tighten, but she refused to allow herself to move forward. Physical affection hadn't been part of the Tucker way. She waited.

"Let me help you, Madeline," the man said. Something in his voice caught Sarah's attention, and she looked at him more closely.

"You remember Dugan Hayes, don't you, Sarah? He became the chief of police just before you...well, he's been the chief of police for about twelve years. I don't know how he happened to be at the hospital, but he very generously insisted on giving me a ride home."

"Hello, Mr. Hayes," Sarah said, even though she only had a vague recollection of a big, gruff man hovering at the very edges of her childhood memories. He hadn't been the policeman who had questioned her about Pattie Dubeaux. She definitely knew that much. His brown eyes were too kind and too filled with concern when her mother winced as she shifted her weight, leaning on his arm as she climbed from the car and took the crutches from him.

"Are you...all right?" Sarah asked. What she really wanted to ask was *How did this happen?* but after what she'd heard about Cass, she didn't want to ask any questions in front of a stranger, and to her Dugan Hayes was a stranger, even if her mother obviously trusted him.

Madeline looked up at Sarah and smiled. A bit too brightly, Sarah thought. "It's just a sprain, dear. I'll be fine in no time. It's nothing. Everything is fine."

It had been her mother's favorite phrase for as long as Sarah could remember. "Everything is fine," or sometimes "Everything will be fine," or "Everything will work out." That blind optimism had filled Sarah with despair at times, but now was not the time to dwell on such things.

"Thank you for bringing her home, Mr. Hayes," Sarah said to the man, and immediately wondered at her own presumption. Maybe Mr. Hayes brought her mother home all the time. Maybe he had more of a right to be here than Sarah did. After all, he had obviously been here in Gold Tree these past twelve years while she had not.

"Yes, thank you, Dugan. I'll be fine now." Her mother's smile was genuine, but her words were an obvious dismissal.

"I'll help you inside."

Immediately, Madeline shook her head. "I want to learn to get around by myself."

"All right, I'll check in on you, Mad," the man said gruffly. He turned to Sarah and tipped his hat. "Nice to see you back, Sarah." Did she imagine the censure in his voice?

Maybe, and maybe it was just her imagination. This town, her memories of it, colored everything suspicious. She turned to her mother and started to suggest they go inside, but Madeline had pasted on a smile and was waiting for Dugan to leave. Only after he had driven out of sight did she look at her crutches with any purpose.

"I'll help you," Sarah offered.

Her mother shook her head. "No, I meant what I said to Dugan. On my birthday this year, I promised that I would learn to stand on my own two feet. At fifty-three it seemed to be about time."

What could a person say to that? "At least let me carry that bag."

Madeline stopped trying to push her crutches forward. She turned to stare at her eldest daughter and handed over the plastic hospital bag that was dangling from her fingertips. "Some medicine and a new wrap," she said.

"Does your ankle hurt?"

"A little. Not much."

And although Sarah wasn't buying into that—her mother's ankle beneath the wrap seemed to be round and puffy as a grapefruit—she said nothing. Everything had always been fine in the Tucker household. Everything would continue to be fine. So what had that telephone conversation she'd had with her mother been about? And what had happened with Cass?

WHAT AM I DOING? Madeline thought. *I'm doing what I always do, what I've always done, the very thing that jeopardized my children's happiness. I'm hiding my head in the sand, pretending, lying. But how did a person stop lying when the truth could hurt worse than a lie?*

She struggled into the house with Sarah, wary eyed, hovering at her side. Sarah who had once, many years ago, been bright and bubbly. Before everything changed.

But by the time Madeline had made her way inside, by the time she moved to the chair, she was beyond thinking about anything but collapsing, getting rid of the dratted crutches.

Sarah came up behind her, slid an arm around her back and relieved her of her right crutch. "I've got your weight. Let go of the other one," she told her mother.

Madeline clung to the crutch. She was the mother.

Wasn't she the mother? A little voice inside her laughed mockingly. It had been a long time since she had acted like a mother, far longer than the twelve years Sarah had been gone. She clutched the bit of metal and foam even though her entire body was shaking.

"Let me help, Mom," Sarah said. "Please."

Tears threatened to spill and Madeline closed her eyes. Sarah was home. At last she was home.

She let go of the crutch, her palm pushing it away so that it clattered to the floor. Her body sagged and Sarah caught her, the two of them jerking slightly before Sarah managed to stop their momentum. Sarah gently lowered her to the old blue and rose easy chair with the lumpy stuffing.

Madeline felt as if she had been beaten up and given a gift at the same time. "Thank you," she said. "Thank you for coming," she amended so that Sarah would know that that was more important than these past few seconds. "I didn't know if I should ask. I still don't know if it was the right thing to do."

"What happened?" Sarah asked.

"I don't know. Cass has been unhappy for some time. After your father died, it got worse. After her eighteenth birthday, worse still. Something's going on. She's secretive, she argues. I think…I think she's going to run."

Madeline looked up at her daughter.

"Like me," Sarah whispered.

"Like you, but different. You went on your own, you had reasons I understood. This I don't understand, so I can't let it go."

"I was told that Cass was here when you fell, that she was the one who called…"

The unstated question hung in the air.

So, I won't be allowed that pretense, Madeline thought. "Cass didn't push me if that's what you're asking. We argued. I was nearly at the bottom of the stairs, following her as she was headed for the door. I missed the last two steps."

"She didn't stay."

"But she solicited help," Madeline said. "Luke was here in no time. He's a good friend. I watch his son when he's at work. Now, because of my clumsiness I won't be able to chase after a toddler for a couple of weeks. He'll need help." She stared at Sarah.

Sarah blanched. "I'm not very good with children."

Madeline's heart clenched. Another mistake she had made. Another mark on the "bad mother" scorecard. Sarah had been pregnant when she left town. She'd miscarried, a message that had been passed along in a hurried, broken-voiced phone call. Obviously, there were still scars associated with that time.

"Of course," Madeline said. "I'm sure he'll find other help." But, she didn't want just anyone taking care of Danny. He had become like a grandchild to her. Who knew if she would ever have grandchildren of her own? Asking Sarah to come home and help with Cass had been more than she had the right to ask, given the circumstances. She had not protected her eldest daughter from things she should have protected her from. There was no changing that, no going back. All she could do was move forward and make the best of things. Since R.J.'s death she had decided that she would finally find some sort of a backbone and do what she could to pull her family back together. To save what little she could save. If that were even possible.

In spite of her determined smile and attempts to help, Sarah's eyes held a wary, haunted look, and Cass had run.

"Will you help with Cass?"

"I barely know her," Sarah began. "Not that that's in any way her fault. I was the one who left. I should know her, but I'm not sure I *can* help. What would you have me do?"

Madeline looked to the side. "I don't know. I don't know what's wrong with her. She won't tell me."

"You said she was becoming…like me." The last two words came out on a whisper.

Yes, Madeline had said that. She had said it knowing Sarah would misinterpret and think she was referring to the clairsentience, the powers that had shaped her oldest child's life and had doomed her in so many ways.

"Did you mean it?" Sarah asked.

Madeline lifted her chin and stared up into her daughter's troubled gray eyes. "I meant it. She's like you. She's alone."

Sarah sucked in a breath. "You know that wasn't what I thought."

"Yes, but it's the same in some ways, isn't it? She's fallen in with a bad group, I think. There are people taking advantage of her. You know what I mean."

Madeline glanced down to see that Sarah's fists were clenched, her knuckles were white. "Yes," Sarah said.

Turning away, Sarah paced the room. She moved to the window, folded her arms around herself and looked outside. "I can't promise anything. I'm not a counselor. I could make a total mess of things."

"Things are already a mess. Will you try?"

"I said I would. Where is she?"

Madeline's heart fell. "I don't have a clue."

Sarah sucked in a breath and Madeline heard how shaky it was. "Maybe she'll come home tonight," Madeline said.

Nodding, Sarah moved away from the window and came to stand beside her. "When you called me, something was already wrong or you wouldn't have asked me to come home and help, but Cass was still here. What happened to make her run?"

Madeline pursed her lips. "Nothing, really."

"Don't do that," Sarah said. "Something did happen, and if I'm going to talk to her, I have to know what the problems are."

Madeline fingered the old brocade of the chair. She plucked at a piece of loose stuffing. "I told her you were coming home to talk to her."

Sarah blinked. She looked suddenly, sad. "Well, I guess that clears things up. At least I know this isn't going to be easy," Sarah said, giving a shaky laugh.

Madeline wanted to say that she was sorry. It seemed that she'd been wanting to say that to Sarah for most of her daughter's life. But sorry didn't change the fact that she had not protected Sarah from R.J.'s greed, from the stares and finger-pointing and demands of the locals or from the boy who had gotten her pregnant. And, no, it didn't change the fact that she had lied to Sarah to get her home and was now asking her to step into a very sticky and ugly and possibly humiliating situation where she would have to face her sister's repudiation.

"She won't listen to me. She might, in time, listen to you."

"I'm not going to be here forever," Sarah said gently. "How long are you staying?"

Sarah bit her lip. "Long enough to get rid of the property Dad left me. Long enough to try with Cass."

That might be almost no time. Madeline's heartbeat picked up, desperation taking hold. She didn't know how to change things, but she wanted to, terribly.

"If she doesn't come home tonight, I'll have to go out looking for her," Sarah said. "Any idea who might help me? Friends of hers?"

"Maybe Luke…" Madeline began.

"Is she in that much trouble?"

"I don't know, but Luke always knows a lot of people. People talk to him. They tell him things."

"Does he share those things with you?"

Madeline shook her head. "Luke doesn't gossip, and he won't compromise his position, but if I asked him to help you as a friend and fellow parent, he might. I just wish I knew that Cass was safe." She couldn't help the hopeful look she turned on Sarah.

"I can't," Sarah whispered. "I haven't, not in years. It's gone. I don't feel those things anymore."

Biting her lip, Madeline nodded. "I'm sorry. That wasn't what I meant. I wouldn't have asked you to do that." And if it were true that Sarah had lost her abilities, then she was glad. Even as a little girl her child had always hated the gift that made her so different from others.

"Will you still look for her in a more conventional way?"

"Yes. And if I have to, I'll ask Luke for help. Of course, that might not be necessary. Maybe Cass will come home tonight."

SARAH HOPED THAT CASS would come home tonight, not just because she wanted to know that her sister was safe but also because she didn't want to have to spend any more time with Luke Packard than necessary. There was an intensity and virility about him that she found disturbing. A man like that saw too much, and she never let men get too close.

But she didn't want to think about that. Fortunately…or unfortunately, there were other distractions. For the past hour her mother's phone had been ringing incessantly. Most of the people had been supposedly calling to check up on Madeline's condition, but many had also wanted to ask questions about Sarah.

Once when her mother had dozed off, Sarah had picked up the phone.

"You're evil. What you do is unnatural. It's not right and it's a lie," the caller said.

Sarah stared at the receiver, unable to speak.

"Don't stay," the caller continued. "We don't want your supernatural disgusting garbage polluting our town."

A loud click sounded in Sarah's ear and then the telephone went dead.

Bile rose in her throat. Memories of other days, taunting children, parents who wouldn't let their sons and daughters play with her rolled through Sarah's mind. She hadn't experienced any of that in years, but it didn't matter. It was all new again.

Quietly she turned away from the telephone.

"That wasn't Cass, was it?" Madeline asked, hope evident in her slightly raised voice.

"Just a wrong number, Mother."

Had there been an edge in her voice? Her mother looked at her as if she doubted her word, but then she nodded, resignation in her eyes.

Long after she had gone to bed Sarah lay staring out

her window. Cass hadn't come home. In the morning she would have to talk to Luke.

She had a feeling he was one of those people who didn't believe in her gift. No, it was more than a feeling. It was something in his eyes. Luke was a practical man, one who liked peace and order.

Sarah's presence was disturbing his peace and order, and come morning, she would disturb him even more.

She remembered his fierce amber gaze, remembered how she was afraid to touch him for fear that she might feel something she didn't want to feel. Truth be told, she liked untroubled waters, too.

But with morning's light untroubled waters wouldn't be a possibility. She was going to renew her acquaintance with Gold Tree and with a man she was pretty sure could pose a danger to her peace of mind.

CHAPTER FOUR

LUKE SAT AT HIS KITCHEN table the next day looking out the window and watching trouble walking toward him. Sarah Tucker was dressed in blue jeans and a white blouse, her long slender legs eating up the ground between her house and his.

"Just any other woman," he told himself, even though he knew that wasn't true. She was different on many levels, and he didn't just mean those rumors that were circulating about her and giving people something to gossip and argue about.

There was something vulnerable in her eyes even though her raised chin dared him to call her weak, and her tentative smile declared that she was braver than anyone else on the planet.

He knew all about brave smiles and vulnerable eyes. He saw them whenever Luke's alcoholic father had beat the crap out of him and then walloped his mother when she tried to intervene, Luke's mother had done her best not to cry out or show fear or pain, all for his sake. Heaven knows that if she had begged, his father would have been pleased and the beatings would have gone easier for her. It still ate at Luke that he had made things harder for his mother by being so obstinate and never being able to keep from mouthing off to his old

man, not even when Luke's arguing incited his father
to hit Luke's mother harder.

And then there had been his wife, Iris. Quiet,
innocent, adoring Iris who had only wanted him to love
her....

Luke almost let out an oath, then realized that his son
was sitting in his high chair smiling at him.

"Sorry, big guy. Dad has to watch himself." Around
Danny and around Sarah. Mostly around Danny,
because he intended to steer clear of Sarah whenever
he could. He didn't get involved with women anymore,
especially not vulnerable ones.

Danny gurgled and looked at him with adoring eyes.
He was worth it. Oh yeah, his kid was worth every
second of minding his p's and q's, but Danny was absolutely all the innocence he could handle.

A deep bark caught Luke's attention and he looked
up to see that Sarah had stopped at the edge of the road
to hug that big nondescript mutt of hers. The dog gave
her a big slurpy lick and she smiled, a genuine smile.

"Later, sweetie," she said, blowing the dog a kiss and
continuing on her way toward Luke. There was a determined look in her eyes.

Luke groaned, then picked his son up in his arms and
went out to meet the day and the lady.

SARAH LOOKED TOWARD Luke's house, a white cottage
with the wraparound front porch and green shutters of
her dreams and saw the man himself coming toward
her, a little round-faced, chubby-cheeked, dark-haired
child on his hip.

The child giggled and slapped at his father's face,
bouncing slightly in Luke's grasp. Without missing a

step, Luke readjusted his hold, making sure the little boy was safe. He spared a glance for his son, one so filled with emotion and concern that Sarah's heart hurt to watch. She would never experience that kind of emotion, never have a child, never allow herself to love anyone that hard. Some people just weren't cut out to have relationships. The thought wasn't new.

Luke looked directly at her, eyes wary, slightly judgmental. It was the look of a man who had seen a lot of bad things and didn't trust too much.

Sarah understood. She was wary herself, but she was here to ask a favor, one she wasn't sure she had the right to ask.

"Good morning," she said. "I hope I'm not intruding."

"Not a problem," Luke said. "What can I do for you?"

She hesitated. Ideally, her mother would be here, initiating this conversation, but Madeline had had a restless and pain-filled night, and when Sarah had awakened to find her sister still missing, she hadn't been able to bring herself to wake her mother with the news or to wait any longer for results.

"My sister," Sarah began. "She still isn't home. My mother's worried. I need to find her, and I need help."

For a second it seemed as if Luke hugged his child tighter, as if thinking about what it would be like to have a missing child, but then he straightened his shoulders and nodded.

"Come on," he said, turning. "Come inside. We'll talk."

She followed him into his kitchen, watching as he put the little boy in his high chair and deftly and gently wiped his face. "How much do you know about what your sister's been doing?" he asked, still concentrating on his son.

"Not much. My mother told me that Cass has been upset lately."

"I'd say that's true. She's been pulled into the station once or twice."

Sarah sucked in her breath, obviously audibly, because Luke turned and focused his attention on her. "She was just with the wrong people at the wrong time. It's not a crime," he clarified.

"No, it's not." Sarah had some experience of being with the wrong people.

"I don't like carrying tales," Luke said, "but I'm sure this is somewhat worrying for you and Madeline. I've heard a few rumors about Cass, some as late as last night, and I have some idea where she might be. I'll ask around if that will help."

Something shifted inside of Sarah. A slight sense of relief crept in. "Thank you. I appreciate it."

"You understand that it's not illegal for an eighteen-year-old girl to leave home. I can't make her return."

Sarah blinked. How much did he know about her own situation? "I wouldn't ask you to do that."

The little boy gurgled and Luke smiled down at his son, picking him back up into his arms. "This is my son," he said. "Danny, meet Ms. Tucker."

Danny blew a bubble, and Sarah's heart tripped. It had been so many years since she had lost her baby. She had been Cass's age when Jed Sturgeon had convinced her that he thought she was something special and seduced her. Then he'd spread the word that he had made it into the psychic's pants without her even having a vision and realizing that he was handing her a line of crap.

She had been waiting to run for years. The resultant pregnancy had only added to her desire to go. For a while she had been petrified about having a baby, the usual fear, she supposed, of a young girl being pregnant and alone, combined with her own special terror that she would pass some of her weirdness to the child. She had wanted to lose the child, and then when, alone on the road, she actually *had* lost her baby a feeling of desolation swept over Sarah. It was subdued by years of dealing with the grief, but it was still there, a dull ache.

She supposed the loss of her baby really shouldn't bother her anymore, but she was rarely in the company of children and when she was it was impossible to keep from wondering what her baby would have been like had he lived. She would never marry, never have another child she might inadvertently pass her cursed "gift" to, and that made it so very difficult to be around children.

But that was not this little boy's or this man's fault.

"Hi, Danny," she said, pasting on a smile. "He's a cutie," she told his father a bit awkwardly.

"Yeah, he's that," Luke agreed. "But then I'm his father. I don't expect everyone to feel the way I do. You don't have to like my son, Ms. Tucker."

Had her discomfort been that obvious? She raised her chin. "He's adorable," she insisted. "And I appreciate you asking around about my sister. I'd better go and let you get to work. Mother told me that you work days most of the time."

She didn't wait for his response. His eyes were too piercing. Her reaction to the man was too unexpectedly strong, and the sweet smell of the little boy tore at her heart.

"Ms. Tucker? Sarah?"

Sarah turned and looked at Luke.

"I don't like to say this," he began, "but there were some ugly things going on in town last night."

"Ugly?"

He shrugged. "Nothing important. A few drunken arguments."

She had a bad feeling she knew what was coming next.

"About me again."

"Yes. People remember things, or maybe they remember them incorrectly. Other people take exception."

"Are you asking me for the truth? About whether or not I can find people? Whether I have special powers? Whether I really did find Pattie Dubeaux dead down by the lake?"

Her voice felt hollow, strained.

"I'm not asking you anything, Sarah," he said, his voice dropping low and surprisingly gentle given the stark, direct look in his eyes. "I'm just suggesting that you be careful."

She frowned and nodded. "I'll watch my back. As for the other, if I were capable of locating my sister through psychic connections, I wouldn't do it unless it was imperative. It's…intrusive. It's frightening. I don't believe in that stuff."

"Neither do I." His voice held more venom than his statement merited. Sarah raised her chin and looked directly at him, but she couldn't figure out the reason for the steel in his voice. She remembered the caller last night, the warning. Could it have been Luke? Probably not. He seemed more direct than that. He wouldn't have muffled his voice.

Still, something kept her from telling him about the telephone call. What could he do, after all?

"I'll be careful," she promised. "Very careful. Believe me, Luke, I don't have any interest in stirring up trouble or even in spending much time talking to people. I have a couple of things to take care of here in Gold Tree, and then I'll be gone again. I'd rather not get too involved in local affairs."

Especially affairs that concerned tall, handsome, brooding men who confused and attracted her.

But as Sarah walked back toward her mother's house, she could feel Luke's gaze on her. Hot, disturbing, volatile. She resisted the temptation to return and ask him why he had sounded so angry when he had said that he didn't believe in psychics, but she knew that the temptation to find out the reason would persist.

LUKE WATCHED SARAH GO and cursed himself for noticing the vulnerable slope of her slender back, for admiring the way her dark hair swept her shoulders or the way her jeans caressed the curve of her ass.

Mostly he cursed himself for having allowed her to hear how much he was affected by the very word *psychic*. She said she didn't believe in that stuff. Good, then, but apparently history didn't bear her out. He'd heard plenty last night about Sarah and her ability to find people and things through touch. Her presence certainly stirred people up.

And it made him remember Iris even though he didn't want to.

Luke carried Danny into the bedroom and began to dress his son for the day. He looked into Danny's eyes and saw the woman he had married.

He and Iris had been friends. She'd known about his awful home life and she'd sympathized. She'd even known that he had not ever been able to commit to a woman because his views on marriage were colored dark by his father's and mother's relationship. He hadn't wanted to care about anyone the way he had about his mother and watch her get hurt.

He'd hurt other women with his inability to love...and he had cared about hurting them. Iris had assured him that she was glad they were just friends. She'd suggested they would make a great couple, no need for emotions. He'd liked her and had been happy to finally have one normal relationship. He'd asked her to marry him, uttering no words of love.

For a while the arrangement had worked, he'd thought. But while there had been no romantic love on his part, Iris had felt it all along. She'd finally confessed that one day. Her heart had broken when he couldn't reciprocate her love. He'd hated himself for that, for not realizing how she'd felt about him, for letting things go too far. And then they had found out she was pregnant.

At first he had thought the hope a child represented would be enough. He'd tried to give her what she needed, but the trying had had the wrong effect. She'd felt humiliated and depressed that he didn't love her. Eventually, she'd gotten angry and had turned elsewhere for comfort and support. To friends, to one friend in particular.

Iris had embraced her supposed psychic friend with all the fervor that was so lacking in her marriage. She had grown to hate Luke. Sometimes he thought she'd wanted to withhold their child from him to get even for his inability to love her the way she needed to be loved.

She'd grown to hate the baby in her womb, but she'd gone through with the pregnancy and given birth. Two days after coming home she hadn't been feeling well. He'd insisted on taking her to the hospital and she had insisted on calling her friend instead. When he'd argued, she'd begged him to give her just this one thing.

He had. And when the friend declared that she was fine, just a little tired from the birth, Iris had refused to even consider going to the hospital. She'd railed at him, screamed down the house when he'd tried to touch her.

In the end he had let her have her way. He'd left her alone. He'd gone outside to try to outrun her cries and his guilt for all he had done to her.

She died from a blood clot, an aftereffect of the birth, and he now had to live with that fact. Danny had to grow up without a mother.

So the venom in his voice when he'd told Sarah that he didn't believe in psychics had been real. His aversion went beyond not believing.

But she hadn't claimed to be one. In fact, she had insisted she wasn't psychic at all.

He ought to remember that. He had no right to place blame on Sarah for what had happened to Iris, and he had absolutely no right to look at her with anything even close to interest, no matter how much she attracted him. He had a way of hurting women, and he had no intention of ever allowing another woman into a position where he could hurt her again.

Thank goodness Sarah didn't plan to stay in Gold

Tree. Maybe if he helped her find Cass he could speed up the process and be free of the disturbing thoughts she was making him think.

I CAN'T GO BACK, Cass thought, staring out the smeared glass of the second-story window. *I don't want to go back.*

Which wasn't exactly the truth, but it was close enough. For most of her life, her existence had been colored by her sister's reputation. In the early years she had wanted to be like Sarah, to be noticed like Sarah, to matter.

Cass circled the tiny creaky room she was inhabiting. She moved over to the mirror, cracked in two places, and stared at her distorted reflection.

"Look what you've become," she said to herself. "Or what you haven't become." She had never done anything remarkable, never excelled in anything. Her parents had been aware of that.

Not that her mother didn't love her. Cass knew she did, but her father had barely noticed her existence. And then when she had only been six years old Sarah had gone, and even her mother hadn't noticed her as much then.

Cass had been an afterthought in everyone's lives, and she had obviously been nonexistent to her sister. Oh, Sarah had sent cards and letters and gifts, but she had never once come to see her. And then when their father, R.J., had died, he had left his house to their mother, his business to Sarah. He had left nothing to Cass.

"So what did you expect?" she asked her reflection. "That something would change? Or that you would discover that he'd loved you all along and had just neglected to say so?"

Mom had been loving. Even in the face of Cass's mean-spirited snottiness her mother had seemed to care, but she couldn't change things. She couldn't make Cass important or hide the fact that Sarah was still her first concern.

Cass had sought her own kind of friends and she had found them. Misfits, troublemakers. She knew them for what they were and she was glad to be a part of things.

Then she had met Zach, and for the first time in her life she had felt wanted, needed, exciting, pretty.

Her mother's worries had fallen on deaf ears. Zach was a dropout. He had no job. He was unreliable. They'd argued. Cass hadn't cared.

She'd suspected that Zach was in some kind of trouble, but she hadn't cared about that, either. Until he'd hit her the first time.

Of course, that had been her own fault. She'd tried harder to please him.

But he'd started to look at other girls.

They'd fought. He'd hit her again. She and her mother had argued again. It had gone on and on like that.

Then she'd missed her period and discovered she was pregnant. Something stopped her from telling Zach.

She'd started to argue with her mother almost daily. She'd begun to say hateful things. It was almost as if she couldn't stop herself.

She longed to be able to talk to her mother about the baby, but instead they just argued, so much that Madeline grew distraught and tripped and fell.

"You did that," Cass whispered to herself. "You caused it."

Suddenly all the ugly things in Cass's life had closed in. She wasn't special, wasn't pretty. She had caused her mother to fall. If Madeline had been higher on the stairs, the fall could have been fatal.

Cass pressed in harder against the broken, stained mirror, trying to disappear inside her reflection. She was pregnant and unlovely. She had her friends, but they didn't really count. She was alone.

And she could never go home again. She couldn't be admirable like Sarah.

"I hate Sarah," she whispered, her words muffled against the cold glass. "I hate you."

A harsh laugh slipped from between Cass's lips. Sarah couldn't hear her. Sarah had never been around to listen.

"I'm glad." She knew that Sarah was in Gold Tree and she couldn't wait for her sister to go home. She hoped, really hoped Sarah wouldn't decide to show off her so-called powers and look for her.

The very thought made her ill. The last person she wanted to see was her sister.

CHAPTER FIVE

LUKE WAS PORING OVER paperwork on his desk the next day when a shadow blocked his light. He looked up to see Dugan Hayes, the chief of police, staring down at him, a troubled look in his eyes.

"Problem?" Luke asked.

"Maybe." Dugan gave a curt jerk of his head, indicating that Luke should follow him into his office.

Leaving his paperwork behind, Luke walked into Dugan's office and closed the door. He waited.

Dugan stared at him as if trying to read his mind. He didn't rush into anything. It had been one of the things that had appealed to Luke when he had interviewed here. Dugan had been around a long time, and he wasn't a hothead who made rash decisions.

"Looks like we've had a little excitement in town lately," Dugan finally said.

"It'll probably blow over." Even though Luke wasn't so sure. Things had been quiet, possibly even dull in Gold Tree for some time. There had been the usual problems, teenagers racing their cars too fast, underage drinking or adults who had imbibed too much and needed to sleep things off. There had even been some hints of drug use on a small scale. Those were the kind of problems every police officer routinely worked to keep in check. But this thing that Dugan was referring to was just plain weird.

When word got out that Sarah was back, there had been a few murmurs about the fact that she had been the girl who had once located a dead child's body. Just neighborhood gossip.

Then a former classmate of Sarah's had started talking about how strange Sarah had been, how as a child she had never looked people in the eye, had talked to animals and hid herself away except when she was having a vision. The woman's neighbor, a newcomer to the town, had immediately called the woman a liar and suggested that even talking about such stuff was evil. An argument had ensued and had been taken up by the women's husbands at a bar last night.

Soon a small group of people were taking sides and the mood of a certain segment of the town was turning ugly. Sarah's return was being blamed for the bad blood between neighbors. There had even been those who suggested that she had used some special voodoo to engineer the feud, trying to get back at those in town she didn't like.

Luke and Dugan had been staring at each other silently. "You don't think anyone seriously believes that Sarah is evil, do you?" Luke asked.

Dugan looked to the side, his thumbs in his belt loops. "When she was a little girl, there were parents who wouldn't let their kids play with her."

Luke uttered a word he usually tried never to say, then he calmed. "Why?"

Dugan blew out a breath. "I guess they were afraid. The day she found that little girl...it was eerie. Everyone had been looking for Pattie, but because she had last been seen playing in her backyard, the concentration had been on that immediate area. Then Sarah said that they needed to look by the water. She pinpointed the exact spot. Her voice was chilling, not like a child's voice at all. She collapsed immediately after Pattie's body was found and slept for the better part of two days. There are people who'll always remember that, I guess. And the fact that, after that, her daddy added a new service to his business—Sarah would try to find lost items for a fee."

Bile rose in Luke's throat. "Did she really find anything?"

Dugan shrugged. "Sometimes. Doesn't matter."

"I suppose not. What matters is that she's at the center of a heated controversy. People who are at the center of things sometimes get hurt."

"Yes, and her sister's missing. There'll be speculation about that."

"I'll do my best to squelch it."

"This is going to hurt Madeline." Dugan's voice was hard. "I don't know if it was a good idea for Sarah to come home."

Something akin to anger slid through Luke, hot and tight. And definitely unfair. He had been thinking the same thing only a bit earlier.

"It isn't Sarah's fault that people are talking."

Dugan looked straight at him. "I know that. And I'm not blaming her. She's got the right to come home if she wants to. I know that Madeline asked her to come, but if anything happens to Sarah, the very fact that Madeline invited her…"

He left his sentence unfinished. What was the point in saying more? Madeline would blame herself for putting

Sarah into this position. Given the fact that she was already worried about Cass, the situation wouldn't be good.

"I don't want to see Madeline hurt." Dugan said the words with some force, causing Luke to study the man's expression.

"I know you're good friends."

"Yes. We're friends. We've been friends for years." Dugan's voice was bleak, but then he cleared his throat.

"Help me keep an eye on them. I don't want any of the Tucker women to get hurt."

Neither did Luke, but…

"Is this in an official capacity? Is it an order?"

"You know I don't have the authority to assign personal bodyguards to citizens without cause, so no, mostly this is a friendly request from someone who respects you and knows that you don't like to see innocent people get hurt. Living right next door, you're in a unique position to stand watch. I'll be watching, too. There's probably no real threat, but this way we'll be sure."

Luke nodded, but inside he was disagreeing, digging his heels into the dirt, trying to stop this thing. He did not want to spend more time with Sarah Tucker than was necessary.

But now he didn't really have a choice.

SARAH RAN FASTER, HER legs stretching out in what had begun as a bid for exercise but had turned into an attempt to outpace her thoughts. Still, even racing, she couldn't outrun the truth.

"All right, let's take it down," she said to Smooch, who was galloping along in front of her with a lopsided gait.

Immediately Smooch slowed, matching his pace to Sarah's. He glanced back at her with total loyalty in his eyes. Was that a trace of sadness as well?

"I'm sorry, Smooch." Smooch loved running above all things. She loved running, too, but her heart just wasn't in it today and she had a nagging feeling that there was something she needed to be doing. She knew what it was, too. She just hadn't talked herself into doing it yet.

Sarah slowed still more and concentrated on breathing normally, on looking as if she wasn't flustered or concerned in any way.

The man coming toward her carrying the grocery bag was the fifth person who had looked at her as if she were a bug under a microscope…or an accident victim. Most people walked or drove right past, but there were enough staring or slowing their cars to gawk that she knew things must have been said about her.

Instantly old reflexes kicked in, and the urge to hunch her shoulders, avert her eyes and shuffle past was almost overwhelming.

"Not going to happen," she whispered to herself. She'd spent twelve years dragging herself out from under that heavy anvil. She'd spent far too much time learning to like herself.

She smiled at the man. "Good afternoon," she called.

For a second she thought he was going to look around to see if anyone was watching. Instead he mumbled a nearly unintelligible and obviously reluctant greeting and moved on, not making eye contact with her.

"Idiot," a female voice said.

Sarah turned around. A rather young and pretty blond woman was crossing the street to meet her.

"Do I know you?" Sarah asked.

The young woman shook her head. "No, my name's Jemma. I work at the police station, so I've heard all about you. Don't mind Paul. He's a fool. He's one of the ones who think you're going to harm his idyllic view of the town in some way."

Sarah blinked. "How would I do that?"

Jemma shrugged. "Who knows? Maybe by starting a colony of those who dabble in the black arts or something. Mostly I think he's just afraid that you're going to open up your father's old shop and start some sort of a psychic detective agency."

The woman's smile seemed genuine, but it was obvious that her comment was also a bit of a question. The very thought of going back into "the business" made Sarah shudder. On the other hand, the thought of having anyone judge her, should she decide to do just that, made her hackles rise.

"So, are you?" the woman asked.

Sarah tried a half smile, a light tone. "Who knows what the future might hold?"

The woman studied her for a second and then laughed. "Is that a joke? I like that. Keep everyone guessing. Works for me. We need some fun around here. It's far too dull for me."

And far too intrusive for Sarah. She wondered if things had been different, if she and Jemma might have become friends. As it was, she just wanted to get out of Gold Tree. The past was already closing in on her, and though she didn't intend to let anyone intimidate her this time, she didn't want to stay longer than she had to.

"Oh well, better get back to work. I see Luke

coming." She rolled her eyes. "He's a complete hunk, but totally not into me…or any woman here for that matter. He's a widower, and I think he may be one of those only-one-woman-for-me types. Just so you know."

Startled, Sarah sucked in a deep breath and wondered if she had been sending out some invisible I'm-interested-in-Luke vibes. She frowned at Jemma. "Thanks for the warning, but the last thing I need in my life is a man."

Jemma chuckled. "Okay, that makes one woman in town who isn't interested in getting into Luke's bed. Ooh, gotta run. I was due back at the office two minutes ago, but I really had to come and say hi and see if what some people were saying was true." She waited expectantly.

Sarah wanted to sigh. "What are they saying?"

The woman reached out and almost touched Sarah's hand. Sarah instantly felt a pain behind her eyes and edged away, a reflex action she had perfected over the years. Jemma blinked, but other than that she appeared to not even notice. "They're saying you used to be able to tell things about people by touching them or something they owned. Is it true?"

Sarah felt her breath freeze in her lungs at both the near contact and the audacity of this woman. She started to take another step back but knew that would only make her look like the timid person she had always been when she lived here.

Instead she looked at Jemma and then beyond her to Luke. She ignored the fact that Jemma was still holding out her hand as if she might try to touch her again.

"If I could tell something about you, it would probably be that Luke is going to ask you why you're standing around here on the street corner talking to me when you're supposed to be working," Sarah finally said, managing a small teasing laugh. She was happy that the laughter wasn't too shaky.

Jemma pulled her hand back. "Hmm, guess maybe people were wrong. You aren't psychic, are you?"

"No." Just a little more intuitive than others, she thought. A bit more inclined to follow hunches to their logical conclusions. That wasn't the same as being psychic.

Jemma frowned, and then she unexpectedly smiled. "Disappointing, but that's okay. You could have slapped my face for being rude, but you didn't. Nice meeting you, Sarah."

She turned to walk away. "I'm out of here, Luke," Jemma called. "Duty awaits."

Duty wasn't the only thing waiting, Sarah thought. She finally admitted what it was that she needed to do. She needed to talk to Luke. Her sister had still not returned home.

The possibilities for what had happened to Cass were frightening, even though she knew from experience that her sister might be all right. Eighteen years old suddenly seemed a lot younger than it had when she had been the one leaving home. A vision of a little dark-haired girl with big, dark, adoring eyes kicked in to her memory. She needed to know that Cass, the little girl in her memories who was all grown up now, was safe, and she needed to assure her mother that all was well.

"I was looking for you," Luke said suddenly,

studying her, his gaze so intense she almost took a step back.

Sarah stared back. A jolt went through her, and she knew it had nothing to do with her quest for Cass. Too bad. Her physical reactions to this man were immaterial. "You have news?"

"Not exactly. I've asked questions, talked to a few people. Although I haven't been able to nail down her specific whereabouts yet, I can tell you that Cass is definitely still in the area. She appears to be safe."

Sarah released a deep breath. A vision of that little innocent dark-haired girl tugged at her heart again. Gratitude toward the man who had brought her some hopeful news filled her. She looked up and realized how close she was standing to him. Not close enough for her to feel the heat from his body, yet it still seemed that way.

The uniform, she told herself. *It's just the appearance of authority that makes my breath come short and quick when he's around.*

"Thank you," she managed to say. "It helps."

"How about yourself?" Luke asked suddenly.

"Myself?"

"No one's bothering you, are they?"

"You don't mean Jemma, do you?"

His lips tilted slightly. "Jemma's nosy. Sometimes she's annoyingly rude in her quest for information, but she's not dangerous. And she's mostly good-natured."

Yes, that's what Sarah had thought, too. "No, no one is bothering me." Other than that phone call, which had probably just been some drunken customer at The Crazy Pig. Most people were ignoring her. In fact, the only person who was bothering her, appearing in her dreams and fantasies, was standing right in front of her.

Too bad, Sarah, she thought. *Move on.*

"Is your son all right?" she asked suddenly. "Mother is worried. She's used to taking care of him. I think she thinks no one can do as good a job as she can."

His lips tilted even more, and Sarah fought to keep from noticing how handsome he was. "She's right. Madeline is good with children."

It was the first time anyone had ever said that. It wasn't a thought Sarah had ever had. Her mother had been a shadow when she was a child...but she *had* called to get help with Cass.

"I guess she is."

"Tell her he's fine," Luke said. "Tell her he'll be better, though, when she's better."

Sarah smiled then, for real this time. "I'll tell her." She turned to go.

"Sarah?"

She looked over her shoulder into those eyes that probed too hard, analyzed too deeply. It took all she had to keep staring at him as she waited.

"You would tell me if anyone said anything or did anything to frighten you, wouldn't you?"

People had been frightening her all her childhood. She had never had anyone suggest it was okay to talk about such things.

"I know some people are looking at me strangely. They distrust me. They know what happened here when I was growing up, and they're not sure what to make of me."

He gave her a curt nod, his jaw tightening. She wondered if he was one of the ones who wasn't sure what to make of her.

"Do you really think anyone would try to harm me?"

She asked the question, knowing he would take it to mean physical harm, even though she knew full well that there were many kinds of harm in the world.

"I don't think anyone would assault you," he said.

Sarah realized that maybe he did acknowledge that there was more than just the physical way of hurting a person. That meant he thought things through more carefully than she was used to. It meant he might see things in her that she didn't want anyone to see ever.

Sarah tried not to follow that thought. "I'll be careful, Luke, and if anyone should do anything that would require the law to get involved, I promise I'll report it." She just wasn't sure Luke would be the one she would tell, she thought as she walked away. He intrigued her, attracted her. He even appeared to have some idea of what made her vulnerable. But in her experience, the men who knew a woman's vulnerabilities were the most dangerous.

MADELINE SAT IN HER ROOM and stared down at her still-puffy ankle, although it wasn't the ankle that was bothering her so much tonight.

She was restless, anxious, in need of productive activity. She needed to find some way to deal with all her worries.

The computer beckoned.

She shouldn't. She had stayed away from her online pen pal for several weeks. It wasn't healthy, this business of venting to a man in this seemingly anonymous setting.

But he would listen, she knew. He wouldn't judge. He wouldn't push.

She hobbled over to her desk and sat down. She clicked on her mouse until her message window opened up and typed:

Dear Fisherman Pete,
I've gone and done something stupid—sprained my ankle—and it couldn't have come at a worse time. My daughter, Cass, has run away from home just when my daughter, Sarah, has come home after years away to try and connect with her sister.
Bad timing, the story of my life.

His response came quickly.

We can't always time things the way we want to. Accidents happen.

With her they happened too conveniently, she thought. She replied:

You always make me feel better. Thank you.

Is the ankle bothering you? he responded.

A little, she wrote back. Mostly fear that my daughters won't connect is bothering me, that Sarah will go away and that will be the end of it forever. I'll lose both her and Cass.

And you're worried about being alone? he asked.

No, she had been alone for years in spirit, if not in fact. She and R.J. hadn't had anything resembling a real marriage, not even from the start. She typed:

It's fear of not having been able to right the mistakes I've made as a mother.

Mistakes can't always be righted. I've learned that, he wrote.

Madeline closed her eyes. She'd learned that, too, but this time... She responded:

I have this opportunity. I don't want to waste it. I've spent my life being timid. This time I want to be bold, to change the world, to turn back time....

His reply came immediately.

How far?

Her breath snagged in her throat. Her lungs seemed to stop working.

Just far enough to make things right for my children, she typed.

There was a long pause. She could tell he was typing, but when his answer came it was shorter than the wait would have justified, as if he had typed, deleted and typed again.

We all want to make things right for our children. Sometimes it helps if they just know that we want the best for them, that we would change the past for them if we could.

She knew what he was trying to tell her. Changing the past wasn't possible. She typed:

I have to try. I have to succeed.

And then what? he asked.

Then we'll see. I might leave home and go wandering. I might run away from myself, she replied.

Alone???

Unless my children need me here, then yes, alone, Madeline wrote back.

By choice or by necessity?

If you're asking if I have friends, I do, she replied.

I wasn't accusing you of not having friends...

She smiled a sad smile, then typed:

I guess I knew that. After all, you're my friend.

After a long pause, he finally responded:

I could tag along...

She touched her palm to her heart and replied:

No. Thank you, but no. I've been married. I won't get involved with a man again, even a man who is a good friend.

Another long pause, then he wrote back:

All right, but...don't do anything rash, all right?
Don't leave without telling me. Don't rush away.

I won't, she replied. If I go, when I go, you would be
the first to know. Good night, Fisherman Pete.

"Good night, Dugan," she whispered as he signed
off. She touched the computer screen as she said
goodbye to her friend. During the course of their correspondence, Dugan had once slipped and called her by
a nickname only he would know. She didn't think he
even realized it and she wasn't about to mention it. No,
Dugan would never know that she knew who he was.

He would never know that she still cared for the man
she had loved since she was a silly young girl. Or that
the mistakes she had made in her life had all started
with him.

CHAPTER SIX

CASS FELT AS IF SHE were shrinking inside herself. She sat on the rickety chair set back against the wall and pulled inward, trying to pretend she wasn't who she was and that her life hadn't taken the turn that it had. How had she ended up staying at Penny Mickerson's uncle's deserted farm?

Because I have nowhere else to go but home, she thought. Home didn't feel like an option right now. Especially since Sarah had arrived. These past few months Cass had been more messed up than usual, and she didn't need to emphasize that by going home to be compared to perfect Sarah who could run away, stay away for years without even visiting and still come back to open arms.

"So, Cass, when are you going to bring your sister around?" Bates McCoy, Penny's cousin asked as if he had read her mind. "Luke Packard has been asking a lot of questions, looking for you, supposedly for that sister of yours. What's that about, anyway? I thought she was psychic or something like that. How come she doesn't just know where you are? I heard that when she touches people or things, she can see stuff the rest of us can't." He laughed.

"Shut up," Penny said. "Think what that would be

like, to have a window into other people's minds. That's
so…incredible. What do you think, Zach?"

Zach, who had just stopped by, smiled a hazy smile.
He moved over to where Cass was sitting. "I don't
know. Is your sister really what they say she is?" he
asked. "How about sharing what you know, babe?" He
looked at Cass with a hint of interest. Very few people
had ever been interested in her. In these past few weeks
Zach hadn't seemed very interested, either, but right
now he was.

Still, Cass didn't answer. She clenched her hands on
the seat of the chair. For the past two days she had been
trying to avoid all the talk of Sarah. Sarah. Sarah.
Didn't anyone want to talk about anything but Sarah?

"Wow, I wonder what it would be like if someone
like that got high," Rob, Penny's boyfriend, said.
"Would she have super visions? Has your sister ever lit
up, Cass?"

She ignored the question. Sarah doing drugs. Who
knew what Sarah did?

"Maybe you could ask her about her visions, Cass."

"I don't think so."

"Why not? Maybe she could teach us things. I'd
like to be able to have visions. Maybe it's the kind of
thing she could show us how to do."

"Yeah, Cass, ask her for us," Bates said.

"Yes, Cass, do it," Penny agreed.

The coaxing and whining became a buzz. A huge
popping thud broke through and Cass jumped. She
looked at Zach who was rubbing his hand. The wall
now bore a fist-sized hole in the plaster.

"Shut up, everyone. Just shut up," Zach said, turning
dark and angry in the sudden and unexpected way he

did a lot lately. "On second thought, it might be a real bad idea to talk to Cass's sister. I've heard a few things, too. Sounds like she might be the prissy kind who would call the cops if she saw somebody lighting up a joint. She could buy all of us some jail time if we pissed her off. Ain't that right, babe?"

Cass turned away. She got up and left the room. She didn't know what Sarah would do if she saw something illegal going on. She didn't know anything about Sarah, except that everyone wanted to talk about Sarah and that Sarah didn't do the kinds of bad things that Cass had always done.

"What's wrong with Cass?" she heard someone ask in the other room. Rob. He was good-looking but a little slow and bewildered. Like everyone, he was here because he was a misfit.

"Is something wrong with Cass?" he asked.

Cass ran her hands over her abdomen. She remembered those last moments when she and her mother had squared off. And she bit down on her lip.

Once again, she had messed up, and now Sarah was sending Luke to check up on her. Sarah was doing the right thing, being good and admirable.

She heard footsteps coming that way. Heavy boots. Zach. She looked up to see him leaning against the door frame.

"Those stories about your weird sister are true, aren't they? She *can* find stuff, can't she? I've been slipping around, listening. You know that I need money. I have to find some source of cash. Not for them, though," he said, nodding back toward the other room. "I don't want to share. This would just be for us, babe. Just us, pretty thing."

She wanted to believe him. She *had* believed him in the beginning when he had called her names like that, but lately…it was harder to believe. She resisted the urge to rub her cheek where the last slap had fallen.

"So," he said, moving nearer, the clump of his boots somewhat ominous on the creaking wooden floor. "Tell me…you're not anything like your sister, are you?"

Red rage blew through Cass, but it wasn't rage against Zach. Sarah was the cause of it. Always, Sarah.

It had been that way for so long. Cass was thoroughly sick of it. Things had been bad these past few weeks. Now they would be worse. She could tell by the look on Zach's face that all she had to do was tell him yes and Zach would court her. He would be kind to her again. He would pretend to love her.

Maybe he would promise to give up the drugs.

She looked up at him and saw the twitching, the way his fingers moved restlessly, the slightly crazed and desperate look in his eyes. He would not give up the drugs.

"I'm nothing at all like Sarah," she said coldly. "And I never have been."

A long pause. "Damn," he said. "Damn. Do you think your sister really is what they say she is?"

She looked up at the hope in his desperate eyes.

"I don't know. I don't want to know."

"Maybe I want you to know."

There was menace in his voice. She didn't answer.

"Think about it," he said. "Find out, because I want money. Soon."

And then he clumped away and slammed out the front door.

Cass sat down heavily on the bed. She lay down and

wondered what would become of her. She wished for many things. Mostly she wished that Sarah would go back to where she came from.

Almost as much as she wished she weren't pregnant.

IT WAS DARK WHEN Sarah headed for the door. Her mother's voice stopped her.

"You're leaving, Sarah?"

The slight trickle of fear in her mother's voice got to her. She didn't remember her mother ever worrying about her, but then most of her latter years at home had been spent in school or working at the shop. She and Madeline had seen each other only at meals. They hadn't talked very much. When her father had ordered her to work, Madeline had never objected.

So, the fear that Sarah was leaving…was it really fear? Sarah wasn't sure. She had never been a mother. Still, the years of thinking about her own baby gave her the merest inkling of what it might have been like to experience full-blown motherhood. Watching the way her friends in California interacted with their children had shown her how frightened a parent could become when worried about a child. Perhaps she was lucky knowing she would never feel that kind of fear—

"Sarah?"

"I'm sorry. I'm just taking Smooch for a walk. It's been hours since he had one. I won't be gone long. Is there anything I can get you or do for you before I go?"

"No, you're right. Your dog needs attention. I'll see you later."

Her mother would be alone in the house. From the sound of things she'd been alone a lot since her husband had died.

"You're sure I can't get you anything?"

"No, I've got some stitching to do. It's amazing what a demand there can be for custom-made clothing. No one does that kind of thing now."

It was how her mother had always made extra money and obviously how she still supplemented her income in the months since R.J. had died. Sarah remembered that her own clothes had always been homemade. Somehow she had forgotten that fact.

"All right." Sarah stepped outside the house into the darkness. She called to Smooch and heard his snuffling.

A smile lit her face. "Did you miss me?" she asked.

A flash went off, illuminating the night, and she shrieked.

Footsteps moved closer and Smooch started barking and jumping around.

Another flash went off. Sarah realized that someone was taking pictures.

She saw Luke's porch light come on just as she saw a slight hunched figure move nearer.

"Wayland Gartner, Ms. Tucker," a man said, snapping another picture.

Smooch barked again. Spots swam in front of Sarah's eyes, but she could see enough to realize that Luke had come through the gate and was descending on the man.

"What the hell are you doing, Wayland?"

"Pictures for the paper, Luke. You know Sarah coming back is news in a town this size."

Sarah looked up to see that some of the neighbors were gathering outside her gate. Her shriek must have gotten everyone's attention.

Luke swore. "Damn it, Wayland, couldn't you just have asked the lady if she wanted her picture taken?"

"I wanted candids, not posed."

"And your reason for swooping down on her at night?" Luke took a step closer to the man. He didn't look anything like a police officer now, dressed only in jeans with no shirt. His muscled skin shone bronze from the faint porch light.

Sarah blinked and looked at the people gathered here. Luke must have noticed her reaction. "Go home," he told everyone. "There's nothing important going on here. Wayland, you didn't answer my question."

"I tried today but she was running when I first saw her. The next time she was zipping along pretty quickly, too. I only got shots of her back disappearing around a corner."

"Yeah, what's she scared of?" someone called. "She got secrets? I heard she can locate stuff just by mind control. A person who can do that…well, it makes you wonder. Is she doing something wrong in that house?"

"Shut up, Barry," Luke said, without even looking back to see who was talking. "What in hell do you think she's doing in her house? Making magic potions? Making a voodoo doll with your name on it? She's taking care of her injured mother, that's what she's doing, and it looks like all this noise disturbed Madeline."

It was true. The light from the house had gone on, and Madeline was standing in the doorway. "Sarah?" her mother said, her voice sounding frail.

"It's all right, Mom," Sarah said. "It's just a mix-up. It seems I'm a celebrity and people want to know what I'm up to."

Madeline targeted Wayland with a frown. "She was walking the dog," she said with some bewilderment.

"Got that, Wayland. Barry? Walking the dog. Now, let's all go home before this gets ugly," Luke suggested.

The crowd silently moved off, except for Wayland.

Luke turned and gave him a warning look. "I don't like you attacking my neighbors," he told the man. "Your job is your job, Wayland, but this is not Hollywood, Ms. Tucker is not an actress and you are not a member of the paparazzi. I can't stop you from taking pictures if you want to, but right now you are on private property. Don't force me to make an issue out of that. You scared Sarah."

Wayland had the grace to look a bit ashamed. "My apologies, Ms. Tucker. I'm just trying to get a good story. You happen to be what's happening here in town right now. You're different. That makes you news."

"Wayland, please." Madeline suddenly spoke.

Sarah turned. "It's okay, Mom."

"Yes, Wayland is leaving. Aren't you, Wayland?" Luke asked.

"Guess so. I'd still like a story," he said, staring at Sarah. "I wasn't living here twenty years ago. I'd like to know your side of the story."

Sarah froze. "I'm afraid I was very young," she said carefully. "I can't give you a story."

"But…"

"Wayland," Luke said. "Enough. This is the lady's house. It's a closed issue."

Wayland frowned, said good night and walked away. From the stubborn set of his jaw, Sarah knew it wasn't a closed issue for him. Her past was about to be dredged up in full, or at least as much as old newspaper clippings and the quotes of citizens who could remember that time would allow.

Her distress must have been written on her face, because Luke stepped closer. "Are you all right?" he asked.

She nodded stiffly.

"Madeline, you should be inside sitting down," Luke continued. "Go rest your ankle, all right? I'll go with Sarah while she takes her dog for a walk."

Sarah started to protest, but she heard the gratitude in her mother's voice when she acquiesced and went back inside. She might not know much about Luke, but she knew he was a man of his word. He would not leave her side until his task was done.

When it was just the two of them, she turned to him, trying to ignore his bare chest. "Your son?" she asked.

He touched a white contraption at his waistband. "Baby monitor. He's sleeping, and as long as we don't go very far, I'll hear him."

They confined their walk to the immediate area. Back and forth, back and forth. His proximity, his near nakedness, disturbed her, entranced her. He seemed so comfortable with his bare back and chest while she was so…aware of his maleness.

"You don't have to do this," she said suddenly. "I'm sure no one would harm me. I'm not a threat."

"You'll have to excuse people a bit. Just two months ago a couple moved into a neighboring town. Seemed perfectly normal, even had kids, a playground set, a dog, the whole nine yards. Turns out they were making crystal meth. That kind of thing is very dangerous, very volatile. It ruins the area environmentally, not to mention giving the town a bad name. People have been a bit jittery and suspicious of strangers since then."

"But I used to live here."

"Yes."

And she had not even been close to normal in the eyes of the citizens. Moreover, she hadn't come back in twelve years. They had no idea what new weirdness she might have been involved in during the time she'd been gone. They probably doubted her reasons for being here now, she thought.

"I appreciate your concern, but you really don't have to look after me. I'm an adult," Sarah said.

They were at her gate. "I know that. It's pretty clear just looking at you," he said, his voice deep. "You're also my neighbor. At least for the time you remain here, you are. And I don't mean to sound sexist, but you're also a woman. I have some personal experience of women being harmed by men, either intentionally or otherwise, and it's stayed with me. Madeline is my friend. She watches over Danny, and he's the light of my life. You're Madeline's daughter. I don't want anything bad happening to you while you're here. I don't want to live with the thought that I stood by and let something happen that I might have prevented. My apologies, Sarah, if I make you uncomfortable, but I plan to make sure that you're safe until such time as you return home."

He stood there staring at her, his amber eyes making promises when she knew she could never allow herself to trust the promises of a man. Heat seemed to shimmer between them. For a second she thought he was going to lean closer and touch her. For a second she thought that she wanted him to touch her even though she never allowed anyone to touch her.

Her breath kicked higher. The moon came out from behind a cloud. Sanity took hold.

Sarah stepped back. "Thank you," she said. "I'll try not to be too much trouble."

And then she quickly moved back into the yard, released Smooch, the walk abandoned, and escaped into the house. She might not be trouble, but Luke…he was a five-alarm fire. Potent, mesmerizing, sexy as hell. Her last thoughts before going to sleep were *Please don't let him touch me ever*, followed immediately by *Please let him touch me soon.*

CHAPTER SEVEN

"IN ANOTHER DAY OR two I should be able to chase a two-year-old around, don't you think?" Madeline asked Sarah.

Sarah watched her mother limp across the kitchen to the coffeepot. She noted that, leaning against the counter, Madeline kept most of her weight on one foot.

"Maybe a little longer than that," she said, rising. "Here, let me pour that for you. You're going to fall and spill hot coffee on yourself."

"I'm fine." Madeline's voice was low and tight. She placed both palms on the blue counter. "I'm not helpless. I can do some things right."

Automatically Sarah stopped. "I know you can. I didn't mean that you couldn't."

Madeline's shoulders slumped. She gingerly turned. "I'm sorry. I don't know why I said that. Yes, of course I'd love some help. I guess I'm just a little out of sorts. I'm used to taking care of Danny. I've heard that Luke is moving him around from place to place. I think Jemma's watching him today, and it's all because I was stupid enough to fall."

"He's at the police station?"

"Well, it's not like there are ever any hardened criminals there, but…"

"Would you like me to ask Jemma if we could bring him over here for a while?"

"You have things to do," Madeline pointed out. "Besides trying to find Cass, I know you wanted to decide what to do with the business."

Which she was avoiding, Sarah admitted. She didn't want to think about having to walk into the building that had been her prison, even to decide whether she wanted to sell it. Maybe tomorrow she would do that.

"Let me give Jemma a call," she said.

Ten minutes later, Sarah pushed open the door to the police station. It was a small office, but every head turned and stared at her. Apparently they were expecting her, and they knew who and what she was. Not for the first time in her life, Sarah was grateful that she wasn't a blusher.

She stepped up to the front desk. "Hi, Jemma. Is Danny ready?"

"Well, there's a bit of a problem," Jenna conceded. "Luke just came in, and now Danny is clinging to him and won't let go. I have a feeling that all this dark blue on these hatchet-faced guys is scaring him. Luke is in that first room on your right, calming Danny down. Perhaps you should go back there."

So she was going to have to face Luke and a baby at the same time. Maybe she could wait right here. Stupid thought.

"Thank you. I will." Sarah moved toward the entrance of the room Jemma had indicated. She glanced up to find one of the men watching her. He looked familiar, like one of the boys who used to taunt her with crude comments. Tom Williams, she thought, remembering his name. He had probably been one of the boys who had egged Jed Sturgeon on in seducing her. Now he was in charge of protecting people?

She felt suddenly sick, but ignoring the man, Sarah went in to find Luke and Danny. The little boy was tucked into his father's shoulder, hanging on with both hands.

"Shh," Luke was crooning. "Nothing's wrong. Everything's fine. Daddy's here."

Uh-oh, Sarah thought. Madeline was going to be very disappointed if she came back empty-handed, but the little boy looked as if nothing was going to drag him away from Luke.

"Won't be long," Luke said to Sarah, swaying back and forth.

"For…?"

"Sleep. It's naptime. He'll be good to go with a little shut-eye. The guys look too big and scary when he's tired. Madeline will be a welcome break for him."

Sarah noticed he didn't say that *she* would be a nice break, but he was probably right. Babies probably had some sixth sense about people who had no experience.

Luke looked at her over his son's head. "If I'd known about this earlier, I would have brought him to Madeline's myself."

Sarah shrugged and smiled. "It was kind of a spur-of-the-moment thing. Mom was afraid Danny was getting substandard care."

Luke laughed. "Sounds like Madeline. Anyway, I'll carry him."

Which meant that he wouldn't have to worry about the weird psychic woman holding his son. People had always been funny about that stuff. Some people wanted her to hold their babies, thinking that she could somehow see into the future, find out if their children would marry happily or make it into Yale. Others didn't want her near their children, for fear she would somehow infect them or cast a curse on them or something of that ilk.

It was ridiculous and okay, sometimes it had been painful at the same time. But she didn't know Luke, so she wouldn't repeat any of that to him. Moreover, his presence would mean that she wouldn't have to get too close to that sweet little boy. Children were easily damaged. Sarah's very heart hurt at the thought of being the one to bring pain or embarrassment into a child's life. So, even though a part of her longed for a child of her own, that wasn't allowed.

Like it or not, people here thought she was weird. That weirdness, the things that set her apart from others, prompted people to misunderstand or even fear her.

No child should ever be subjected to that kind of situation. If her child had lived, he would have grown up with constant reminders that his mother was an outsider. Maybe her baby would have been an outcast, too. Protecting the innocent was so important. She would never risk harming a child in any way, and she would risk everything to battle anyone who tried to harm a vulnerable baby.

Although, Sarah welcomed Luke holding his little boy, the warm baby smell of Danny made her long for something she would never allow herself to have.

"I would never hurt him," she said, and she nearly clamped her hands over her mouth. Had she really said that? Was she saying it for Danny or for Luke?

Luke looked at her strangely.

"I didn't say you would." But he didn't hand over his son, either.

IT WAS MORE THAN obvious that Sarah wasn't comfortable around children. Luke was okay with that. In his two years with Danny, he'd run across people who were kid people and those who were not. Sarah obviously wasn't a kid person. In fact, she looked almost scared when he drifted too near and her arm nearly brushed against Danny.

Luke shifted his son to the opposite hip, away from Sarah.

"He's gorgeous," she said softly. "His eyes are so unusual."

Yes, they were almost violet, the color of Iris's eyes, Luke thought. "Thank you." His voice was tight, more abrupt than he had intended.

Sarah raised a brow. "You're welcome."

At just that moment, though, someone came running at them full force from Sarah's side. Luke's immediate reaction was to step between Sarah and the person barreling toward her, but he was holding Danny.

The man, Harris Ornette, stopped right next to Sarah. Luke realized that she had taken a step out, too, as if she had been afraid the man might run right through her and into him and Danny. A protective move from a woman who was afraid of babies.

"Sarah," the man said, reaching out to grasp her arm.

She gasped, loud enough to be heard. Her body stiffened. The man looked down at his hand, then carefully removed it from her arm. He took a couple of steps back as if distancing himself from possible danger.

"Mr. Ornette?" she asked, her voice slightly choked. "Is that you? What's wrong?"

"I've lost my dog. I had her with me this morning and then she darted away chasing a rabbit. I've been looking for her all morning. I don't know where else to look."

The man was clearly frantic. He looked as if he might be considering grabbing Sarah by the arm again, but he crossed his arms in front of himself as if to keep temptation at bay.

Luke cleared his throat. He stepped forward, moving up next to Sarah. "You can post notices in the town, Harris. I'll let everyone know that you're looking. Is it Blue?"

"Yes, but notices don't do much…Sarah…"

Glancing at her, Luke couldn't help noticing that her pretty gray eyes were big and frightened.

"Your poor dog," she said. "I understand how you feel, Mr. Ornette, but I…what you want…I—"

"You're not going to do it, are you?" Harris's voice turned angry. "I heard you had gotten snooty, but I didn't believe it. You have a dog of your own. How would you feel if he got hurt or something bad happened to him?" His voice was filled with menace.

"I'm truly sorry about Blue, Harris, but you're not issuing a threat, are you?" Luke asked.

"No…" It was Sarah's voice, not Harris's. "It's his dog, his friend…"

Luke's radio beeped. "Yes?" he said. He listened. Then he blew out a breath and looked at Harris.

"Your wife called the station, frantic to find you before you got to Sarah and did something you would regret. It seems Blue's at home. He came back on his own."

Harris looked as if he was going to cry with relief. He gave a tight nod. "Thank you," he said to Luke. He said nothing to Sarah. Then he turned on his heel and left.

Luke looked down at Sarah, who almost seemed to wilt. "You all right?" he asked.

"I'm good," she said. "I'm glad he got his dog back." He watched as she visibly gathered herself, lifted her chin slightly and pasted on a smile. She turned beautiful, expressive gray eyes on him, and he felt something roll over in his stomach. He had a terrible urge, a hunger to do what Harris had almost done. He wanted to touch her. He wouldn't.

His son had no such compunction, however. He waved his chubby arms, just missing Sarah's cheek. "Dog," Danny said, thrilled that one of his favorite words was being thrown around. "Bah." Another favorite word. Who knew what it meant?

His little arm waved harder.

Luke took a step back, preventing the inevitable collision.

"Sorry."

Sarah nodded. "He's a baby, and obviously happy. He's sweet and adorable. I'll bet you're proud." The words were complimentary, even sincere, but there was sadness in her voice.

This woman…she was too complicated, had too many issues trailing her around. She was, as he had noted often, vulnerable.

And he was becoming fascinated with her. Stepping out in front of him and Danny to protect them, feeling sorry for a man who had shocked and scared her because he had lost his pet. What kind of a woman was that?

He didn't want to look too deeply.

"Danny's my life," he said simply, and that said everything. His commitment to Danny was all he could handle, because he knew that in this one relationship, this one with his child, he would never ever fail to do what was needed. All others…well, just look how he had failed those in the past.

"We'd better get you home," he said abruptly.

"Yes, Mom will panic if I don't get Danny there soon."

But that wasn't the home he was referring to. Whatever Sarah Tucker had come here to do, he would do everything in his power to help her do it, to fulfill her goal, because the sooner she did that, the sooner she would leave for her home in California.

And he really needed her to leave, because he really wanted her to stay.

ZACH LOUNGED BEHIND THE high wall of a fence across the street.

"Wow, did you see that?" he asked no one in particular. "When Harris grabbed her, I thought she was going to faint or throw up, and it was obvious that she knew the guy. She didn't seem afraid of him at all. It was his hand on her arm, the touching part, the part everyone keeps talking about."

Yeah, he would have to think about that. There was something to the rumors after all. A person who saw visions because of physical contact. That was the ticket.

He'd heard that having her touch an object would work just as well.

She was a person who could find things. He really could use someone who could find things.

"I'll bet she could find what I need," he muttered, fading into the bushes as the sound of footsteps came close.

It was getting harder and harder to get the cash to buy what he needed. His dealer had gotten really stingy with the amounts lately. Zach was pretty sure he was cheating him or cutting the stuff or something. The highs just weren't as high lately.

But if I had plenty of money I could have all I wanted, he thought through his red rage. *Where could a guy get a lot of money without drawing too much attention to himself?*

"Not sure, but I'll bet she could find some of the stuff. Have to think about this. Really have to think about this."

But he was starting to feel terribly sick. His hands were shaking, his knees were weakening. His whole body…

"Later. Gonna do it later," he said. He would figure things out later. He didn't know how, but somehow Sarah Tucker was going to help him find all the money he needed to get all the drugs he wanted.

What he had to do was figure out some way to make her do what he wanted….

CHAPTER EIGHT

THE NEXT DAY, A WOMAN backing out of a shop door nearly bumped into Sarah, and the old familiar chest-crushing panic threatened. Sarah slid away.

But why panic? she thought. When Harris had clamped his hand on her arm, she hadn't felt anything other than the initial shock of being grabbed and a searing spike of pain in her head. She'd felt nothing of what she used to feel…which was wonderful.

For years she'd been telling herself she had lost her powers, that she had managed to submerge or disconnect them. Over time she had even allowed herself small touches, minor swipes, mere hints of skin brushing skin just to test things.

But she'd been so nervous each time, her body shaking with the fear that a vision would hit, that she hadn't been sure the tiny touches had been completely without incident.

"Nothing," she told Smooch, even though her head ached a bit. "I'm free and clear. I was scared, but I didn't see one thing. Not a single vision." She was normal, or as near normal as someone like her could ever be.

Admitting that she could never be completely normal was a tough one. The truth was that she *had* once had visions, and they had changed her. She could never forget them or what they had taught her, and no matter what she knew, there would always be people who would still see her as that weird psychic woman.

And while we're dealing truth, she thought, *think about Luke.* She did. She had. He was too much for her to handle. She was too attracted to him. Jemma had said he didn't want a wife, and Sarah definitely didn't want a husband. But a man that compelling and enticing could get past her defenses. He could hurt her…and she could hurt his child.

"Time to clear things up and go," she decided. She'd done enough dragging her feet. Today she would take the next step toward finding Cass and then she would face the shop.

EVEN THOUGH SHE DIDN'T want to think about where she was headed, she knew just who she needed to talk to. Luke had limitations on how much he could butt into people's lives. What she needed right now was a person who didn't much care about ethics or anything beyond getting answers.

Sarah took a deep breath. She took Smooch along for companionship and comfort and false bravado.

"I wonder what I'm going to have to trade Wayland for information," she told her dog.

Smooch cocked his head and barked his response. He panted in the heat, his tongue hanging out.

Sarah laughed. "You know, Smooch. You look a little like Wayland, but at least you're panting for a good reason. Still, I guess I shouldn't complain. I'm asking for his help. I hope he's willing to cooperate."

It took only a few minutes to make her way to the

offices of the *Gold Tree Weekly*. She could see Wayland through the open window. He was camped out behind a computer screen. There was no one else there. Before she went inside, she found a shady, grassy spot behind the building for Smooch to wait.

Then squaring her shoulders, she walked through the office door. "Hi, Wayland," she said.

He blinked as if caught off guard, then quickly recovered and stood. When he started to shake her hand, she sat in the chair in front of his desk. She might be cured, and maybe they were going to do business together, but she wasn't sure she wanted to get too chummy with this man.

"You came, after all," he said, sitting down. He allowed his gaze to traverse her body. "Yeah, there is something about seeing your name in print, isn't there, pretty lady?"

Sarah restrained a shudder and tried not to concentrate on Wayland's lascivious looks but on his words, which were even worse. When she was young, she hadn't realized the power of the press until someone showed her the story that had been written about Pattie Dubeaux. Even to a young girl, it had seemed somewhat obscene to be concentrating on the drama of a psychic when a child lay dead and her family would be forever grieving.

"I'm not here for a story. I'm looking for information myself. I thought you might be able to help me."

Wayland grinned. His mouth was overly large, his gums too pink, and it wasn't a pretty sight. "Sarah, come on. You can't come in here and tell me you want information and not at least give me a story of some sort."

She sighed. It wasn't as if she hadn't expected this, and it wasn't as if she would have to be here in Gold Tree for years living with the results of the story. But her mother and sister would.

"What kind of story did you want?"

He stood, paced the floor. "I want it all. What it was like when you first realized you were different from other kids, what it was like to aid in a search, what you've been doing, psychically speaking, for the past twelve years."

"I want to know anything you know about my sister," she said. "For that I'll give you an exclusive on what I intend to do with Tucker's Lost & Found Emporium just as soon as I decide what I'm going to do with it."

"No deal. People will know about that soon, anyway. It's not personal and not nearly as newsworthy as what I asked for."

Sarah felt a slow sizzle growing within her. Even though she had been prepared for this, the fact that the man wasn't going to be happy unless he bared her soul to the town angered her. Still, she didn't have much in the way of ammunition.

"I have pictures of the shop from years ago, even before my time. I have photos from my childhood and, when I open up the shop I'll let you in one day ahead of everyone else to explore on your own. I'll give you what history I know. That's the best I can do."

She stood to go.

"Why would you think I even know anything about your sister?"

"I don't. But you get into places other people don't. You're nosy, you probably see things other people might miss."

He rocked back on his heels, then loomed forward.

"All right, let's start with the history of the Emporium. For that you get this bit of information. Your sister has been seeing a guy named Zach Claxton. I'm not sure where he lives right now. His mother threw him out of the house, but if you find Zach, you might locate your sister."

"That's all you know?"

"That's all I'm telling you until you get me a better story." His expression didn't change. Sarah couldn't tell if he really did know more or if he was just bluffing. This conversation with Wayland had most likely been a waste of time. But she at least knew the boy's name. That was a start, someplace to wade in.

"I'll send over the information when I get it together," she said.

"I'll be waiting."

She held back a shiver and did her best not to rush through the doorway. Still, by the time she got to the back of the office and untied Smooch, she was eager to get out of sight of Wayland. She hurried around to the front of the building and ran smack into the wall of Luke's chest.

He caught her and steadied her with his hands on her arms. Sensation flowed through her, streamed through her, hot and fast and impossible to stem. She felt... power, strength, anger, something else, something stronger. She breathed in and felt herself surrounded by Luke's scent. She was close, close enough that if she leaned forward slightly, her breasts would brush his chest. Dizziness, longing assaulted her.

Danger, run, don't let anyone wield power over you, she thought.

Immediately she wrenched herself back, nearly stepping on Smooch, who was dancing around the two of them.

Her chest was heaving. She felt as if she had just gotten off a scary amusement-park ride, one that had sent a rush of exhilarating adrenaline through her. At least what she had felt had been normal.

She almost wanted to laugh at that. Her reactions had been more intense than any she had ever experienced before, but she didn't feel like laughing.

"Are you out of your mind?" Luke's amber eyes flashed dark. Apparently he didn't feel much like laughing, either.

"What do you mean? Why are you here?"

"I was on my way to see you. I happened to see your dog down the gangway. Then I saw you and Wayland, and I heard what he said through the window. You're not going to trust that guy, are you?"

Sarah glanced behind her toward the window. "He'll hear you," she said, starting to move forward.

He reached out as if to stop her, then pulled his hand back. "You're right. This is between you and me. I don't want it in the newspapers. You hear me, Wayland?"

"Loud and clear, Luke." A laugh followed.

Luke frowned and started to walk. Sarah trotted to keep up. "I don't know what business of yours it is if I go ask Wayland some questions about Cass."

"Anything you say to him is on the record for starters."

"I didn't say anything important."

"You would, eventually, or it would get twisted into something you wouldn't recognize."

"Why do you care?"

They were a block away from the newspaper office now. There was a park on the corner. He nodded toward it, and they moved together into the trees. Luke stopped and turned to her. "You may live in California, Sarah. You may think you're a woman of the world, but you don't know men like Wayland. It isn't because he's a reporter, either. It's because he's a man without principles. A man like that isn't always going to treat you fairly."

"You think I haven't dealt with men like that before. I have. My father was one of them. He wasn't the only unprincipled male I knew, either. You think I don't know what kind of man Wayland might turn out to be?"

"You were bargaining with him."

"I wasn't going to tell him anything important."

"If you tell him something that isn't interesting enough, then he'll print something that sounds more interesting."

"Lies?"

He held his hands out. "Embellishments."

"I could deny those."

"Yes, and he would print a retraction, a correction. How often do you read the correction section of the newspaper?"

She frowned at him. "I get your point, but…why do you care?"

He didn't answer for what felt like forever. "I don't like men who take advantage of people, especially women. And if he hurts you, you won't be the only one hurt. What affects you, affects both Madeline and Cass. You may be alone in California, Sarah, but you're not alone here."

He stared into her eyes, and she wanted to believe him, but it wasn't possible. All her life she had been alone, even in the midst of her family. She was the only one she could depend on. Still…

"You might be right about one thing," she said. "I don't want to do anything to cause Mom or Cass grief while I'm here. I just thought Wayland might help me find Cass. He told me she was seeing a boy named Zach Claxton. Do you know where he lives?"

A string of curse words flew from Luke's mouth even though he uttered them beneath his breath. "I know about Zach, and, as of this morning, I know where Cass is. I got a tip about her whereabouts, so I drove out there and spoke with one of her roommates. Penny's evasiveness was more revealing than anything she said. Cass is most likely there, but she doesn't want to be found, so think long and hard before you take the next step, Sarah."

"She's my sister."

His expression softened slightly. "Yes, she's family, but sometimes members of families can hurt each other more than strangers can. And sometimes there's no going back once the harm has been done."

They stood there staring at each other, troubled eyes into troubled eyes. Sarah knew about harm that couldn't be undone.

"You know what you're talking about, don't you?" she asked.

He hesitated, but in the end he gave a curt nod. "I do. My father was an abuser and because of my stubborn ways, he hurt my mother. I knew that, but I just kept challenging him. I was the cause of her pain so many times. Later, I did things and said things and left things unsaid and undone that harmed my wife irreparably in many ways. Be careful, Sarah."

Then Luke turned and walked away, leaving her standing there.

He was right. She needed to be careful. About Cass, about anything she might say that would affect Madeline's life here, and absolutely about Luke. She wanted to know more about him, but everything she learned only showed her that he was a man she ought to steer clear of.

He was a man who could hurt her, and she had a very strong suspicion that if he hurt her, he would suffer just as much as she did.

CHAPTER NINE

DUGAN HAYES WATCHED Sarah Tucker stalking down
the street, her hands shoved deep in the pockets of her
cutoff jeans, a pinched look on her face. Her head was
bent as if she were struggling against a strong wind, but
there was no wind, so the worried look on Sarah's face
had Dugan seriously concerned.

Not in a professional capacity, either. He might be
chief of police, but he had no reason to suspect Sarah
of anything. Her sister, maybe. Cass had been living on
the edge for a while, but Sarah? She was a lot like her
mother, and Madeline was…no more his business now
than she had been thirty-two years ago when he had
been hopelessly in love with her.

Except he still worried about her. He had been
thinking about Maddie a lot lately—ever since his wife
had died a year ago and Madeline's husband had
followed mere months ago. He'd seen enough to know
that she was unhappy, and he suspected that some of
that had to do with her children. His own kids could
keep him tossing and turning at night even though they
were both grown and long gone. And Madeline had
always been a worrier.

Sarah looked very much as if something was wrong.
She turned down Great Pine Road and Dugan's concern

took a turn for the worse. There was nothing much down that road except for Sarah's father's old business, the one R.J. had turned into an obsession. The place where everyone knew Sarah had spent a lot of her time, the place R.J. had left her and which everyone in town knew she hadn't gone near even though she had been in town several days already.

Leaving some space and turning the corner exactly where Sarah had, Dugan watched her from a distance.

SARAH HAD PUT OFF GOING to Tucker's Lost & Found Emporium for days, but now that she had decided to go, she had hoped she would be able to handle the situation with a certain amount of detachment.

She had been wrong. Already her palms were sweating and her throat was closing up. She felt dizzy and sick.

But she kept walking toward the building, angling nearer. What was she going to do? How was she going to feel when she got there?

"I'm going to feel nothing," she whispered. The building was just a building. It held no threat, nothing that could hurt her now.

She would just walk by, do the thing that she dreaded doing, and it would cease to have any hold on her.

Simple. Easy. Wonderfully cathartic. No big deal.

But the drums were pounding in her head. Her father's voice was yelling in rhythm with her steps. *Sit down. Sit down. Shut up. Shut up. Help me or else. Help me or else. Or else. Or else. Or else. Or else.*

Sarah clutched at her sides. She folded her arms across her chest, trying to hold the fear in, to keep it from escaping and growing larger.

Just two-and-a-half more blocks.

She pushed on.

Just two more blocks. The buildings she passed were a misty blur.

Keep going. Keep going.

Just one-and-a-half more blocks.

The terror clamped down on her throat. The fear exploded. She veered sharply off to the left, picking up speed, trying not to run. If someone should see—she didn't want anyone to see—they would know that she was still a freak.

And then she stopped thinking and just ran.

DUGAN WATCHED AS SARAH ran full force away from the building. She turned and fled, her dog galloping ahead of her. It was not the first time in her life he'd seen her do that. As a child, she had often been seen running away from here.

He knew where she would go. She had a special place in the woods where she went to hide. He'd followed her there once to make sure she was all right. And then he'd never told anyone about her special place. He certainly didn't intend to start now.

But her terror…it made him angry, and not just for her sake.

Without even thinking, his steps turned in a direction he seldom allowed them to take. He allowed himself to do this today because if anyone had seen Sarah and mentioned her fearful run to her mother, Madeline would be worried sick.

If she was worried, then he wanted to be there for her, even though he had no right.

It wasn't a long walk to the Tucker house. He

knocked tentatively, then waited a long time. When she swung back the door, his attention immediately went from her still-pretty face to her still-swollen ankle.

"All right if I come in?" he asked. "I don't want to keep you standing."

"Dugan?" She nodded, her hands fluttering. "Come in. Sit, but really I'm fine. I'm getting better every day. In fact, I'm thinking seriously about going back to my job at the Midnight Diner."

"So soon?" He both loved and hated the fact that Madeline worked the late shift two nights a week at the diner. He loved it because he could go in there under the pretext of getting a cup of coffee and catch glimpses of her whenever he wanted to. Hated it because other men could do the same...and did. It didn't matter. She didn't give any of them the time of day, at least no more than friendship called for.

"Hey, a woman has to make a living. Stitching clothes isn't enough, and I won't be able to watch Danny all the time next year when he goes to pre-school."

"I guess you're right," he agreed. Damn R.J. for leaving her with pretty much no money. Damn R.J. for a lot of things.

"Dugan, why are you here?" Madeline asked. There was a trace of concern in her voice.

"I worry about you, Madeline. I always have."

"Don't, Dugan." Her voice broke.

"Why not? R.J. is dead, Essie's been dead for more than a year."

"I'm not capable of what you seem to want from me."

"Because of what happened nearly thirty years ago?"

"No. Maybe just a little, but no. I was as much to blame as you were for the fact that you ended up married to Essie and I ended up married to R.J."

"I loved you even when I married Essie. I think she knew, even though I never said it."

Maddie groaned. "Dugan, don't. I was the one who left you to date R.J. because he was wild and handsome and adventurous, and I thought I wanted adventure."

"And I was the one who dated Essie on the rebound and got her pregnant, so that we had to get married."

"But you didn't make me marry R.J. I did that on my own."

"Why did you marry him?" He'd been wanting to ask that question for years. If Sarah hadn't come home and he hadn't been so worried about Madeline, how much longer would it have taken him?

She shook her head. "I got swept away. I felt betrayed by you, and I was angry and scared and he…he wanted me. I went along."

Dugan laughed, a bitter sound. "You never go along with me."

She gave him a sad smile. "I didn't like marriage very much. I didn't like having a man control things, and Dugan, I don't think I can get caught up in a relationship again. I'm not very good with men, and with all of the mistakes I made with you and R.J. and then with my daughters, I just don't want to get involved anymore."

He opened his mouth to protest, but she shook her head. "I can't, Dugan. I don't want to."

"All right, Madeline, but just so you know. I still care for you. I always will."

"Thank you," she said, and she sounded as if she meant it. "Is that why you came to see me, to tell me that?" she asked.

"The time seemed right. R.J.'s been gone six months, and maybe I was rushing it, but I didn't want some other guy to get there ahead of me again."

"Dugan." There was pain in her voice. "No other man will. There won't be any other man."

"I don't like you being alone. I worry."

She laughed then, a very small laugh. "I worry, too. In fact, I'm worried now. Sarah's been gone a long time, and there are people in town who haven't been nice to her. She won't say anything, but I hear things. I hope nothing's happened."

"I saw her. She was out walking, but no one was bothering her."

The look in Maddie's eyes softened. "That's good to know."

Dugan felt better about coming here. At least he had relieved her mind.

It should be enough. It wasn't. He wanted more for Madeline and for himself, so he kept her chatting about inconsequential things.

But when he finally saw Sarah coming down the street, he excused himself, said goodbye to Madeline and went on his way.

He wondered if he should go up to Sarah and maybe hint that she needed to tell Madeline if she was going to be later than usual.

Not that he had any right. All he had was his job, and it was time to realize that, and take more of an interest in his work and less of an interest in the Tuckers...if that was possible.

TEMPTATION COMES IN many forms, Sarah decided later that evening. When she came back from walking Smooch after dinner she saw Luke sitting on his porch with Danny on his lap. He was rocking the little boy in a swing, his arm draped about his child. Danny lay against him, totally trusting, his tiny hand resting on Luke's chest.

It was a domestic scene, not passionate or fiery or anything that should arouse desire in a woman. But looking at the protective gesture of the man to the child, reading the love so evident in the relationship, something dark and hot and needy flowed through her.

She glanced up and looked straight into Luke's eyes. He was staring at her, concentrating on her. For a short while she could swear he was going to get up and walk across his property onto hers. Anticipation rose within her even though she knew she shouldn't want any such thing.

Then he stood up, took one last look, turned and moved back into the house. Sarah felt herself sag. She couldn't say whether it was with relief or regret, and she wasn't sure she wanted to know.

When she went inside, her mother was waiting. "Everything all right?" Madeline asked.

"Couldn't be better." Which was such a lie.

"You're sure?"

Sarah dredged up a smile. "Absolutely."

A pinched, concerned look crossed Madeline's face, but then she nodded. "That's good then. Everything's fine."

The two of them stood there smiling at each other though Sarah wasn't happy and Madeline didn't actually look happy. Then Madeline nodded again. "All right, I guess I'll go get something done." She waited, as if she wanted to say something more, but in the end she left the room.

Sarah felt lost and hollow. She wished she had asked her mother if she could bring Smooch inside, but she had a feeling Madeline would say yes even if she wanted to say no, so it was probably best not to bring up the subject.

Instead she concentrated on her reaction to the shop today and on what she could do about that. She had walked out into the woods after that experience and just concentrated on breathing. The memory of her father locking her in a small closet when she hadn't done what he wanted was something she had shut away in a part of her mind. She'd thought she'd learned to deal with it, but the closer she'd gotten to the building, the more it had felt as if invisible walls had been closing in. In the end, she had panicked.

But that wasn't going to fly the next time. She could probably sell the place without going inside, but if she did that, that fear would forever own her. She was just going to have to spend some time preparing herself… and then she was going to eventually have to walk into the building and face down her fears.

She promised herself that before she went to bed. Turning off the light in her room, she wondered if Luke was still awake or if he was in bed, too.

"Stop it, Sarah," she told herself, and then she did her best to make her mind a blank, though the thought of Luke lying naked under a sheet stayed with her for a long time.

Tomorrow would be better, she promised herself. She would conquer her fears about the shop. Maybe she would even face the fact that she and her mother needed to talk. She would definitely stop thinking about Luke.

CHAPTER TEN

CASS LAY IN BED, FEELING the room roll and shift. Whoever called it morning sickness hadn't bothered telling her body that. It was the middle of the night, and she was sick and terrified. The other side of the bed was empty. Zach had not come over tonight.

Relief drifted in. Yesterday, Zach had been at the house, and she'd found him rummaging through a drawer when she came in. He'd stuffed something in his pocket and cursed at her when she'd asked what he was doing. His eyes had been crazy.

Fear and disappointment mingled, adding to her nausea. Zach had been the first guy to ever pay any special attention to her. He hadn't seemed to care that she was a plain vanilla kind of person, that she wasn't the special Tucker.

Lately, though, he was a scary stranger, and she wanted to get away from this town and from Zach. But get away to where? Home when she had messed up so bad?

A tear ran down Cass's cheek.

"Stupid idiot," she said from between clenched teeth. She turned into the pillow and her stomach lurched. Breathing slowly, she got things back under control. If she were home, her mother would be watching her with those wounded, judgmental eyes, fussing, expecting too much. So why did she miss her and need to hear her voice? Cass wondered. It didn't make sense, did it?

Slowly, Cass reached out and picked up the phone. She dialed. Waited. And waited. Of course, it would take her mother a while to get to the phone.

Guilt nudged her. Why couldn't Goody-Two-shoes Sarah pick up the phone?

Of course, she knew the reason. Her mother talked about Sarah all the time even after all these years. She had heard of her sister's tendency to sleep through everything about a thousand times. Her mother had often wondered aloud if it played into her "gift."

Cass had never had a gift.

"But now I do," she whispered, running her hand over her flat belly. A shameful gift, but it was all hers.

Zach appeared in the doorway, startling her. "Hey babe, I want you to do something for me," he said, as if they'd been in the middle of a conversation. "Stop messing around and go see your sister. I really, really need her to help me find some money. A lot. Fast." He pulled at the hem of his shirt while he talked, his fingers moving fast. His eyes darted around the room as if looking for money in every corner.

"I told you I can't talk to my sister."

Zach's brows drew together. "Sure you can talk to her. You can convince her. We need the money."

But he didn't know about the baby. She hadn't told him. She didn't want to tell him.

Slowly she shook her head no.

"Yes. Do it." His voice rose, grew stronger, higher.

Cass had been holding the receiver against her stomach. Now, as if for the first time, Zach noticed it.

"Who are you calling? Are you calling the cops?"

Fear rose, acidic and overwhelming. Her mother's voice could be heard on the other end of the line. "Hello, hello, hello."

"Tell her you want to talk to Sarah," Zach commanded.

Desperate, afraid, sick, Cass tried to rise to get to the bathroom, to get away from Zach. She stumbled and fell.

"Tell her," Zach yelled.

Cass couldn't hold on. Nausea overtook her.

"Bitch!" Cass heard Zach yell, followed by the sound of the telephone crashing into the wall, the buzzing of a dial tone.

"What the hell is wrong with you? You talk to your sister tomorrow," Zach said, then she heard his heavy footsteps down the hall.

Cass lay there on the floor, cradling her belly and wondering what she was going to do.

In the end she called her mother back and pretended she was fine. She wondered why she did that if she didn't really care what her mother thought about her?

"Because I don't want her to look for me. I don't want her to find me," Cass said to herself. Life as she had known it was over. From now on it was just her and the baby, and that was the way she wanted it.

SARAH DREAMED THAT something was poking at her, jabbing her shoulder. She tried to turn over.

"Get up! Get up! Wake up, Sarah. Please wake up."

That voice hadn't been by her bedside in years, not since she had been very small. This was a dream. This had to be a dream, but the voice was so loud and sounded so scared.

She turned onto her back and blinked, nearly blinded by the overhead light streaming down. Her mother stood there, leaning against the nightstand.

"What?" Immediately Sarah sat up. "What is it?"

"Cass. Something's wrong with her. Really wrong. I knew it. I knew it all along, but I didn't say."

Madeline swayed. Immediately, Sarah slid her legs over and patted the bed. Her mother turned awkwardly and sank down.

"Tell me," Sarah commanded.

"I think…" Madeline's voice broke. "I think Cass is pregnant. She didn't say, but…she's been seeing that boy."

"Zach?"

"You know?"

"I heard. A little. Not much. Tell me."

Madeline shook her head. "I don't know much, but I'm sure he's bad. I feel it." Madeline's voice was strained.

To another person, explaining something with the phrase "I feel it" would have been to invite ridicule, but Sarah understood perfectly.

"We fought about him," Madeline continued. "That last night I told her I didn't like her dating him. She'd been coming in all hours even though I'd tried to stop her. I warned her that she was going to end up pregnant, and then she started yelling. It was ugly. I reached out for her and I tripped and fell."

And Cass left you there, Sarah wanted to say, but she didn't. Madeline had purposely skipped over that part. She'd looked away the same way she'd looked away from lots of ugly things over the years.

"Mom, it's the middle of the night. Why are you telling me this now?"

"The phone rang a few minutes ago. I didn't hear Cass's voice, but I heard Zach. He called her a bitch and then there was a crash and the phone went dead. Then Cass called back and told me she and Zach had had a lover's tiff, but they had made up, he had gone home, and she was fine. I don't believe her."

Madeline was twisting her hands together. "That night, when I told her she might end up pregnant, if you could have seen her face…I think she really is pregnant. That's the hold he has on her."

Sarah nearly doubled over. An unmarried eighteen-year-old pregnant girl—history repeating itself.

"If what you say is true, about Zach swearing at Cass and then the phone going dead, she might be in danger," Sarah commented.

"I don't know what to do," Madeline said. "There's probably nothing to be done, really. I just don't know."

Sarah wondered if that was what her mother had told herself when her oldest child was being kept a virtual slave by R.J. Anger and bitter resentment had Sarah fighting her own nausea.

Somewhere in town Sarah's pregnant sister might be being abused by a man. And even if Cass didn't want help, Sarah intended to do something.

"I'll get Luke to take me there in the morning," she said. "I'll do something."

"You'll find her?"

Sarah was grateful to be able to answer truthfully. "Luke will lead me there."

So much for putting all thoughts of Luke out of her mind.

WHEN LUKE GOT UP the next morning and went out to get the morning paper, Sarah was sitting on his doorstep like a gift that had been left there just for him. Smooch sat next to her, his head in her lap, his tail wagging as she petted him, her hand caressing his fur over and over. Lucky dog.

Luke exchanged a look with Smooch, who almost seemed to smirk. Idiotic thought.

The urge to sit next to Sarah, to put his arm around her and just sit here in the cool morning sunshine, breathing in the scent of roses from Madeline's garden, was strong.

Luke resisted. He crossed his arms over his chest and looked down at Sarah.

"How long have you been here?"

"About a half hour. I heard Danny through the open window and settled down to wait."

"You could have knocked on the door."

She shook her head. "No. I wanted to catch you before you headed for the station, but what I want— what I *need* is for you to take me to see Cass, and we can't do that until Danny is taken care of, anyway. I didn't want to intrude on your private time with him."

Her thoughtfulness touched him immeasurably. Danny was his world, his heart and soul. Luke truly appreciated how much other people enjoyed being around his child and he couldn't be more grateful for the offers of help to babysit when he had to be at work and away from Danny, but there were times when he wanted to be alone with his son, to be selfish about sharing him.

"Thank you." He hunkered down next to her, giving in to the urge to get closer for just a second. "But breakfast is over. Danny and I have had our private time. He's playing with his toys right now, but I don't want to leave him alone. I'll get him, and then we'll talk," he said, then disappeared into the house.

"Uh-oh," Danny said, turning toward his father when Luke walked into the kitchen. His face was a chocolate mess, and Luke realized that he had gotten into the cookie jar. Now what? Sarah was waiting, he was already dressed for work and Danny looked as if he needed a dunk in the tub. He should have taken Danny outside with him. Ordinarily, he never left his son alone, not even for two seconds, but he'd been distracted by the sight of Sarah sitting on his steps.

Which just goes to show you that you ought to get the woman out of your thoughts, he reminded himself.

Well, she was there now big-time. He ought to tell her to come back later, but he couldn't ignore the look in her eyes. She was asking him to take her to Cass, which meant she was dealing with some serious emotional issues.

"Sarah," he bellowed, scooping Danny up football fashion. "You might want to come inside. Looks like I'm going to be a few minutes. Dad emergency."

He headed toward the bathroom with Danny giggling. In the back of his mind Luke couldn't keep from thinking about what would have happened if he had raided the cookie jar as a child when his father had been in a rush. Two black eyes. No, make that four. Two for him and two for his mother.

The thought nearly made him sick. His mother had always paid for his mistakes, even when there wasn't a damn thing she could have done to prevent them.

Danny was never going to know that kind of a father. Everything in his son's life was going to be perfect. No mistakes, no people in town giving him pitying looks, no questions about what life at home was like.

He looked up just as Sarah came around the corner. Everyone except Sarah claimed she was a psychic. They talked about her, whispered about her. They remembered things from her childhood. She hated it.

Luke felt for her, but Sarah was never going to be more than his neighbor's daughter. He couldn't want her to be more. Danny had to be everything.

"Oh, my. What happened? Is Danny all right?" she asked.

Luke flipped Danny right-side up just then, sitting him on the closed toilet lid, and Danny giggled.

"I'd say he's fine. Just full of cookies. I think he ate them all."

"Except for the one he's holding," she said with a low, sexy chuckle.

"What?" Luke looked down. Danny had produced another cookie from somewhere.

"Cook," Danny said. He offered a piece to Sarah.

A smile transformed her face. "How very generous you are."

"Eat," Danny said as if directing her. He started to push the other piece of cookie into his mouth.

"No," Luke said firmly. "You're going to be sick." He took the cookie from Danny.

Immediately, his child got that big-eyed, tearful, puckered-lip look that promised tears. He looked completely wounded, as if someone had just hit him or taken everything of value from him.

"Luke?" Sarah asked, and when he turned to look at her, she was wearing the same look as Danny was.

A tear trickled down Danny's cheek. Luke's heart cracked a little.

Sarah moaned slightly. "Oh, he's crying. Maybe you should give the cookie back?"

There was nothing Luke would have liked to do more. He hated disappointing his child. That woebegone expression slayed him every time, but he had learned one or two things over the past two years.

"Can't do that. If I give it to him and he's sick, I'll hate myself later, because then there won't be a tear or two. There will be utter physical misery. A parent has to be strong and do the right thing."

"I suppose you're right." But Sarah still looked brokenhearted. She was biting her lip. "I wouldn't want him to be sick. What's the right thing now?"

"Clean him up fast. Take his mind off his troubles. Excuse me while I get a cloth to wash him." Sarah was leaning against the sink. The cabinet where the cloths were kept was right beneath her hips.

She slid slightly to the right in the few inches of space that was available to her, and Luke reached past her legs to snag a cloth. He tried not to notice how the womanly scent of her filled his nostrils, how soft her skin looked.

"Got it," he said, but his voice was a bit too raspy. Quickly, he cleaned one of Danny's little hands. "Can you hand me that rubber duck?" he asked Sarah. "If I give him something to hold in the clean hand, I won't have to worry about him touching anything dirty with that one, so that we have to start the whole process over again."

Sarah leaned over the tub, her pretty rear end outlined against her skirt, which rose up slightly as she leaned. She turned and handed him the duck, her fingertips grazing Luke's palm. Heat arrowed from his palm up his arm and shot straight down to his groin.

He jerked and nearly lost his grip on Danny. When he turned, his son had already smeared the clean hand.

Damn, damn, double damn. Quickly Luke put Sarah out of his mind, cleaned up Danny, carried him into the next room and changed his clothes. At last he could get Sarah out of his house and out of his mind.

"All right, let's walk over to Bea Reynolds. That's where Danny is spending today. On the way you can tell me what happened that made you so eager to see Cass that you felt you had to camp out on my doorstep."

Sarah thinned her lips, but she nodded. Okay, that had been a bit snotty on his part, he realized. It wasn't her fault that he was thinking indecent thoughts about her. She hadn't done anything to invite that kind of attention. Patiently, Luke waited while Sarah gave Smooch a hug and let him back into her own yard. Together they began to walk down the street.

A woman, a man and a child, he thought. But this woman and this man didn't fit and never would.

"I think Cass is in serious trouble," Sarah said. "I'm not really sure, but my mother thinks she's pregnant and that Zach Claxton is the father. She thinks Zach may be abusing Cass in some way."

Luke felt his heart turn into a rock. His jaw tightened. "That could be trouble if he's the father of her unborn child. A guy like Zach likes to have power. The baby gives him a certain amount of power over her."

"Will you tell me where Cass is so I can go see her?"

Luke turned to face Sarah and shook his head. "If there's a chance Zach is there, then no."

Her pretty brows drew together. "I have a right to know where my sister is."

"I didn't say you didn't. What I said was that I wouldn't tell you where she is. I don't want you walking into that guy's territory alone. I'll take you there myself."

And no doubt he would regret doing so. Anywhere a guy like Zach was was definitely not the kind of place for someone as classy and delicate as Sarah. "You're sure you have to go? I could go there alone."

"You told me you already did."

"Yes," he agreed. "I spoke to Cass's friend Penny but without the force of the law behind me, she wouldn't talk about Cass."

"If I went there alone, I could just claim the right of family."

"Forget it. I'm not telling you where she is. If you go, you go with me at your side."

For a moment she stared up into his eyes, her gray eyes dark and worried. "I don't like men who try to boss women around."

"I don't, either," he agreed. "What time do you want me to pick you up?"

CHAPTER ELEVEN

"YOU'RE GOING TO DO what?" Dugan asked Luke, rubbing his hand back through his thinning hair.

"I'm taking Sarah Tucker over to the old Mickerson farm. That's where I think Cass is staying."

"Mad know about this?"

"I think Madeline may have initiated it, or at least concern for her and Cass may be the reason why Sarah wants to go."

"And you're telling me this why?"

Luke grimaced. "You know why."

"Because there might be trouble?"

"I'm not saying there will be, but if Cass is there, she obviously doesn't want to be found, and if what I believe to be true actually is true, and Zach Claxton shows up—"

Dugan swore. "That guy's an ass. Why do you think someone as pretty as Cass would take up with some jerk like that?"

Luke blew out a long breath. "I don't know. Who can tell why a woman gets involved with any man? I'm sure there are good reasons at the start, or that there appear to be good reasons."

Dugan swore. "Yeah, a lot of that going around and has been for years. Women getting stuck with men who aren't good enough for them. Madeline has to be worried. She's had a lot of pain in her life and she deserves some peace of mind."

Raising his head, Luke stared at his boss. Dugan wasn't the kind to discuss feelings.

"Well, maybe Sarah will be able to talk Cass into coming back home. That might make things easier for Madeline."

"Yeah, that would be good. Don't let either of her daughters get hurt though, Luke. I wouldn't want Madeline to have to live through that."

Luke hadn't realized he was staring at Dugan until the man turned slightly pink. "You're worried about her, too," Luke commented. He understood his own reasons for his concern. He was Madeline's neighbor, and she had been taking care of his child. But what was Dugan's reason?

"Yeah," Dugan said. "Just do what you have to do, Packard, and forget that we talked about any of this."

"Dugan, don't worry about it. I'm glad you share my concern."

"Well, I'm not glad about it." Dugan walked away, leaving Luke to wonder what that meant.

SARAH SAT IN THE PASSENGER seat of Luke's SUV, his off-duty car. A family-man's vehicle, she thought, with a child carrier strapped tightly into the back seat. Luke was a family man, a man who would risk everything for his son.

And she was a woman who could easily turn a child's existence into an absolute nightmare. What kid would want someone like her to show up at school parties or field trips? Worse, what kind of mother would want to subject a child to ridicule from his classmates?

Not her. Never her.

Stupid, stupid, she told herself. *Stop thinking about things like that. Concentrate on Cass. Just Cass.*

"Is it far now?" she asked.

"It's out on the edge of town," Luke admitted. "Down some dirt roads. I have to warn you that it's a bit of a shack."

"How did you find out about it?"

Luke's jaw tensed. "Sorry, can't tell you that. I got it from a confidential source."

Immediately panic set in. What kind of a crowd was Cass hanging around with? "I thought you said earlier that you heard Cass was okay."

"I did."

"And you had to pay off a source to divulge her whereabouts? Someone who doesn't want anyone to know? Is this person's life in danger? Is Cass's life in danger? Is someone holding a gun to her head?"

Luke stopped the car. "You think I'd take you into a place where I thought you might get shot? If I even thought there was a hint of illegal activity or a cache of guns or ammo in that place, your pretty little butt would be back home and I'd be going in with a warrant and a cadre of officers."

Okay, so maybe she had overreacted and things weren't as bad as she had thought. Sarah had been doing her best for days to ignore the fact that if she hadn't thrown away her clairsentience, she might have been able to find her sister unaided. Luke's comment about paying off someone for information had sent her into an irrational panic.

"I'm sorry. No, I don't think you would do that," Sarah said. If there was one thing she did know about

Luke, it was that he was a man of honor, even if he had made that sexist "pretty little butt" comment. She could ignore that...maybe. Or at least ignore it for now. Men did not comment on her butt. Men did not treat her the way they treated other women, and they never had.

"I'm sorry," she said again, not sure what she was sorry for this time.

He slammed the palm of his hand against the wheel. "Look, don't be sorry. It was a kid who told me where to find this place, okay? A kid who thought I might pay him for information. I didn't. I bought him a meal and promised not to reveal his identity, because one of those people in that house is related to him and wouldn't take kindly to him squealing. It's as simple as that. I don't think what's going on in the place is particularly savory. It may not even be legal, but there's no hard evidence to support that fact, so I can't barge in there and steal Cass home. On the other hand, I don't think anyone is holding your sister hostage. She could leave if she wanted to. Be prepared for her to tell us both to get lost."

"You think I was stupid to ask you to bring me?"

"No more stupid than I was to go along with the thing." He turned off the dusty road and pulled up in front of a tall, narrow frame building with a definite tilt to it and no paint. Two bony mud-colored dogs lay in the dirt. There were no screens in the open windows.

"Go away," someone yelled from the house. "We haven't done anything. You're not allowed here if we haven't done anything."

Sarah stared at the place where her sister was staying. She couldn't tell Madeline about this hovel. Her mother would be devastated, especially given the fact that she thought that Cass was pregnant.

"We're getting her out of there. I'm going inside even if I have to break down the door," she told Luke.

"Great. This is a hell of a great situation," he said.

LUKE'S ORIGINAL PLAN had been to simply be here for Sarah if she needed help, but now that he was here and things were already getting hostile, his plan had changed. He would be first up the stairs. He'd be the one to pound on the door and try to get Cass to come out. In a purely unofficial capacity, of course.

At least that was what he told himself just before Sarah ducked under his arm and trotted up the stairs ahead of him. She rapped on the door. "Cass! Are you in there, Cass?"

The door swung open. "I told you to go away," a tall, too thin, lank-haired young man said. "I'd leave right now if I were you."

Luke stepped forward, taking up part of the space in the doorway. "You're not threatening the lady, are you?"

The man's eyes narrowed. "You can't do anything to us. You got no warrant and no reason to be here. Zach told me that when he was here last time."

Bingo. Zach had been here, and Cass and Zach were an item. If Luke could just keep this guy talking, they might find out something they needed to know.

Again, that was the plan until Sarah stepped over the threshold. Luke wanted to groan. He didn't. If the guy didn't think about the fact that Sarah was trespassing, he might not do anything rash.

"Cass *is* here, isn't she?" Sarah asked. "I'm sure of it."

Instantly, the man took a step back, his eyes growing

larger. "You see her?" he asked. "You've had one of those premonitions, haven't you? You've got the sight."

His voice sounded half choked, half frightened.

Sarah blinked. She cast a look Luke's way, frowning, but she didn't refute the man's words. Probably because if she did, the guy might toss her out in the dirt and she wouldn't get to ask any questions.

"I know she's here," she repeated. "And I'm going to see her." She began moving farther into the house. Luke stayed at her back. No one was getting close enough to threaten her in any way.

The skinny guy started running deeper into the bowels of the building. "Cass, your sister found us! She's here."

The smell of the place was almost overwhelming as they moved down the narrow dark hallways. Cooking smells, rotting food, cigarette smoke, urine. Out of the corner of his eye, Luke saw Penny Mickerson, who had answered the door the other day.

"This is my uncle's place, and he's going to be pissed if he finds out the cops have been here," she told him. "This isn't good."

Luke looked down at some garbage on the floor and couldn't agree more. This was beyond "not good." He tried to imagine how he would feel if Danny grew up and ended up living in a place like this. Cass and the girl standing before him…they were just too young to be in such downtrodden circumstances.

"You have a home?" he couldn't help asking.

"Yeah. Here. It's nicer than where I grew up. Now get her out of here before Zach comes around or something bad happens," she said, nodding toward Sarah, whose steps had slowed despite the fact that she was still moving forward.

Luke would have liked nothing better than to get Sarah out of here. She looked like a clean, sweet, white rose blossoming in the midst of sludge. The thought that anyone might threaten her because she was here trying to do something good ticked him off. He moved forward and closed in behind her again, shielding her.

"Do you know where Cass is?" he asked Penny.

But Sarah stopped at that moment and he bumped into her, throwing her off balance. Immediately, he reached out and looped an arm around her waist, catching her to him to steady her.

She was soft, her rear end pressed up against him, her hair catching against his lips. He breathed in the scent of warm woman, and a rush of desire spread through his body.

As soon as she was planted firmly on her feet, he let go.

"Thank you," she said, and he wasn't sure if she was grateful that he had caught her or that he had freed her afterward.

But a scream sounded to the right, and both of them turned. Cass was barreling in from another hallway. "What are you doing here?" she demanded. "Did Mom send you?"

Sarah turned to face her sister. "No one sent me," she said quietly. "But Mom *is* worried about you."

"Oh, that's rich."

"I mean it."

"I'm sure you do. But having *you* imply that my brief stay with friends in the neighborhood is causing Mom sleepless nights when you disappeared off the face of the earth at my age is truly laughable."

Sarah blanched and took a step back, bumping up against Luke again.

"Did you bring her?" Cass demanded of Luke. "What did you tell her?"

"What should I have told her?"

"Nothing. You don't know anything. I haven't done anything illegal."

Luke shrugged. "If you had done anything illegal, we wouldn't be talking. You'd be read your rights and be in the squad car. I didn't bring the squad car, and I'm not your enemy, Cass. I have no interest in seeing you get arrested and every interest in your well-being."

"You brought *her,*" Cass accused.

"Looks that way."

"I asked him to bring me, Cass," Sarah said.

Cass moved closer. Her hair was a bit wild, she was too thin and there were dark circles under her eyes. She got up in Sarah's face.

Sarah's jaw went rigid and she paled slightly, but she didn't budge. "This was my doing," she repeated. "We've been worried all along, but after the phone call last night we were worried still more. Mom needs to see you."

"And you mean to be the good daughter and bring me home. To show your concern."

"This isn't a contest, Cass. I needed to make sure you were all right. I wanted to see you firsthand, and yes, I do want you to come home, and also yes, I am doing this partly for Mom."

Cass's brows drew together. "Aren't you the concerned daughter? You haven't taken an interest in your family for years, but now you're suddenly taking an interest? What's that about?"

Suddenly it seemed as if people were coming out of the woodwork. Besides Penny and the man who had opened the door, several more people began to filter in. They stood there watching as if a play were being acted on a real life stage.

Nothing new to Luke. In his line of work he was used to gawkers, but Sarah glanced to the side and trembled slightly. He'd just bet she was used to gawkers, too, but it clearly mattered to her. He had to give her credit for standing her ground.

"I'm worried, Cass," she repeated.

"Save your worries. I don't need or want them. And I'm not leaving. This is my home now. I want you to leave."

The two women stood there staring at each other. Same brown hair with golden streaks, gray eyes of different hues. Sarah's height and age should have given her an edge, but Cass's anger was apparently the more powerful emotion. She would not be moved.

Slowly, Sarah turned away. She looked up at Luke with anguished eyes and nodded. "All right," she said, and started to leave.

Luke wanted to touch her, to take her arm and offer his support, but she was so magnificent standing on her own in the midst of adversity. Taking her arm would be to steal some of her dignity.

When she had moved past him, he fell into step behind her.

She stopped at the end of the hall and looked around him at Cass. "I really *am* worried about Mom. She cares about you, and I'm sorry I never came home. I really am. I wanted to at times, but I just couldn't. I don't expect you to understand that. I did try to write as much as I could."

For a second Luke thought he saw Cass flinch, but he might have been wrong about that.

"Yeah, well, if you're so concerned about Mom, don't eat her out of house and home, because she's not making too much money. Dad left the shop to you, and that, rat hole that it was, was what paid most of the bills. Maybe you should think about that." Cass turned and moved away. Five seconds later, they heard a door slam.

Sarah took a deep breath and walked back through the house and out the front door. Luke opened the car door, but he didn't speak. Somehow he didn't think she would appreciate any comment he might make at the moment. Her jaw was rigid, her breathing was shallow.

He drove on in silence back toward Gold Tree. They were nearing the town when he saw her turn toward him out of the corner of his eye.

"Do you think my mother is having financial difficulties?"

"Cass is young, Sarah. She's temperamental."

"I know that, but that's not what I'm asking."

He hesitated.

"Luke?"

Luke slammed the heel of his hand against the steering wheel. "Damn it, Sarah, what kind of a thing is that to ask a man? To speculate on his neighbor's finances?"

"You care about her. You would have noticed a thing or two. And if you really care, you'll be concerned if she's struggling. You pay her to keep Danny."

"That's not just for her."

"But partly?"

Luke swore beneath his breath and pulled the car over. This woman exasperated him, frustrated him and drove him nuts on all kinds of levels. He didn't want to go staring into her eyes again, but this was too important a topic and she was too distressed for them to have this conversation while he was driving.

"Look, Sarah, I don't know your mother's situation completely, and I would hire her regardless of that situation. She's good for Danny, and that's good for me. But…all right, if I had to guess, I'd say that she's probably not hitting the jackpot lately. That's purely speculation based on the state of her house and the fact that she can't be making that much money selling clothes and working at the diner two nights a week. It probably doesn't mean a thing. Forget it."

But looking into Sarah's worried eyes, Luke wondered if this woman ever forgot anything. And he knew how rough remembering could be….

THE DRIVE HOME WAS mostly silent. Sarah couldn't help thinking about what Cass had said about her mother. Was it true?

Most likely.

Had she known it all along?

Maybe on some level. Otherwise, why had she started sending her mother checks the minute she'd heard that her father had left her the shop? Madeline would hold on to the checks for weeks before cashing them, but eventually she would cash them and send Sarah a receipt. Sarah hadn't been offended by the receipt, because after all, money was so easy to put in an envelope and send off when you had it. The face-to-face stuff was what was hard.

Cass had been there for the hard stuff, and Sarah had not. She'd closed her eyes so she wouldn't see what she didn't want to see, so she wouldn't have to dig deeper, move closer, come home.

Sarah turned and looked at Luke, whose gaze was on the road, that square jaw hard as usual, his expression unreadable.

He had known about Madeline, and he'd done something to help when Madeline's own child had not.

Shame mixed with gratitude.

"Thank you," Sarah said softly.

He turned his head. "No problem. Cass is going through a difficult time. I hate to see her heading down the wrong road. I'm glad you tried and I was happy to help."

"Yes, thank you for that," she said, "but I meant my mother. Thank you for helping her."

He shrugged. "I told you already—"

"I know, but that doesn't matter. You saw a need. I should have talked to my mother about her financial situation."

His jaw tightened. "You live thousands of miles away."

"No excuses. I don't believe in excuses. My whole life people have justified unjustifiable things with excuses. If I go that route, I'm not better than them."

Luke gave a quick nod. "All right. But I still can't take your thanks. When a man is trying to raise a child alone, every bit of help counts. Madeline loves my son. I can't begin to put a price on that."

Sarah thought about that. Her mother had always seemed to be such a retiring, timid woman. A woman who had stayed in the background when Sarah was growing up. But there was no denying that she loved Danny Packard. Remembering Danny's sunny ways,

Sarah was glad her mother cared for him. It didn't change her own awkward relationship with her mother, but it changed something.

"He's a terrific little boy," Sarah said.

Luke smiled, and even from this angle it was a wonderful thing to behold. A woman could become addicted to seeing that smile. It would be a good idea to remember that and do her best not to start wanting things that could never be.

So when Luke pulled up in front of her house, Sarah quickly thanked him once again and hopped out of the car. She took two steps and nearly walked right into a man who was standing there.

Searing pain scalded her. It was all she could do not to grab her head. Somehow, she managed to keep her hands at her side.

"You're Sarah Tucker, aren't you?" the man asked.

Sarah looked up at the elderly man who was nervously twisting at the stem on his watch.

A bad, dark feeling rose up in Sarah. "Yes. I am."

"You're the one who finds things." The pain in Sarah's head grew. She ignored it.

"I don't do that anymore."

"I need you to help me. I'll pay." He reached for his back pocket.

Sarah wanted to stop him, to keep him from pulling out his wallet and taking this to the next step. "I'm sorry. I can't. I'm not able. I'm not what you think I am."

"You don't even know what I want." His tone grew slightly belligerent. His brow was drawn together in irritation.

He reached out toward her, and Sarah's head began

to throb harder in the way she had gotten used to of late. No, she didn't know what he wanted, but she knew she couldn't start this again even if she was mentally and physically capable of it, which she no longer was. She didn't want to have her powers back, especially since in her "finding" days most people had not been simply looking for a misplaced book or article of clothing. More often than not what they had wanted was for Sarah to do something life-changing, maybe lifesaving. Those had been the scary things, the threatening things, the things that had turned her life inside out in ways she didn't want to remember.

"How much?" the man asked. "What would it take for me to buy you?" He took a step forward.

Sarah took a step backward, and the man moved forward again. She'd seen this before. He probably wasn't even aware of what he was doing. People acted this way when they were distraught and desperate. That didn't make it any less frightening.

"Please take the money," the man said. "I'll give you whatever you want." He started to move forward again, but just then Luke stepped between him and Sarah.

"She can't, Harvey. Go home."

"Yes, she can. I've heard."

"Then you've heard wrong. People talk. They make up stories, stretch the truth. She said she can't. You have to take that as a solid no. Doing more than that would be wrong. You know that."

The man's shoulders slumped, and Sarah felt small and wrong herself. Whatever he had wanted had been important to him. If she could have managed it…

She remembered her failures and even the successes

that had felt like failures when what was found wasn't what was wanted…the times people had gone home more heartbroken than when they arrived. It had been a tremendous burden for a child to break a heart like that…beyond frightening, because what was often wanted was for her to save a life, and she had barely managed to save her own. The possibility for bringing even more pain into a person's life than they had come to her with was the stuff of nightmares.

"I'm sorry. I'm truly sorry," she told the man.

"Luke?" the man asked, as if willing to try again.

Luke shook his head and the man shuffled off.

Once the man was gone, Sarah wanted nothing more than to disappear inside the house, but she knew that wasn't an option. She owed Luke something.

CHAPTER TWELVE

"Go inside," Luke said. "And promise Madeline that I'll bring Danny by to see her soon."

Sarah started to turn, but then she shook her head. "You deserve to know about what just happened. If you spend this much time with my family, you have the right to ask."

Maybe, but he didn't want to. It would be opening doors that were probably better off closed. But staring at Sarah's ashen face, he saw that she was right. He couldn't let it go.

"This kind of thing happen often in your life?" he asked.

"Not in years, or at least it didn't happen until I returned to Gold Tree."

"But there's a chance it will happen again." The thought that there might be a line of supplicants demanding that she help them ticked Luke off.

He must have been frowning, looking like a thundercloud in that way he knew he had, because Sarah touched his sleeve. Softly, barely making contact.

He felt it down to his toes. He wanted it, and so he moved away just a fraction of an inch.

Sarah lowered her hand and shook her head. "I can't really blame people. They're usually desperate. They

need something no one can provide and so they'll take
any chance that they can, even approaching someone
like me. That's what this was about."

Luke swore.

Sarah blanched, but then she pasted on a brave
smile. He spent a lot of time with people dealing with
uncomfortable situations and he knew an attempt at
bravado when he saw one. She gave a small laugh.

"Well, I can see by your reaction that you haven't
spent too much time hanging out with psychic women.
This isn't unusual. It just…happens."

Luke didn't laugh. This kind of thing didn't happen
to him, and damn it, he didn't want it happening to
Sarah, either. Not when he could see that it upset her.

"It's not really funny," he told her.

She nodded. "No, I guess not. I never was good at
jokes."

"You don't have to be," he told her.

She looked up at him. "What do I have to be?"

He shook his head. "You don't have to be anything
you don't want to be."

"Sounds like something you tell your son."

Finally he smiled. "It is." But as he strode back
toward his house, it was Sarah who was on his mind.
He had told her she didn't have to be anything she
didn't want to be, but what did *he* want her to be?

SARAH WENT INSIDE the house and shut the door. She
could hear humming coming from the kitchen. Nice
humming, happy humming.

She moved toward the sound and peered in the
kitchen door. Her mother was baking, still slightly off
balance but working hard. It must be painful for her

mother to get things done when her injury had still not completely healed, but she was trying.

Cooking was a nurturing act. Sarah latched on to that thought. When Sarah had been a child, her mother had always been cooking, puttering around the house, sometimes sewing. Sarah had thought of it as hiding out, because Madeline never dissented with anything her husband did. Instead, she tended to those kinds of chores. Had she been hiding out by maintaining her post at the stove and the sewing machine? And was she suffering financially? Sarah had been buying food, but what about everything else?

The shop had been a paltry thing. Her father had worked odd jobs off and on over the years. She'd assumed that he'd left her mother at least some money, but Cass's words brought doubts to her mind.

A responsible daughter would do something more. Something helpful, something useful, something that would make a difference.

Sarah closed her eyes, knowing what she had to do. She steeled her mind. And then as quietly as she could, she took the keys to the shop off the hook where they were kept, retraced her steps and left the house heading for her old haunt. The shop had to be assessed, prepared to be sold so she could help her mother. She had to stop being a coward and go inside the place. This time there would be no detours.

LUKE WAS JUST HEADING off to the grocery store and to pick up Danny when he saw Sarah emerge from her house, speak to her dog and then let herself out the gate.

There was a grim determination in her expression and no spring in her step. Her fist was clenched around something and he could see the silvered end of a key that had to be cutting into her skin.

It didn't take a genius to know where she was headed, not after that conversation with Cass. What he didn't understand was why she looked as if she was heading off to a funeral.

He also didn't understand why he was moving out the door to meet her, but he was.

"I'm heading into town. Mind if I tag along?" he asked.

She glanced up, a startled look in her eyes, as if she had been thinking so hard that she hadn't heard his approach. One delicate shoulder lifted. "That's fine. I'm just going to check out the shop, see what needs to be done if I plan to sell it, that kind of thing."

"I see." So she was going to put the shop up for sale. That meant she would be leaving town soon. No doubt that was a good idea even if he didn't feel very good at the moment.

They walked on in silence. It wasn't that far to the shop. As they got closer, her expression grew more grim. Suddenly she turned to him.

"How did you end up in Gold Tree? Do you like it here? Were you a police officer in your old town?"

Ah, nervous chatter. All right, if she needed to talk, he'd talk. Everyone around here knew a few things about him, anyway.

"I was a police officer in a midsize town called Ace City before I came here. My wife died right after Danny was born, and I wanted to start somewhere new, to raise him in a smaller place where people would know who he was and care about him."

She gave a tight nod and walked on. Two minutes

passed. They were only a block away from the shop. "I'm sorry about your wife," she said. "I really am."

"Me, too."

"I hope…I hope you've found what you were looking for in Gold Tree."

Had he? He supposed he had. People seemed to care about Danny and himself. "Yes," he said as they came up to the shop.

Sarah stopped in her tracks, staring at the little store with the crooked sign. She didn't make any move to go inside.

"I thought I would never come back here," she said. From the sound of her voice, she'd hoped never to return. He didn't know what that was about, but he knew what she meant. He would never go back to his old home, not the one where he grew up or the one he'd shared with Iris.

Sarah took a visible breath and stood taller. "Well, I guess I should go inside and get the lay of the land. I'm not doing any good standing outside, am I?" Her words were barely a whisper.

Luke didn't have a clue what was wrong, but he knew something was. Any kid who'd grown up in a dysfunctional family developed a sixth sense about such things. When he was eleven, he could tell when his father was in a silent rage simply by opening the door of his house. There was something about the atmosphere…just as there was something about Sarah right now.

He wanted to tell her that she didn't have to do anything, but she had already unlocked the door and was carefully stepping over the threshold.

"There," she said as she took one step inside. She

turned and smiled at him, a look of utter satisfaction and accomplishment on her face.

He wondered what a man would have to do to get her to smile like that all the time. He wondered what it would be like to feel that smile against his lips, against his skin…

Stop it, he warned himself. "Things don't look too bad," he told her.

There was a hodgepodge of items in one corner, recycled junk, some decent stuff that might be genuine antiques and a number of craft items as well. A vintage sewing machine shared a table with a set of dollar-store dishes. Dust lay thick over everything.

"How does Madeline feel about you selling the place?"

She looked to the side. "I don't know. I didn't tell her I was going to. I didn't even tell her I was coming here today."

"The structure seems to be in relatively decent shape," Luke said, glancing at the ceiling, examining a wall.

Sarah nodded tightly. She circled the room slowly, but Luke got the distinct impression that she wasn't really seeing the room.

She passed the door to the next room but, instead of going inside, she turned abruptly. "It looks like everything is fine," she said, circling the room again. "I suppose I'll shovel the place out or maybe I'll just sell it as is, contents and all. Maybe someone will want all this junk."

"Could be. Come on. I think there's probably some plumbing in the back. We'd better look at that," Luke said.

She stopped dead in her tracks. "Yes, there's a

bathroom. Not much else. A small room and a closet."
Her voice had grown even more strained. Luke glanced
at her as she stood glued to the floor, her face positively
ashen.

"Sarah, what's wrong?" he asked.

She shook her head. "Nothing."

Which was a lie if ever he'd heard one. "Tell me."

"No, nothing." And taking a visible breath, she
entered the next room.

"Oh, it's different. It's so different. Mom's been
here. I can tell." There was a white worktable set up,
blue gingham curtains at the window. The floor was
pale birch. Everything was tidy, homey. Jars of dried
flowers were here and there. Cheery prints were on the
wall.

Sarah turned to him. "I used to spend a lot of time
here, but it wasn't like this. It wasn't anything like this.
This is so nice. Mom made it nice."

She turned in a big circle, relaxing for the first time.
And then she stared at a picture on the wall. A large
picture. A very large picture with several other large
pictures surrounding it.

Her smile faded. She walked over to the picture and
pushed it aside a bit at the bottom. The room had been
carefully wallpapered in a white-and-yellow-and-blue
pin-striped design. The work was done so neatly and
carefully that unless a person was looking closely they
wouldn't notice that a door had been wallpapered over as
well. But beneath the picture was a small round hole, just
the size of the cutout where a doorknob should have been.

With the picture shoved aside, it gaped. Sarah stared
at it. She put her hand out as if to open the door, and
Luke saw that her hand was trembling.

He looked up. Her face was almost gray. She was swallowing hard. She let the picture fall. It swung down and rattled against the wall.

"Sarah?"

She closed her eyes, and her knees started to buckle.

"Sarah!" Luke yelled, moving forward and catching her. Lifting her up into his arms, he cradled her to his chest. She placed one hand on his arm and he looked into her face.

"Outside," she whispered. "Take me outside. Help me to walk. I don't want to be seen like this. I don't want anyone asking questions."

That was too damn bad, because he had a hell of a lot of questions running through his mind. Lowering her gently to the ground, Luke placed an arm around her waist and took her weight against his body, walking her to the front room of the shop and then out through the front door.

Holding on to her with one arm, he dragged a chair next to the door and gently lowered her into it, kneeling before her. "You're sick?" he asked.

Sarah shook her head. "No, just…no, not sick."

But clearly not recovered. What had that been about? Luke wondered. What in hell had that been back there?

Against his better judgment, Luke touched her, cupped his palm around her jaw. "Tell me."

She looked down and his hand slid against her skin. She was so delicate and fragile-looking. Yet, she had insisted that she be allowed to walk out of the shop. She had insisted on coming here when it was clear as rain-water that this wasn't a place she wanted to be.

"I want to know what's going on," he said. "Something happened back there. What was it if it wasn't illness?"

"This place…I spent a lot of time here when I was a kid. Most of my time, in fact. I just don't like being here."

"You're sidestepping," he told her.

She looked up and stared directly into his eyes. "Yes."

And what could he say to that? The truth was sometimes more difficult to battle than a lie.

Down on one knee, he stared into her eyes and wondered who Sarah Tucker was. Someone complex, someone strong, a million questions wrapped into one woman. She was temptation and therefore she was danger.

"I need to get up before someone sees me like this," she said in her sweetly husky voice.

He slid his palms around her arms, rising and lifting her at the same time. She swayed on her feet. It would be so easy to tilt her forward against his chest, to touch his lips to hers, to hold her.

Sarah's palms came up against his chest. They stood there staring at each other, his heart thudding against her touch.

"We should go," she finally said.

"Absolutely." But it took him a second or two to free her, and even after they had made the short walk home, he could still feel the impression of her palm against his skin.

No doubt about it. It would be a good idea to stay away from Sarah. A woman with secrets in her life wasn't the kind of woman that a man with a child should get involved with, and Luke was pretty sure that Sarah's secrets were just the kind he wasn't going to like. But there was also no doubt about the fact that he wasn't likely to heed his own good advice.

MADELINE WATCHED SARAH approach the house with Luke by her side. Both of them were looking grim, but when Sarah stumbled slightly, Luke automatically reached out and caught her elbow.

Lorena Branford, who had come to pick up a dress Madeline had sewn for her, made a derisive noise. What was a person supposed to say to a noise like that, Madeline thought. She looked at Lorena and saw that the woman seemed altogether too interested in what Luke and Sarah were doing.

"Well, I hope you like the dress," Madeline said, trying to steer Lorena out the door.

"I can stay a minute," Lorena said. "I haven't had a chance to talk to Sarah yet." Or ask her any nosy questions, Madeline assumed.

Just then Sarah came through the door without Luke. She hung a key on the hook next to where the coats would be kept in winter. Madeline hadn't noticed it missing, but now, seeing what key it was, her heart started to thump like a bass drum. Sarah had been to the shop. Sarah hated the shop and always had, Madeline knew. R.J. had made her go there every day after school, on Saturdays and in the summer.

Madeline's hand trembled at the thought that Sarah had been there today. She folded her fingers into a fist to still them.

"I see you were talking to Luke," Lorena said, just as if it was any of her business. "Handsome man, but I'm surprised the two of you get along, with his history."

Both Madeline and Sarah's heads snapped up. "What are you talking about?" Madeline demanded, and instantly regretted it. Lorena loved to carry tales.

She liked to type her neighbors' names into search engines and see what dirt she could dig up. If she had news about Luke, then she had probably gotten it that way.

"Oh, just some stuff about his wife's funeral," Lorena said. "I couldn't find much of the story. Just some little blurb in the *Ace City Times* that mentioned Luke had gone berserk when his wife's friend, who was supposed to be psychic, tried to come into the funeral home. I guess he must hate psychics. I wouldn't get my hopes up," she told Sarah.

Madeline saw her daughter take a visible breath, but Sarah held her tongue. What, after all, could any woman say to a comment like that? If Sarah denied there was anything between her and Luke, it would sound like some sort of defensive lie. If she told Lorena to mind her own business, Lorena would assume Sarah was interested in Luke and that would just encourage her to gossip more.

And what was Lorena talking about? Sarah looked as if someone had hit her. Madeline wanted to spit.

"You got that nonsense off the Internet," Madeline said, trying to make her daughter feel better. "Everyone knows half that stuff isn't even true."

Lorena opened her mouth to object, and Madeline knew she had to shut the woman up somehow.

"You went to the shop?" Madeline asked, changing the subject. She wanted to slap Lorena, to shove her out the door, but if she did, the whole town would know about it in two minutes. Sarah's name would be bandied about some more.

Sarah looked at Madeline. "Yes." The word was clipped.

Madeline could barely breathe. "Why?"

Stealing a glance at Lorena, Sarah shrugged. "I needed to see what condition it was in so that I could decide what to do with it. I've let it sit there too long," she said, her tone light. "It's no big deal."

Madeline noticed that Sarah was playing with a button on her blouse. Sarah had always fidgeted when she was nervous. The shop was a big deal.

"What are you going to do with it?" Lorena asked.

Sarah hesitated. "I don't know. Remodel it. Sell it."

Lorena's eyes lit up. For sure, word of Sarah's plans would be all over town within the hour. In fact, the woman left soon afterward, obviously eager to go spread the news that Sarah had decided to sell the Lost & Found Emporium.

After Lorena left, Sarah turned to look at Madeline, and Madeline tried to suppress the dread that was filling her up inside. She couldn't.

"Don't do it," she finally said.

Sarah closed her eyes. "I'd give it to you in a heartbeat. I never wanted it. I don't know why he left it to me."

Madeline did. She suspected that Sarah did, too. R.J. was a heartless bastard who always had to have his way. He hadn't had enough of punishing his eldest daughter for having the guts to stand up to him and leave town. "I don't want it," Madeline said, and it was the truth. She hated the place, probably almost as much as Sarah did.

Blinking, Sarah looked at her. "I thought you just asked me not to sell it."

Madeline let out a sigh. She sidled over and collapsed on the overstuffed, blue flowered sofa. "I meant don't go back there. I know you always hated it. Do you think I haven't noticed that you've avoided going near it these past few days? If you want to sell it, just…sell it."

"It wouldn't bring very much looking the way it does."

Madeline nodded. "I suppose you're right. Still…"

Sarah paced. "I can't just sell it without fixing it up. I have to get the most money that I can. If Cass has a baby, she'll need money. You will, too, if you're going to help her. The baby shouldn't suffer just because I don't particularly like the Emporium. So, I'm going to fix it up. This is one way I can actually help Cass."

Madeline opened her mouth, then she closed it again. After all, what was there to say? There was a baby at risk here, and babies shouldn't suffer for the mistakes and cruelty of adults.

Madeline nodded. "I'll make dinner." She left the room, silently cursing herself. All her life, it seemed, she had been keeping her mouth shut at the wrong times, not saying or doing the right things. And she had spent a hell of a lot of time in the kitchen cooking dinner to hide her own inadequacies.

Sometimes dinner just wasn't enough.

CHAPTER THIRTEEN

LUKE PICKED UP THE morning paper and nearly sloshed hot coffee all over himself when he read the headline: Sarah Tucker, Then and Now: A Woman of Vision.

A color photo of Sarah taken just days ago ran alongside a grainy black-and-white of her as a cute little kid with long, stringy hair and skinny arms and legs. In the childhood photo she looked innocent and trusting; in the current one she looked wary. He tried not to remember how she had looked the other day when they'd gone to her shop.

He failed. Her life had obviously not been easy when she had lived there. Little kid or not, when people wanted something they often forgot about the needs of others.

He wondered how bad the situation had been back then. He wondered if people had approached her the way Harris Ornette had the other day. Persistently. Without regard for her feelings. A kid, to do that to a child…

Luke looked to Danny, who was making patterns with his O-shaped cereal on his high chair tray. Danny looked up and grinned, completely open and giving and trusting.

"Da," he said, with a giggle.

Luke's eyes misted without warning.

"I love you, buddy," he said, and leaned over and dropped a kiss on Danny's silky hair.

"Wuv," Danny agreed.

A child. She'd been a mere child when all this started, Luke reminded himself. More vulnerable than his mother had been, more vulnerable and trusting than Iris....

Luke forced himself to read the story, to see the cut-and-dried newspaper account of how Sarah had found the little girl's dead body, of how she'd collapsed afterward and of how her father had gone to the store and nailed up the sign the next week advertising that lost items or pets or even humans would be found for a price.

A swearword lodged in Luke's throat. This was not the story Sarah had promised to Wayland. This was worse, and it was going to dredge up a lot of memories. He remembered Sarah's face again at the shop, and turned to his son. "You want to go visit Aunt Madeline?"

Madeline had been hinting that she was ready to go back to work. Now seemed like a good time. For everyone.

Danny's eyes lit up. He squealed with delight.

Luke didn't feel half so delighted. He was getting in too deep with this worrying about Sarah, especially when he didn't believe in her so-called gift and when he had nothing to offer a woman other than pain and regret. He had a way of messing up with women that always left them with gaping emotional wounds, sometimes even physical wounds, and he didn't think he could handle anything personal anymore. He just didn't want that kind of emotional risk for himself or for Danny.

But damn it, he couldn't stand by and watch Sarah get waylaid. It simply wasn't an option.

So to hell with what he wanted or even what she wanted. He had something to say to her and he might as well say it right now.

SARAH WAS ON THE verge of getting ready to go for a walk with Smooch when she saw Luke through the window. He had Danny on his hip, and his long, lean legs were quickly carrying him over the expanse that separated the two houses.

Her heart started beating faster. Should she go meet him? Should she just continue on with her plans to walk Smooch? And why on earth was she even debating the issue? It wasn't as if there was any real reason for her to get all nervous and bothered about the fact that Luke was heading her way.

Except for the fact that she could still remember the feel of his arms around her, his body supporting her. She swallowed hard to dislodge the memory and only succeeded in imagining what it might have been like if things had been different, and they had been touching because they wanted to, not because she was acting like an idiot and he was worried about her.

A groan slipped from between her lips, and Madeline turned from her post at the kitchen sink. "You're not groaning because Luke is bringing Danny over, are you? I know you don't like seeing children all that much, but I promise I'll keep Danny out of your hair."

Sarah shook her head. "Mother, that's not it at all. I

don't dislike children, and Danny is adorable. I just re-membered something I forgot to do is all."

Yes, she had forgotten to stop thinking of Luke as a desirable man the way she was supposed to.

Madeline looked uncertain.

Sarah smiled to reassure her. Her mother blinked and looked almost pathetically grateful. Sarah wanted to kick herself. Had she been that much of an ogre to Madeline? Surely she had smiled at her mother now and then.

But she hadn't, she realized. Why hadn't she?

The answer was too complex to think about now, and besides, dealing with Luke was about all the com-plexity she could handle in one swoop.

His knock sounded on the door.

Sarah tried to figure out what to do with her hands as Madeline shuffled over to answer the door. Her mother's step seemed lighter than it had yesterday, less labored.

There was no time to note anything else when the door opened, and Luke and Danny were there filling up the door frame.

Sarah couldn't help it. She gave the little boy a smile and a wink, lapping up his giggle and letting her heart turn over when he puckered his lips, simulating a kiss. Then she looked up, right into Luke's eyes.

He wasn't smiling. In fact, he was looking some-what upset. She realized that he was holding a news-paper in his hand.

"Come here, baby," Madeline said and she held out her arms. Danny held his out, too. He went right into Madeline's embrace.

That left Luke and Sarah facing each other. He raised the newspaper. "Have you seen this?" he asked.

She slowly shook her head. She had dropped off her paltry few pictures of the Emporium at Wayland's, and he had scoffed at them.

"Inadequate," he'd told her. "I'll need more." But she hadn't given him more. Now, she took the newspaper from Luke, dread filling her heart. It didn't take long to read the article. She already knew the details. The words "wonder kid" leaped out at her. She had almost forgotten that term. "Special talents" was also there, sounding like a compliment although it had often been said with either a desperate cry or a condescending sneer in years past, depending on who had been talking.

She supposed she should thank Wayland. He had left out the more common terms she had been referred to by the children of the neighborhood. "Freak" and "witch" were nowhere to be found in the article, but she had heard them plenty of times, especially as she had grown into a woman's body. Boys had been afraid to get too close, as if she could read their minds and know their sexual secrets. She had also heard rumors that some of them thought that sleeping with her would curse them in some way. That was why Jed had won so much money when he had managed to get her into bed. His bravery had not gone unnoticed by the other boys.

Sarah swallowed hard, struggling past the revulsion that filled her.

"This will make things worse for you, won't it?" Luke asked, his voice strained.

"It won't be anything I haven't dealt with before," she told him. "Even when I was young, I had to fight against looking for people. I refused to do it." She wouldn't mention that her father was the one she had to fight hardest against, and that he had punished her for it. "I just…couldn't."

"No one should be asking such things of you," Luke said, his voice filled with anger.

She looked up, surprised. "Because it's not possible," she supplied for him.

"Yes," he agreed. "But even if it was, to ask a person to do that…after what you had seen…"

Tears clogged her throat. She couldn't remember anyone ever saying that to her, not even her mother. Although she did remember Madeline holding her that day, smoothing her hair, singing to her. It was an old memory, but one of the last close memories she had of her mother.

Sarah bit her lip. "Thank you," she said.

He looked taken aback. "For what?"

"For understanding."

He shook his head. "I don't. I don't understand a bit of it, and the truth is that I don't believe in what they're saying, but I know right from wrong. Asking a child to look for missing persons is wrong. Asking you to live through that again is cruel."

He leaned toward her as he spoke, and for a second Sarah thought he was going to touch her, reach out and pull her close. She swayed toward him slightly. Then Danny's laughter brought her back into the moment. She took a step back.

Luke turned to look at Madeline and Danny. He cleared his throat and then looked at Sarah again.

"If anyone harasses you, I want you to send them to me. You don't have to handle this alone. If things get worse and people start asking questions, I don't want you to feel that you have to put up with such things. You can call on me."

"As a police officer?"

He smiled slightly. "Well, I can't arrest anyone unless they break the law, but as a mere man I can remind them that they're overstepping themselves."

"As a man," she repeated. Stupid to say that. It only reminded her that she was constantly on the verge of overstepping her boundaries with Luke. "I'll keep that in mind."

He nodded and turned to Madeline. "Would it be all right if Danny comes over here tomorrow for the day?"

Madeline's smile turned bright. "Oh yes, that would be wonderful. Then we could get back to normal. Won't that be nice?"

Luke agreed that it would be nice. A bit too enthusiastically, Sarah couldn't help thinking. Was he wishing his life would go back to the way it had been before she had arrived?

And was he going to regret his offer to intercede on her behalf? She hoped there wouldn't be any reason for him to do that. Surely even with this newspaper article, the passing of years would have dented people's beliefs in her abilities to work miracles.

She certainly hadn't worked any in a long time.

IT WAS STILL MORNING when Cass's sister came outside walking her dog. Zach watched from the cover of some trees. He saw her speak to the dog and the dog look back at her as if he understood what she was saying.

A human-dog conversation ensued.

"Doesn't mean anything," Zach muttered to himself, but he'd read the newspaper article. He'd found a newspaper lying on the street when he wandered into town today. It looked like maybe Sarah was the real deal—psychic. She was different from everyone else in this hick town. She had powers.

He wanted power, but he'd never had any. All of his life he'd been nothing and nobody. He'd had no father, his mother didn't care anything about him, his teachers didn't feel like fooling with someone too stupid and stubborn to learn. He'd spent more time in the principal's office than he had in the classroom until he'd gotten old enough to drop out of school.

But now things were different. He was on his own, master of his fate. He could have what he wanted, and he wanted a lot.

If he had power....

His conviction that Sarah was the answer to his problems grew. There had to be a way to make her help him. He had to figure out what that way was, and he would.

But at that moment, she turned and stared at him.

He slipped back into the trees and then when he was out of her line of sight, he slipped away, sticking to the shady areas. She had seen him watching her. Could be a setback...or maybe that would be a good thing. Shake her up, scare her. It could work if he needed it to.

OKAY, PROBABLY THAT WASN'T anyone, Sarah thought, watching the place where the man had been standing. He was probably just some resident she'd never met, someone who had read the article in the newspaper. Revulsion filled her soul. She had so wanted to avoid all of this attention.

But when she turned to walk away, she saw Geralind

Stoddard, an old friend of her mother's, watching her. "That was your sister's boyfriend, wasn't it?" Geralind asked. She was holding a copy of the newspaper in her hand. "I was just coming to show this to Madeline since she doesn't subscribe."

Sarah nodded. "Luke brought it over."

Geralind shrugged. "Good picture of you." She stood there for a minute as if trying to decide something. "Do you still see things? Madeline doesn't talk or doesn't know."

For some reason the woman's nosy question didn't bother her. At least she was being straightforward about the whole thing, and she wasn't looking at Sarah as if she were a scary oddity.

"I don't think I can do it anymore," Sarah said. "I haven't. Not for a long time."

The older woman nodded. "Too bad. I lost my favorite earrings last week."

Sarah nodded back. "Yeah, I've done that from time to time. That's tough. Good luck finding the earrings."

"Are you staying long? What are you going to do about the shop?"

"Restructure it, remodel it. Sell it."

"Hmm. Probably need a permit then." Geralind started down the street. "If your power comes back, let me know. I really miss those earrings."

For some reason Sarah wanted to smile. She couldn't for the life of her figure out why. She needed a permit to remodel the shop and she didn't have the slightest idea how to go about getting one, but if she didn't she would be breaking the law. Moreover, her sister's boyfriend, the one everyone said was big trouble, had been watching her. Both of those things pointed to one conclusion. If she needed to deal with a stalker or discover whether her remodeling plans were potentially illegal, there was one place she had to go.

"And don't feel so cheerful about it, either," she ordered herself as she turned her steps toward the police station. "You are so very temporary here. He is so completely not for you."

Her heart flipped about a bit, but that was ridiculous. She chose to ignore it, and simply headed across town.

When she pushed open the door of the police station, it looked as if half the town of Gold Tree was crowded inside. There was a cake on one of the desks. *Happy One Year Anniversary, Luke!* it said.

Luke was surrounded by what seemed like a lot of women and as many of the officers who were on duty, all urging him to make a speech and cut the cake.

"Welcome to the fan club," Jemma said.

Sarah blinked. "Fan club?"

"The Luke Packard fan club. Every woman in town has a membership card. You remember what I told you."

"Yes."

"Yeah, even if you're not looking for a man, you have to admit that Luke has a nice package."

Sarah fought the urge to look at Luke, especially the part of his anatomy Jemma was referring to. Thank goodness she wasn't a blusher.

"I'm just here to ask Luke a question," she said, trying to keep her voice even.

"Oh. All right." Jemma's tone implied that she'd heard that excuse before.

"It's business."

"Yes." Jemma didn't bat an eye. Sarah wondered exactly how many women had claimed to be here on business to see Luke. A lot, apparently.

She sighed and placed both palms on the counter in front of Jemma. "Look, I need some information about building permits, I think, and I'm not sure who to ask. I also think someone might have been stalking me today. I could be wrong, but it felt a lot like stalking. I'll come back later, but that's what this is about."

Jemma studied Sarah for a moment. Then she gave a quick, efficient nod, stuck two fingers in her mouth and let out a piercing whistle. The whole room turned.

"Luke," Jemma said. "Sarah needs to see you on business. It's important, so stop eating cake and get over here."

No one said a word, but Sarah could have sworn that if it hadn't been too obvious, the women would have stoned her.

"Pretty cake," she said by way of apology.

Luke immediately turned professional and walked over to Sarah. "Hello, Sarah."

"Sorry to interrupt," she said. "Truly."

He shrugged. "Things happen. How can I help you?"

She tried to ignore the watching crowd. Probably most of them were thinking the same thing that Jemma had. Embarrassment flooded her body, which was just so stupid. She really did have business to discuss with Luke.

"It can wait a little bit," she said.

Luke looked over his shoulder, then back at Sarah. "I don't make a point of choosing pleasure over business. Mind if we take this outside?" Not waiting for her response, he turned back to the obviously disappointed crowd. "Thank you for the cake," he said solemnly, then led the way out of the station.

"I didn't mean to interrupt your party," Sarah said as the door shut behind them.

"A police officer is always on duty even when he's off duty. If there's a problem, the problem has to come first. And for the record, I was looking for an excuse to leave. It was really nice of the ladies to bake the cake, but…well, it was nice of them."

He frowned, and she reminded herself what Jemma had once said about Luke not being interested in the women in town. She wondered what had happened to his wife and wondered if he still mourned her. But there was no time to contemplate such things and no reason to, either.

"What can I do for you?" he asked, with the concerned look that probably had women telling him all kinds of inappropriate things.

"I need to know about what I can legally do with the shop, permits and such."

He nodded. "Jemma probably could have told you that, but I'll be glad to help."

"And I think Zach Claxton was spying on me today."

Instantly Luke froze. He took her by the arm and started to lead her down the street.

"Where are we going?"

"Somewhere we can really talk. I'm going to need to know a few things. We're going to make some plans, and all of this might take some time."

CHAPTER FOURTEEN

LUKE LED SARAH DOWN the street toward his house. He considered taking her to a restaurant, but that was too public. He needed a private place where they could talk. Maybe her house?

"Your mother know about this?" he asked.

Sarah jerked. "No, and I'd rather she didn't. Mom's already really worried about Cass. This would just make things worse."

"Do you have a problem going to my house?" he asked.

She hesitated. Luke stopped and looked at her. "Bad idea," he said. "I didn't mean it that way, so you can quit looking like I just suggested you and I were going to do something social. We'll go to the park out on the edge of town." He started to turn.

"I didn't think you had something social in mind," she said quickly, standing taller, taking the stubborn stance he was beginning to recognize and admire. She raised her chin when she did that, a sure sign she had made a decision to be brave. He wondered if she knew she did that. "Jemma already told me that you weren't interested in any of the women in town."

Luke blinked. "She said that, did she?"

Sarah looked distinctly uncomfortable, and he

wanted to smile. "Not because I was showing an interest in you or anything," she clarified.

Okay, he couldn't help himself. He had to smile.

"Of course not. Never thought that."

"It was just…all those women with the cake…she assumed that was why I had come to the station. I assured her that I wasn't interested."

"Good to know. Now, about that park…"

She shook her head. "It's summer. There will be children there. And I'd just keep wondering if Zach was hiding behind a tree listening. Your house is fine. I doubt this will take long, anyway."

Luke nodded. They moved on. Just before they got to his house, he decided he had to say one thing. "For the record, about what Jemma said…I just have a bad track record with women, so I don't get involved."

Sarah cocked her head. "Well, that makes two of us. I have a bad track record with men."

He let that sink in. "Well then, I guess we don't have anything to worry about." But as he opened up the door, let Sarah inside and walked in behind her, safety was the last thing on his mind.

Without the insulating factor of his child, Sarah became the focal point of the room. She was slim and pretty, her dark hair brushing her shoulders as she moved. When she turned and looked up at him, he focused in on those gray eyes flecked with blue. He'd seen those eyes hurt, defiant, scared and he didn't want to see that look in her eyes ever again.

He wanted to take Zach Claxton and bang him up against a wall, because if Sarah had come to the station for help with the man, she was worried and feeling threatened, and it wasn't acceptable for a man to frighten a woman.

A part of Luke wanted to take Sarah in his arms and hold her up against his body, promise he'd never let anything happen to her or her loved ones, but that would be a mistake.

What she needed right now was to feel safe and if he held Sarah she wouldn't feel safe because she'd know that he wanted her. No matter what his reservations were, no matter what was right or wrong. He wanted her skin against his. He wanted his lips covering hers.

"Luke?" She was looking worried. Damn, he had done that.

"What did Zach do?" The question came out like a growl.

Despite his grumpy, overbearing attitude, she didn't hesitate answering. "He didn't really do anything. I just looked up and he was there outside my house, staring at me. He kept staring for a few seconds. It was eerie. He was a little wild in the eyes. Then he slipped back into the trees, and that was perhaps the eeriest thing of all. The way he did it, as if he was being so secretive, even though he knew I had seen him. He didn't try to say anything to me or approach me. He was just watching."

Luke's heart started to thud angrily. "Did you see what direction he took?"

She shook her head. "No, he just seemed to disappear. I didn't know who he was at first. Geralind told me who it was, but by then Zach had gone. If I'd known who he was, I would have chased him and warned him about beating on my sister."

Her chin hardened, her eyes grew dark.

Luke swore. He couldn't help himself then. He

stepped forward and grasped her chin between his
fingers, gently, but enough to still her and get her attention.

"Do not go chasing after Zach, Sarah."

She frowned harder. "But Cass—"

"I mean it. The guy's a jerk, and I think he may be
under the influence of drugs at times. If he comes near
you again, even if you just see him again, run to the
station and find me. I'll go after him. As it is, I'm going
to start looking for him, but I don't want you near him.
He could hurt you."

She shifted, her soft skin sliding beneath his fingers.

Luke suppressed a groan. "Sarah? Promise me," he
said.

She looked up, straight into his eyes. "How can you
go after him," she asked, "when he hasn't done anything illegal?" Her voice was a whisper.

"He scared you," he managed to say. "He may be
stalking you. Maybe I can't arrest him, but I can talk
to him."

"Okay," she said in a whisper, driving him mad.

"Promise me, Sarah," he told her again.

"All right, I promise I'll come find you if I need you,"
she said, nodding. For some reason he didn't understand, her eyes misted over. They were the saddest, pret-
tiest eyes he had ever seen, and he knew he was doomed.

He framed her face with his hands and he brought
his mouth to hers, brushing her lips with his own. She
was warm, sweet and so very soft.

"Thank you," he said.

She rose on her toes and kissed him back. "Thank
you," she said. "No one's ever offered to protect me
before."

Those words nearly killed him, and the feel of her against him slayed him entirely. He swept his arms out and around her and crushed her against him. Awkwardly, clumsily, as need filled him.

She clung to him, and he slanted his mouth over hers, over and over. She returned kiss for kiss. The heat was filling up Luke's soul. He didn't want to hurt her, and with a need like this, someone was bound to get hurt.

"I want you, damn it," he said.

Suddenly she froze. She placed her palms against his chest as if to push.

A moan of regret rushed through his body. To let her go now...

He had to let her go.

Taking a deep, ragged breath, Luke stepped back, steadying her with his hands and then letting go completely.

"I'm sorry," Sarah said. "I didn't mean to do that."

To kiss him or to stop, he wondered. But he couldn't ask. Instead he shook his head. "I didn't mean to start anything, either," he said. "That wasn't why I brought you here. I'm sorry, Sarah."

"It's just because things have been so tense lately," she said lamely.

He shook his head, raked his palm gently down her face, then pulled away. "I'm not going to lie and say it was that," he argued. "I've been attracted to you from the start even though I haven't wanted to be."

She wrapped her arms around herself. "Because of the psychic thing."

A word he rarely uttered slipped from his mouth. "Because I don't intend to start a long-term relationship ever again. I can't do that anymore, but I knew I wanted you too much to be smart."

She kept her arms around herself, but looked to the side. "Okay, I understand that. I was attracted to you, too, and I don't want to let things get out of hand. You have Danny to think about. Having women come in and out of his life can't be good for him, and then there's my reputation as the weird psychic lady. Having his father get involved with someone like me…well, that would follow him all his life. As you can see, the notoriety never ends. It's better that you and I not start anything for lots of reasons."

Her voice grew stronger as she spoke. He knew it would be best to listen to her, because she was right. This thing between them was burning too hot for things to end in anything but ashes. Still, there was one thing he had to say.

"Danny likes you," he told her. "I'm not worried that you're going to hurt him."

"I like him, too," she said with a tiny, sad smile. "But I don't agree that I won't hurt him. I lived so much of my life with this…reputation, so I'm used to the notoriety and the name-calling, but there isn't a day that goes by that I wish I hadn't been born this way. It's why I'll never have a child of my own, because I would never risk passing this so-called gift down to another generation. And it's why I would never willingly expose a child, any child, to that kind of scrutiny. I would never willingly hurt Danny, but if he were old enough to know better I could embarrass him just by being in his life. It's part of the reason I haven't pursued Cass harder. I think perhaps she doesn't want to be associated with me, and I honestly can't blame her for that. What must it have been like growing up and hearing the stories about your weird psychic sister?"

She gave him a smile, and it was the most determined effort at a brave, flippant smile he had ever seen. Then she started to turn.

He caught her hand. He raised it and pressed his lips against her palm, burning a kiss there.

"You'll tell me if Zach bothers you or if you even see him?" he asked, releasing her.

She pressed her palm against her throat. It was all Luke could do not to grab her and kiss her again. "I'm a woman of my word," she said as she left.

When the door closed behind her, the silence settled in. Luke leaned back against the nearest wall. She was a woman of her word? She was so much more than that, and every bit of her was off-limits to him, because if he touched her again, he would need to take her to bed. And he had the strongest feeling that if he ever let himself go completely with Sarah, powerful, unforgivable, irreversible things would happen.

It was obvious that they'd both had enough irreversible things taking place in their lives.

He couldn't cause more pain to himself or to her, and he most certainly couldn't do anything risky when he had a child to think about.

The one thing he was going to do, however, was find out what was going on with Zach Claxton.

MADELINE WATCHED HER daughter coming out of Luke's house. Part of her thought that was a good thing. Luke was an honorable man, but the rumor was that he wasn't interested in getting married again. She dismissed that rumor Lorena had mentioned about Luke throwing his wife's psychic friend out of the funeral. Lorena just liked to make trouble, but Madeline suspected the stories about Luke not wanting to marry were true.

Madeline fussed with the pocket of her skirt. She glanced over at Danny, playing contentedly with two stuffed animals. She eyed her telephone, glanced away from it and then walked over to it. Taking a deep breath, she picked up the receiver and dialed Dugan's number.

After going through all the channels, she finally reached Dugan. Madeline's heart started to thump violently, partially because of what she was about to do but also because it was Dugan. She had been mostly staying away from her computer and her transparent charade of a correspondence lately. Fisherman Pete had sent her a message asking how she was doing yesterday, but realizing that she had almost revealed too much of herself that last time, she had only allowed herself a brief, polite response. Calling the man was probably an even more stupid thing to do, but she closed her eyes and held on to the receiver as his voice came over the line.

"Madeline?" Dugan said after she said hello. "Maddie, what's wrong? You never call me."

That was true. She never had, even though there had been many times in her life when she had wanted to talk to him.

She took another deep breath and glanced out the window. "I need to talk to you, but I can't do it right now. Sarah just came home. She's in the yard talking to her dog but she'll come inside soon."

"No problem. I'll pick you up tonight for dinner."

Her heart thumped louder, harder. She wanted to

say something stupid, tell him that this wasn't a date. How foolish. He knew that. He wasn't suggesting any such thing. Just food, just a way to ease into a conversation.

"No, just meet me around back in ten minutes."

A long pause. "Absolutely, Maddie," he finally said. "I'll be there right away. Maddie?"

"Yes?" she answered, gripping the receiver harder.

"You want to tell me why? Why now?"

No, she couldn't. She didn't know why exactly. "Just meet me," she begged.

He was there in no time, standing in her back doorway, filling up the space. He looked good there.

She hustled him outside, following him. It would be best if she didn't look at him, if she just asked her questions quickly.

"I think Luke and Sarah might be starting something." She turned worried eyes to him.

Dugan studied her. "But you like Luke, don't you?"

"Yes, you know I do, but...I'm pretty sure he won't marry her."

Dugan looked to the side. "Lot of that going around."

Her face grew warm. She didn't know what to say. She started to go back inside. He reached out and touched her to turn her around.

Madeline sucked in a breath. She closed her eyes. It had been so long since she had felt his touch. It felt...wonderful.

It felt wrong. Her children were miserable, largely because of her own mistakes. She couldn't think of her own happiness while they were unhappy, and she certainly couldn't risk making another horrendous mistake

of a marriage. Over the years, Dugan had built her up
into some dream woman. If she married him, she was
sure to disappoint him and fall off her pedestal. She
would fail again.

Madeline stepped away and looked up at him.

Dugan blew out a breath. "What do you want from
me, Maddie?"

She let out a shaky breath. "Be my friend."

He winced. "I am."

"And…let me know if you think there's any reason
Luke might hurt Sarah."

"He won't."

"How do you know?"

"I just know."

"What if he can't keep from hurting her? What if she
falls in love with him and he can't love her back?"

They stood there staring at each other, too many
memories and too many lost dreams between them.

"Sometimes that happens," Dugan agreed. "I'll
promise you this. I'll treat Sarah the way I would treat
my own daughter. That means if she's in trouble, I'll
do all I can to help. Trust me on this, Maddie."

"I do," she told him. "I would trust you with my life."

He gave a sad smile. "Well, I guess that will have to
be enough, won't it?"

But as he left her standing there, Madeline covered
her hand with her mouth. She wanted to call him back.

Instead she shut off her heart and went inside. If she
concentrated on making things up to her children
enough, maybe she could stop longing for Dugan.

THE NEXT MORNING CASS was pushing a broom across
the floors that never really looked clean no matter how

much cleaning she did, when she heard the front door open and murmurs coming from the living room.

Her body stiffened. Zach was here. When had she started dreading his arrival? Without thinking, she whirled to face him. She still wasn't really showing, but she was pretty sure that when she did it would be more evident if someone saw her in silhouette. She didn't want Zach to notice her pregnancy, and she didn't really want to think about the reason.

"Hey, babe," Zach said, giving her a brilliant smile. She'd forgotten that smile. It had been so long since she'd seen it.

Instantly, something melted within her. Maybe he'd just been tired lately. Maybe she'd misjudged him.

She smiled back, feeling relaxed and almost happy for the first time in what seemed like a long time.

"Zach," she said.

"Looking stunning today, Cass," he said, sidling up to her. He put his arms around her and dropped a kiss on her lips. She turned in his arms and returned his kiss.

"What you been doing?" he asked.

"You know what I've been doing," she said with a smile. "Same old thing. Working in the grocery store in Ricksville part-time and staying here the rest of the time." *Hiding from my family and waiting for my baby to grow,* she almost said but she didn't.

"That's good. Working. We could use the money," he agreed. "Keep doing that."

Cass managed a laugh. "Why do you say that?" But a part of her knew. She shared her money with him. Actually, some of her money had gone missing last week. She had an awful feeling he had taken it, but she didn't want to ask. She tried not to think about the fact that he had hit her or remember what he looked like when his eyes grew wild from whatever he had taken. Booze or drugs? She didn't really want to know.

"I just want you to know that nothing has changed, Cass. I love you," he said. "I'm sorry I hit you the other day. I'm so very sorry. I don't want things to change between us."

"I love you, too." She said the words and realized that it had been a long time since they had told each other they cared.

"But I think you should go home now," he continued.

Cass's heart did a funny, skipping thump. "Home? Why? I can't go home, Zach. I don't want to go home."

"Cass, it's not because I'm dumping you or that I'm wanting time to fool around or anything. Don't think that."

She hadn't been…until this second.

"Why do you want me to go home, then?"

"I'm working on an idea. It hasn't completely formed yet, but when it does, I'm going to need your sister to make it work. I need you to help me."

Cass took a deep breath. The Sarah thing again. For a minute she thought she might be dizzy. Zach's sudden smile when it had been gone so long, the apology, the love words…

"I know you told me that the two of you don't get along. That's why you gotta go home. You'll patch things up with her, babe, make it right. Words can make a lot of things right."

Words like *I'm sorry I hit you*. Words like *I love you*. Cass tried to dodge the thought, but it stuck. Words didn't mean that much. Her father had used them to get what he wanted. And when he didn't want anything, which was most of the time, he didn't say anything. And Sarah? Her sister had written Cass many words over the years, but she hadn't made the effort to visit.

"I can't make things right with Sarah."

Zach's smile turned into a taut frown. "You can do anything. If you loved me, you would do it, get her to help me."

The sharp tone of his voice sent fear chasing down Cass's spine. "What do you want Sarah to do for you?"

"I told you I don't exactly know yet. I haven't decided, but I know your sister will be the key. She sees things and finds things. She can do stuff that no one else can do. A person like that...I could use her."

The desperate look was back in his eyes. Zach was starting to pull at a thread on the front of his shirt. Over and over, he pulled, his fingers starting to twitch.

"Sarah doesn't find things anymore. I know that much. Penny told me that people have asked her and she's turned them down flat."

"She doesn't help people because nobody has asked her the right way. The right person hasn't asked her. She's got no reason to help strangers. She'd help you."

The edge in his voice grew sharper.

"No, she wouldn't."

"She came here looking for you."

Yes, but Cass still didn't understand why. Maybe Sarah had done it for their mother. Maybe Madeline had done something to convince her, though heaven knows Madeline had never asked Sarah for anything before. The only reason Sarah had even shown up was because their father had left her that property, and even then she had taken her sweet time getting here.

"I don't know why she came here, but it wasn't because she cared. Maybe just to show that she was superior to me, maybe to make herself look good."

"All right, we're getting somewhere now."

Cass shook her head. "I don't understand."

"It's easy. You find out why she did come here. You ask a lot of questions and figure out what makes her tick. Then you'll have the power and you can convince her to talk to me. That's all I'm really asking, babe, for her to talk to me, to really listen to what I need. She could help me."

Not *us,* Cass noticed, but *me.*

She thought about going back home, seeing her mother's sad, disappointed eyes, watching everyone fawning over special Sarah. "I don't want to go home," she reiterated.

Zach whirled and caught her by one arm. He jerked her around and then shoved her hard, sending her spinning away. She tripped and fell against the wall, hitting her side.

Immediately she reached out to protect her abdomen.

Zach's eyes took in her movements. "I don't give a damn what you want," he said, and she realized that it was true. It had probably always been true. "I want access to your sister. I saw her today, but I could tell she wasn't going to talk to me. She was going to turn me away the way she's turned other people away. But I know what she can do. I read the story in the newspaper this morning. She has powers. I want you to convince her to listen to me. You're going home."

Cass fought the fear and the tears that threatened to spill over. She failed.

Zach walked up to her. He cupped one palm around her cheek and rubbed his thumb gently over her skin. He kissed her.

"You're going home, Cass. If you fight me, I'll tell Penny that you have the hots for Rob and she'll throw you out, anyway. And if you don't do what I say, I'll tell you something else. I'll claim my rights to your baby."

She sucked in her breath, and he chuckled. "You think I don't see you looking at your stomach all the time? You think I don't know why your breasts are growing? My mother had half-a-dozen brats, and I was the oldest. She complained all the time about how sore she got when the things started to balloon. I know you've got a baby on the way and you haven't slept with anyone but me. I have rights…if I want to exercise them."

Anger nearly suffocated Cass. "You think a judge would give you custody?" Although she was terrified, she managed to get the words out.

He slapped her hard, and then he smiled. "You think he would give you sole custody? You left your mother lying on the floor at the bottom of the stairs. Your family is weird. You don't have a full-time job, and with the right words I can get you fired from the one you have. A judge might not give me custody, but I could convince him not to give it to you, either. Then your baby would end up a ward of the state. You're going home, Cass, and you're going to help me. If you do, then I'll sign papers giving up all rights to the brat."

He kissed her again, and then he turned and left the house, pulling a cell phone from his pocket. In a minute a beat up black car pulled up and he got inside.

Cass waited until the car had been gone a long, long time. She looked down at her abdomen and then she went into the room she had been staying in the past few days. She sat down on the bed, rebellion filling up her soul.

But she knew she had lost. In just a while she would get her stuff together and head home, like it or not.

CHAPTER FIFTEEN

SARAH SAT OUT ON THE porch with her morning coffee, reviewing her options, and she decided that running wasn't really one of them even though it was what she most wanted to do right now. Since she'd come back to Gold Tree she had made too many mistakes, and the biggest one had been plastering herself up against Luke's body and pressing her lips to his.

The man could give graduate lessons in kissing. Her body still trembled just thinking about what it had felt like to be pressed against the hard planes of his body.

If she stayed here much longer, she would want to kiss him some more. Heck she already did, but at least she hadn't crawled into his bed…yet. She had a feeling that being around Luke for too long would do awful things to her emotions, and she knew getting involved that way wasn't an option. Getting emotionally attached to the man in any way was just begging to have her heart mangled.

It was time to tie up all the loose threads she'd left hanging in Gold Tree, pack up her stuff and Smooch and ride out of town for good.

The decision felt good, but the feeling died almost as soon as it began. Looking up, she saw Jed Spurgeon walking past her house. Instantly, she remembered that long-ago day when she'd heard him laughing and telling his friends he'd won the bet.

He glanced up hastily, and his eyes met hers. She raised her chin and motioned to Smooch to come closer. "If he comes in the yard, Smooch, I want you to bite him really hard, okay?"

Smooch wagged his tail. He had never bitten anyone in his life to her knowledge. But when friendly Smooch followed the direction of Sarah's pointing finger and moved toward the fence and Jed, the man picked up his pace.

"You're crazy," he said. "Keep your dog away from me." He hustled on down the street.

For maybe ten seconds Sarah savored the sensation of having rattled Jed's composure. Then reality set in. Things hadn't changed all that much since she had been eighteen. It really was time to get things rolling. She pulled a pad and a pen out of her back pocket and started scribbling.

1. Stop doing the Fear Factor thing and get the shop fixed up and sold.
2. Go to Cass and try to have a heart-to-heart.
3. Settle things with Mom. Tell her what's been bugging you all these years and finalize things this time. Tell her that you love her.

Sarah looked at the list and scratched her last sentence out. Madeline had never used the words. She probably wouldn't feel comfortable with them.

Sarah took a deep breath and scribbled down two last items.

4. Take out an ad in the paper and announce that you are not a psychic and cannot really find things for people.

5. Say goodbye to Luke and Danny and go back to California.

She looked at her list, pressing her fingertips to the last item with something akin to pain. She realized that she was already beginning to let her life and feelings get entangled with Luke and his child and with her family. That wasn't smart. She couldn't afford that, because once she left here she would be on her own again, as she had been for so many years.

"Well, get things done, then," she told herself and turned toward the shop. She had already spoken to Jemma and had been told that the building code in Gold Tree was very loosely structured and wouldn't prevent her from doing what she wanted to do without a permit. There seemed to be nothing stopping her from marching to the Lost & Found Emporium and getting started other than her own memories and fears.

Even now, she could feel the fear rising, but she started moving down the street. She had barely gone a block when a woman came up to her.

"You're Sarah Tucker, the woman in the newspaper article."

Sarah recognized the hopeful sound in the woman's voice, and her hands started to shake. Her head started hurting more than ever before, so much that she winced. "Yes," she said gently, not wanting to hurt the woman, just wishing she would go away. "But I don't really find things. Even when I did, it

was more a question of logic rather than anything supernatural."

"Oh." Disappointment made the woman slump,
Sarah saw out of the corner of her eye.

"I'm sorry," Sarah said gently.

The woman nodded and walked away.

As Sarah moved closer to the shop, she saw a few
people watching her, talking to each other, even
pointing. She swallowed hard and kept walking.
Wayland's article had obviously stirred up interest.

She was almost grateful when she got to the street
where the Emporium was. This was a part of town
where people didn't live or do much business. Her
father hadn't been much of a businessman, and the
business had been mostly a junk shop, not the kind of
thing the people of the town wanted on Main Street.

Still, now that she was alone she had nothing to
distract her from her purpose. She slowed her steps, approaching the shop as if it were a living entity. It *had*
been that in her mind when she was a child. Her father's
demands had made it that.

Tension clenched her heart till it hurt, but she fought
it. Dealing with this place, getting beyond her fear was
important.

Sarah braced herself. She curled her hands into fists
and swayed as if she were going to make a run and
break down the door.

"Get ready, get ready," she told herself. "This is no
big deal. What are you waiting for?"

LUKE GLANCED DOWN the street. He had already
handled a drunk and he'd broken up a scuffle outside
the diner. Now he was just observing, making sure that

everything was moving along peacefully in the town. It seemed to be. At least there were no visible problems.

"Hey, Luke," a fellow officer called, on his way back in from lunch. Wes Ariston was a good man. Luke turned to say hello as Wes crossed the street to meet him. "Everything going all right?"

"The usual," Luke said. "Can't get much better than that."

Wes nodded and pushed his cap back on his head. "So…nothing unusual going on. Everything okay in your world, too? Your personal world, I mean."

Something in Wes's tone made Luke frown. "You're not the kind of man who usually asks personal questions of fellow officers."

"I know. And we're not just fellow officers. I consider you a friend."

"Same here. That doesn't explain the question. It's not like you."

Wes blew out a breath. "That's because I don't usually have people coming up to me asking what's going on between you and your neighbor. Seems Sarah Tucker was seen leaving your house yesterday and she looked a bit disheveled."

Anger slipped through Luke. "That's really none of your business, is it, Wes? Friend or not."

"It's not," Wes agreed, "but I know you lost your wife a couple of years ago and I know people, especially women, pay attention to what you do. They watch you. And they remember Sarah. After that article and what some people remember about her, they're going to watch you more closely."

Luke wanted to say that he and Sarah hadn't been doing anything, but that would have been a lie.

"Sarah is an adult and so am I."

"That's true, but people remember what went on here when she was a child. I remember. We were in the same class. She wasn't like other kids, at least not after that day Pattie disappeared. Sarah used to get a weird look in her eyes, pull inside herself. Sometimes she wouldn't talk to anyone in class for days. She all but lived in the shop when she wasn't at school, and, believe it or not, she *did* find things or at least she pulled some mumbo jumbo that made it seem as if she did. Six weeks after Mr. Vinnas died, my dad saw her put her hand on a handkerchief belonging to Mr. Vinnas and then Sarah, her father and Mr. Vinnas's adult daughter went to the cemetery and they dug up a box where the crazy old man had kept his money buried next to his wife's tombstone. Sarah's father made her dig the last few shovelfuls herself. She was, if anything, even weirder after that, more withdrawn. She was older by the time that happened, and it wasn't long after that that she left town."

The thought of a young girl being forced to shovel dirt in a cemetery sent the hot sizzle of anger rushing through Luke. He had a bad feeling that Sarah was another woman who had been abused by men. It made her more fragile. That made her more off-limits. He wanted to swear and not stop.

Instead he focused on Wes. "And you're telling me all of this for what reason?"

Wes looked uncomfortable. "I don't know if Sarah is the real deal or if she and her father were hucksters. She talks to that dog as if it were a human. She's pretty as all get-out so I can see why a man would be attracted to her, but she's more than a little strange, and trouble seems to hang about her. I can tell you've already had pain in your life. As a friend, I don't want you to have more. And, no, I don't ordinarily interfere in my friends' lives or even ask questions, but I was here when Sarah lived here. You weren't. You've never seen her go on a hunt. And you weren't here when she left town and her father went on a tear. He claimed she betrayed him. I wouldn't want to see her betray you. I'm pretty sure she's not here for the long haul. Everyone says she's not staying and everyone wants to see if she does something interesting. If you get involved with her, they'll be watching you and gossiping about you. Luke, you've got a kid just about the same age as mine. Do you really want to risk him being subjected to whispers and questions. Do you want to see him hurt?"

"That doesn't even deserve an answer, Wes. You're treading on thin ice here."

"Hell, do you think I don't know that? It's just… there were rumors she was carrying Jed Spurgeon's baby when she left town. But here she is with no baby and Jed not knowing what the story is."

"He could ask her."

Wes looked uncomfortable. "I think he's half afraid to ask. He slept with her on a bet."

Luke did swear then. "What kind of a bet?"

"You don't want to know."

"You're right. I don't want to know, but I need to know. What kind of a bet, Wes?"

"A bunch of guys bet that he couldn't get the psychic into bed. She'd never let anyone get close before, so Jed smooth-talked her, told her the usual lies. This morning she threatened to sic her dog on him."

Luke wanted to applaud the lady. "And Jed's deception…that's why she left town?"

Wes shrugged. "I don't know. Some guy came to town and wanted to pay her father a lot of money to help find his wife. He was afraid she had been murdered. All that happened at the same time. Who knows why she left?"

"Looks like there are plenty of reasons, more than enough blame to go around."

"I know it sounds bad, and it is. That's just it, Luke. A woman like that…she can't be really normal, can she? As your friend, I wanted to warn you."

"And you have," Luke said. With that he turned on his heel.

"I didn't mean to piss you off, Luke. I know it's really none of my business."

"Yeah."

"Mind if I ask you where you're going?"

"I don't know, Wes. I really don't know."

But he *did* know, Luke thought. He didn't want to know any of the things Wes had told him, but the deed was done. He hated the fact that people were gossiping about Sarah, but they were, and yes, he did have a son he had to be concerned with, but right now…he just needed to find her.

He had questions. A lot of questions. And he had a feeling that the answers, if she would give them, were going to drive an even bigger wedge between the two of them, making her even more off-limits. That was probably a good thing.

But it sure as hell didn't feel like it.

SARAH STOOD IN FRONT of the Emporium, gathering her wits and her courage. In the past she had been a coward.

The Reader Service — Here's How It Works:

Accepting your 2 free books and gift places you under no obligation to buy anything. You may keep the books and gift and return the shipping statement marked "cancel." If you do not cancel, about a month later we'll send you 3 additional books and bill you just $5.24 each in the U.S., or $5.74 each in Canada, plus 25¢ shipping & handling per book and applicable taxes if any.* That's the complete price and — compared to cover prices starting from $5.99 each in the U.S. and $6.99 each in Canada — it's quite a bargain! You may cancel at any time, but if you choose to continue, every month we'll send you 3 more books, which you may either purchase at the discount price or return to us and cancel your subscription.

*Terms and prices subject to change without notice. Sales tax applicable in N.Y. Canadian residents will be charged applicable provincial taxes and GST.

If offer card is missing write to: The Reader Service, 3010 Walden Ave., P.O. Box 1867, Buffalo, NY 14240-1867

BUSINESS REPLY MAIL

FIRST-CLASS MAIL   PERMIT NO. 717-003   BUFFALO, NY

POSTAGE WILL BE PAID BY ADDRESSEE

THE READER SERVICE
3010 WALDEN AVE
PO BOX 1341
BUFFALO NY 14240-8571

NO POSTAGE
NECESSARY
IF MAILED
IN THE
UNITED STATES

Today that wasn't going to happen, but she didn't expect to work a miracle, either. It might take a minute or two before she built up enough nerve to go inside the shop.

"What are you doing here?" Luke's voice sounded behind her and she jerked and whirled to face him.

She looked up into his face and saw that his eyes were dark and angry. He was magnificent. Some of her fear dissipated even though Luke was glowering and clearly unhappy. "What do you mean? Why are *you* here?" she managed to say.

"I'm here because the town is buzzing. There seem to be an inordinate number of people who read that newspaper article and want to ask me questions. I figured that if they were asking them of me, they might be harassing you. I came to find out."

"Why are they asking you?" she asked. "I haven't done anything wrong, have I?" Oh, but she had. She had kissed Luke and made her heart ache with longing. That was so very wrong given the fact that he was un-attainable. This time she wasn't fooling herself. She knew better than to hope for something that couldn't be.

"You're my neighbor, temporarily," he said. He looked to the side. "Also, I think you should know that you were seen leaving my house and looking...kissed. I never should have brought you there."

Her heart felt like a stone. She'd been here too many times before. "I understand."

He stepped closer to her. "No, I don't think you do. You and I have some talking to do...about a number of things. I was on my way over to your house, but on my way there I heard that you were headed over here. Why?"

She frowned and stood her ground, crossing her

arms. "I own this place. Do I have to give a reason for coming here?"

Luke blew out a breath. "Don't ask as if I was accusing you of something criminal. You know why I'm asking. I was with you the other day. I saw your reaction to this place. I don't understand the reason, but this place isn't one of your favorite locations."

In spite of herself, she shook her head and smiled. "That was a tactful way of putting things. And you're right. I hate this shop. There are only bad memories associated with it."

"So why come here?"

"When I sell it, I can walk away from it. But who would buy this place in this condition? I have to fix it up, change it, maybe even demolish part of it."

"You could hire someone to do that for you."

"No, I can't. I can't afford to, and besides, I need to do this myself. I ran away once before but the knowledge that I ran follows me. This time it's important that I do this myself."

They stood there staring at each other for a few minutes. "Do you understand?" she asked.

He gave a terse jerk of his head. "Absolutely."

"Are you going to try and stop me?"

"No." But he didn't walk away.

"People will talk if you stay here with me, Luke. It would be best for Danny if your name weren't linked to mine in any personal way. You saw that article. I have a reputation. No good can come of your staying, especially if people know you kissed me. As a public servant, you have a reputation to uphold."

He smiled then. "I do. It may be pompous, but I like to think of myself as a protector of the people—

including you. And as a man, I also have a reputation to uphold. I don't let idle gossip determine who I kiss or don't kiss." He kissed her gently then stepped away. "I'm staying until I'm sure that you're all right."

Sarah swallowed hard. "Thank you." She turned and faced the shop. And then she walked inside.

This time she knew Luke would stay by her side, at least through this. She knew that he had at least a bit of a clue what he was letting himself in for by staying beside her, and she was convinced that he wouldn't criticize her or ask too much of her.

"What are your plans?" he asked.

"I'm not really sure," she said, "except where one thing is concerned. I want to remove the door in the back of the shop, the one that leads to the closet. It isn't really a closet. It's a shed with a dirt floor. Then when I've taken down the door, I want to go outside and destroy the shed." Her voice had grown harsh and hard and raspy. She probably sounded a little crazy and realized it. "This might not be something you want to witness or get involved in."

"Sarah, I don't know what happened here, but believe me, if you have demons to chase and knocking down that shed will help you do that, I'm going to make sure that you get the chance. At the very least I'll hold the public at bay."

"I should probably explain everything to you. If you're supporting me, then you have the right to know what this is all about."

"You can tell me, but only what you feel comfortable revealing. It's not a requirement for my support. And it doesn't have to be now." He took her hand and together they walked toward the back room.

Strength flowed through Sarah. She knew that a lot of it was coming from Luke. She still felt shaky at the thought of facing the back room, but not as much as yesterday.

She turned and glanced at Luke.

"You're sure you're okay?" he asked.

"Yes." Even though that wasn't completely true. She took a step forward and entered the back room. She faced the door at the rear of the building.

"My father was a dreamer. When I was small, I don't remember him being obsessed with his dreams, but then I probably wouldn't have known. Don't children think the best of their parents?"

"Most do, I'm told."

Luke's voice was harsh. Sarah looked at him but his expression revealed nothing. "Go on," he encouraged.

"When Pattie Dubeaux went missing, I was in school that day. Pattie had her desk right next to mine. We were all scared. We didn't understand what was going on. I kept trying to think of all the places that Pattie liked to play and I did think of a few. I think I even told the teacher my ideas, but she didn't seem to be paying much attention. I got more scared as the day went on and Pattie's desk stayed empty. People—the principal and another man I think was the superintendent—came and went into our classroom. Then Pattie's father came in with the sheriff. It wasn't Dugan back then. He wanted to ask us some questions about who had seen Pattie last."

Sarah took a long, deep breath. She realized that her hands were shaking. She tried to stop the shaking by pressing them against her sides. Luke took her hands, pressed her palms together and cupped them in his own. "You don't have to tell me this if it's painful."

It was painful. She hadn't told the story in a long time, maybe never. No one wanted to relive that day. At least no one wanted to listen in an attempt to comfort her. They just wanted to know about the unexplainable parts.

"No, it's all right. I'm all right," she said, taking a small step closer to him. "I got scared, then. Mr. Dubeaux was crying, begging for information about Pattie. I wanted to tell him something that would make him feel better, but all the things I'd thought of seemed stupid and wrong. He came over by her desk and I realized that her pencil had fallen on the floor. It had little poodles on it and a poufy top like the hair on those Troll dolls. Pattie used to play with it when the teacher was talking. I leaned over and picked it up, and it felt…cold. Not cold like a temperature, but cold like despair. At least that's the way it seemed. I was pretty scared and probably imagining things. I dropped it immediately. But as Mr. Dubeaux squeezed into her desk, tears slipping down his cheeks, I started remembering places I had forgotten, things Pattie had told me.

"I don't remember much after that. People told me I looked like I was in a trance. I told Mr. Dubeaux what I knew, but he didn't know the place I was talking about. The sheriff came back and they took me to the police station. They drove me out to the spot they thought I was describing. It was…pretty, a stream back in the woods. Not terribly far from Pattie's house, but secluded. And I saw her. She was floating in the water and muddy and…she was dead."

Sarah wanted to scream, to stop remembering. She realized that she had loosened her hands from Luke's grasp and she was squeezing his hands with her own. Hard.

Instantly she pulled back.

"Sarah," Luke said gently, brushing his fingers across her cheek. "Stop. You don't have to do this for me."

"No. I want you to know why I'm doing this. After that, the stories started spreading about me. My father, the dreamer, began to dream bigger. He tried to get me to find other missing people, but I got sick. I screamed, and he didn't make me do that anymore. But he did ask me to find things. Mostly little things—like lost family jewelry. People from neighboring counties came to ask for my help. I think I was mostly a sideshow. I wanted to stop, I wanted to play with the other kids after school, but my father liked the notoriety and getting paid for what I did, and he kept asking me to find just one more thing. Soon the other kids didn't want to play with me anymore.

"Eventually, business tailed off. I guess the mystique faded and not that many people had things they wanted to pay someone to find. My father grew frustrated and mean. When I was eighteen, several things happened. There was an incident with Jed Spurgeon. I ended up pregnant and scared, and…my father seemed happy that I was pregnant. It made me sick. I know he was hoping that the baby would be clairsentient, too."

She put her head down, struggling for breath.

Luke stroked her hair. "Sarah, you don't have to tell me this. It's all right."

She shook her head. "No. You saw what this place did to me. You deserve to know why. Soon after that a man came to see my father. The man seemed desperate. His wife was missing and neither the police nor the private investigators he had hired had found her. He was convinced she was dead."

Sarah's voice cracked a little, and Luke took her by the arms. He leaned her against him and tucked her under his chin. "Sarah, shh, don't do this to yourself."

She soaked in the feel of him, drew strength. "I need to, I think. Is that all right?"

She felt him nod.

"I told my father I didn't want to find the woman, but I think he was having money problems, and the man was willing to throw a great deal of money at him. My father told me I had to. We argued, and then…"

She swallowed hard. Luke waited, smoothing his hand over her back, over and over. He didn't offer her platitudes, just the strength of his body and his presence.

"My father had attached the storage shed to hold what he considered his more valuable items for sale. But when I refused to do what he wanted me to he locked me inside. It was dark, there were no windows, and I started screaming and begging to be let out. He told me that if I didn't stop yelling he would hit me, and he would hurt China, the dog I had at the time. I stopped, but I was scared. It was completely dark inside the shed. I thought I heard rats or mice. Now and then he would promise to let me out if I would look for the woman's body. Then someone came and called him away. I was scared, but I found a piece of wood and started digging next to the wall until I had a hole in the dirt big enough to squeeze out of. I didn't go home that night. I roamed the streets. The next day I headed west."

She realized that Luke had stopped moving. She pushed back and looked up and saw that his face was a hard mask.

"Your father was an animal, Sarah. I'm sorry I never

knew this about him, because I would have loved to have had the chance to beat the crap out of him."

She tried to smile and nearly managed, but her face crumpled slightly.

"Shh, don't," he said, stroking her face. "Sarah, I have to ask. Did your mother know what your father did to you?"

"I didn't go home, and I wouldn't have told her anyway. She always told me that I needed to mind my father and be good. She seemed fragile. My father told me that if I told her that he threatened me, he would tell her I was a liar and she would believe him because she was a good wife. I think she might have. Mother always has believed the best of everyone. It was important to her that everything turn out all right."

"She would have believed you."

Sarah shook her head. "The thing with Pattie scared her. She looked at me that day as if she had given birth to a two-headed monster. We never talked about what I did at the shop or that I spent my afternoons there while other kids went out for sports or theater or hung out with other kids. And now, even if she would believe me, what would be the point in telling her? I...I don't want to hurt her. It's over. I ended it. Now I just want to destroy this place where my father locked me up."

"All right, then. Let's do it."

She looked at the door that had held her prisoner. She glanced around for something to hit it with.

"Maybe this," Luke said, and he waded through the junk coming back with an old ax.

"Thank you for not suggesting that I let a man do the job for me," she said.

"I wouldn't. You need to feel the thing breaking apart. Be careful with the ax, though."

She nodded, and took a swing. The door split a little, and Luke applauded.

The bell on the door of the shop jingled. "Luke, I saw the open door. What's going on here?" someone asked.

Luke looked over his shoulder. "Just a Gold Tree property owner exercising her right to do what she wants to with her land. Isn't that right, Sarah?"

"That's right," she agreed, but she knew that there was more going on here with her and Luke. She just didn't know exactly what it was. The one thing she did know was that she liked the feeling of him being there with her...and that it wasn't permanent.

CHAPTER SIXTEEN

MADELINE OPENED HER FRONT door and found Dugan standing there looking flustered. She wasn't sure she remembered ever seeing Dugan flustered before.

"Dugan, what's wrong?"

"You need to come with me." He reached out as if to drag her from the house.

"Where? Why? I've got Danny here."

"All right, we'll take him with us." He went over and picked up the little boy from where he was playing on the carpet. He gave Danny a hug and a kiss, then held out his hand to Madeline again.

"I can't just leave without contacting Luke or leaving a note."

"He'll see us. He's already there."

"Where?"

"The shop. It's Sarah."

Instantly, Madeline's heart started pounding hard. "Is she hurt? Is that why you haven't told me what's going on?"

"Mad, I haven't told you because I figured you might not believe me and I wanted you there because I know how you've felt about that newspaper article. Wayland's writing another one."

Madeline frowned. "Honestly, doesn't that man have

anything worthwhile to do with his time? It's not as if Sarah is really news."

Dugan chuckled. "You might change your mind this time. She's taken an ax to the shop and is chopping the life out of part of it. People are saying she's crazy."

Madeline raised her chin. "They're crazy then. Sarah is perfectly sane."

"I overheard her asking her dog what kind of music he wanted to listen to."

"Dugan Hayes, I can't believe you're criticizing my daughter."

"I'm not. I think it's great that she loves her dog that much. I adore Sarah, but people have been talking about her for years. They'll talk more now."

The two of them stood facing each other. Madeline bit her lip. "I always hated the fact that people made fun of her or were standoffish to her or said things about her. I kept thinking that if I just ignored the situation, the people would realize they were being hurtful and mean. I tried to outlast them. And then R.J...."

She stopped talking.

"You don't have to go there, Madeline. I hated that guy's guts and we both know why, but I won't ask you to badmouth your late husband."

"It's not that. I just…can't think about those years."

"Then you don't have to."

"I can't because I didn't stand up to him, because I should have no matter what he told me or threatened. I've failed Sarah, Dugan. I've failed both my children over and over and over. I can't explain, but I tried to protect them with a blanket of peace and comfort, and everything I did ended up making things worse. I never stood up to people."

"You're a gentle woman, Mad."

Madeline uttered a cuss word. Dugan raised his eyebrows, and Danny cocked his head.

"Now look what I've done. I'm swearing in front of a baby. What kind of woman does that?"

"A good woman, Maddie. Everyone knows you love that baby to death."

"Well, I do, but my own daughters…what do they know? Why did you really come to get me, Dugan?"

"I knew it would hurt you to know that people were buzzing about Sarah going off the deep end. But you're a woman people respect. I thought that working the crowd might make you feel better and might make a difference."

His voice softened, and Madeline wished she deserved this man. She wished she could go back and change things that could never be changed.

"Crowd control," she mused. "Defending my daughter. It sounds like a plan, but it's just words. I've spent my whole life trying to make things right with soothing words, and that's never done the trick."

"You have a better idea?"

She shook her head. "No, but you're right. I'm going to the shop. At the very least I will be there supporting Sarah in whatever she chooses to do. If she's insane, then so am I."

"All right, Madeline, let's go see what all the talk is about. Is your ankle well enough for this?"

"It's getting better, but…let's take the squad car. Is that okay? Is it legal?"

"It is now. I'm going to check out a public disturbance. You're doing a ride-along."

"Good. Can we use the lights and sirens to intimidate the jerks who are there to sneer at Sarah?"

"Whatever your heart desires, Mad."

Madeline took a deep breath. She knew that wasn't really true. She had a number of hearts desires she would never allow herself, but this one?

Yes, she wanted to intimidate. For once in her life she wanted to be a—what would Cass call it? She wanted to be a badass.

CASS CLIMBED OUT OF Penny's car and waved goodbye, her heart thudding so hard she thought it might actually force its way out of her body. She carried no belongings since she had left home with nothing and she had been borrowing Penny's clothes since she had been gone. In fact it hadn't been that long since she left home, but it felt as if a million years had gone by. She was, as they said, a stranger in a strange land.

During the time she had been gone, her sister had returned, and signs of it were evident. A big blue dog bowl sat in a corner of the yard. An old car was parked in the driveway.

Cass braced herself. She opened the unlocked front door and went inside. The house was silent.

A set of crutches was leaning against the wall of the living room. The very sight of them made Cass feel ill. She moved to the couch and sat heavily. No matter how much she told herself that she wasn't responsible for her mother's accident, she knew that she was. If they hadn't been arguing so heatedly, if she hadn't said she was going to leave, if her mother hadn't taken a step toward her to stop her, she wouldn't have missed the steps and fallen.

And then Cass had committed an even greater sin by leaving. Cass let that *finally* sink in. She had been avoiding the thought ever since she left. She couldn't do so anymore. What kind of person was she? How could she even think she was worthy of raising a child?

"But if I don't..." She closed her eyes and breathed heavily, rocking back and forth. Zach was her baby's father. Zach had hit her. He'd threatened her.

She didn't want him to have anything to do with the baby.

Running away from her thoughts, Cass wrapped her arms around herself and strode back to the door. There was no one here, and her thoughts were unwelcome companions. Sooner or later she would have to face the music, anyway. Maybe it would be better to see her mother first in a public place.

Where would her mother be? Maybe the diner... maybe she had gone back to work there....

Cass left the house and started down the street.

"Cassandra Tucker, is that you?"

Cass knew the voice, but empty as the street was, she knew she couldn't pretend she hadn't heard. She turned in time to see Geralind Stoddard, her mother's friend, moving toward her.

"Mrs. Stoddard," she said. "Do you know where Mom is?" Maybe if she asked her a question, she could head off any of the million nosy questions Geralind tended to ask.

"On my way there, right now. I thought you were, too. In fact, I'd say a pretty good part of the town is on their way over to the shop right now."

"The shop?"

"Your sister's."

Cass froze. For all of her life the shop had been Tucker's Lost & Found Emporium. It had been her father's, never her sister's, even though she knew that her father had deeded it to Sarah.

"Why?" Cass wasn't sure if she was asking why he had given Sarah something and given her nothing or why everyone was headed to the shop.

"Sarah's tearing it down. With her bare hands, I've heard. Or at least part of it. Everybody's talking about it."

Of course. Hadn't everybody been talking about Sarah all of Cass's life? When Cass had been small, she hadn't minded. In fact, she had looked up to Sarah and wished she could be more like her older sister. She remembered Sarah smiling at her, taking her side when their father criticized Cass. She remembered Sarah sneaking into her room to read her bedtime stories. The only time she ever remembered Sarah getting angry with her was when Cass asked her to make up stories about Sarah's gifts. She had refused that request. Her body had stiffened, and she had told Cass that she didn't want to make up those kinds of stories. Those were stupid stories.

Cass had been hurt. She had begged Sarah's forgiveness and promised not to ask again. Sarah had come into her room later and apologized. She had hugged Cass and read her what she called a real story. Cass had felt warm inside. She had wanted to be just like Sarah.

But then Sarah had abandoned the town and abandoned her family.

People had talked even more, until Cass grew sick of the talk. Her father had lashed out at her, ridiculed her, made sure she knew that she wasn't special at all, that she wasn't worthy of his attention. Her mother had looked sad and had tried to comfort Cass, but most of her attention had been turned toward Sarah.

"What are they saying about Sarah?" Cass asked.

Geralind shrugged. "Depends on who's talking. Some are saying she's gone completely insane. Others think that she knows something the rest of us don't know, that there's something of value buried beneath the shop."

"What does Sarah say?"

"Heavens, how should I know?"

That was a first, Geralind admitting that she didn't know everything, Cass thought.

"Are you coming?" Geralind asked Cass. "Don't you want to see what's going on at the shop?"

Cass shook her head. "This town…" she began.

"What about this town?" Geralind asked, a note of warning in her voice.

"Who cares why a woman is tearing down a shop? Isn't there anything else for people to do or talk about?" Cass's anger spilled out.

Geralind raised her chin and looked down her nose at Cass. "That shop has been there for almost thirty years. In a town this size, all change is meaningful, especially historic change," she said. Then Geralind put her head down and hustled along, not waiting to see if Cass was following.

A stubborn part of Cass didn't want to go. She didn't want to be another one of the masses paying homage to Sarah. She had once worshipped her big sister, and look where it had gotten her. Forgotten, abandoned and in trouble, while Sarah's reputation had taken on the dimensions of James Dean. Now everyone wanted to know what Sarah was up to every moment of the day.

"Well, I don't," Cass muttered, even though she knew her words were childish.

But there was nowhere she wanted to go right now, nowhere she was needed or had to be, and there was one other thought. Zach was monitoring Sarah's every move. He expected Cass to be on top of things, too. If she didn't, he would try to punish her, and there was only one way he could truly punish her that would stick.

She hugged her arms tightly around herself and bent over slightly as if to hide her baby from the eyes of the world.

"Come on," she said to her child, "Let's go see what crazy Aunt Sarah is up to this time."

LUKE WAS VERY AWARE of what was going on both inside and outside the shop. He could hear the crowds beginning to gather, and he could hear them outside the part of the shop where Sarah was tearing away with the ax. Wayland Gartner's distinct voice was among those gathered outside, so it was pretty clear that the moment was going to be given a write-up in the newspaper. Luke knew that given the vigor with which she was wielding the ax, Sarah would break through the wall soon and that then she would be face-to-face with the curiosity seekers outside.

He also knew that this was a very private moment for Sarah. She was battling the demons of her past, memories that had haunted her. She was attacking the ghost of her father or at least what her father had been.

He knew about that kind of need for closure.

She ought to be alone. This was, after all, a private affair. He would leave himself if it weren't for the fact that in her rage and despair she was swinging the ax rather wildly.

He would stay, but if he could, he would send the crowd away. Luke turned to move toward the door.

"Don't go." Her voice was so soft that he almost thought he had imagined it. He looked at Sarah. She had stopped swinging the ax. She was watching him.

"Don't go," she repeated.

"There are people outside. I was just going to send them away."

She shook her head vehemently. "I hate crowds. I hate their whispering and I hate the fact that they and my father stole my childhood from me. They made it unpleasant. But I want people to see this, to see that I'm not beaten or bowed by the whispers or the gossip or the memories. I want them to know that, for whatever twisted reason, this is my place now, and I will do with it as I like. Within the guidelines of the law, of course," she added primly.

He had to smile. "Of course. Do you think they'll realize all of that?"

She seemed to study him, her eyes going dark as she sucked in her lower lip in concentration. "Probably not, but they'll at least know that I'm in a hell of a rage. They'll know that I'm not going to let anyone push me around this time. There's no R. J. Tucker to get me to do things I don't want to do." She grinned at that, even though the grin seemed a bit shaky.

She looked magnificent standing there, the heavy ax resting by her feet, her fist clutched around the end of the handle, her face and voice defiant. He wanted to tell her that he would not allow anyone to try to make her do what she didn't want to do, but what she needed right now was to know that the power came from within her, not from him. And there *was* a definite power radiating from her.

"No man can make you do what you don't want to do," he agreed. "Any man who tried to coax you would be a fool."

They stood there staring at each other, the very air seeming to crackle with heat and need.

"Anything you give you have to give by choice," he said, and he knew he was speaking to himself, wrestling with the desire to go up to her and just look at her, touch her, be closer to her.

"There are times when I want to give, but I don't think I'm capable. I'm scared of giving," she admitted.

An ache started within him, one he knew he wasn't going to be able to assuage because he had meant what he said. Anything she gave him had to be completely voluntary, not coaxed. And she was probably right, anyway. If she gave, what could he give her? Nothing permanent, nothing she needed for more than the moment.

"It's all right to be scared," he told her. "It's definitely all right to say no. Every man should understand the word *no* or he isn't any kind of a man."

She looked up into his eyes as if to judge whether he meant what he was saying. "Thank you," she said. She stared down at the ax, leaned it up against the wall and stepped across to where he was standing. Hesitantly, almost fearfully, she reached out and touched his hand. For a second she stiffened.

Fear gripped him. He leaned closer, wanting to ask what was happening here but fearful of what she might tell him. He didn't believe the stories about her gift, but so many people did. In the end, he couldn't ask. Still, he had to know if she was all right.

"Sarah?" The word was a deep, strangled whisper.

She shook her head. "No, it wasn't what you thought. I'm fine. It was nothing." She smiled up at him through misty eyes, and he realized that *she* had been afraid she might "see" something.

Relief broke through him at her smile. He chuckled softly. "Thank you, I think. So touching me was nothing?"

A soft, gentle laugh broke from her. "Well, not nothing. It was pretty sizzling and it was definitely earthy, electric, maybe even erotic, but it wasn't metaphysical."

He ducked his head. "I appreciate your attempt to save my male ego."

"You're welcome." Her smile grew. "And I meant what I said. Thank you for everything. Most especially for staying. I was a bit afraid to do this and to be here alone."

He reached out and stroked two fingers down her cheek. "You don't ever have to be alone with the scary stuff."

She nodded. A rumbling sounded outside. She turned her head. "Looks like the crowd is getting restless. I'd better get back to business."

"Yes, your audience awaits."

She laughed again, marched over to the wall and took a big swing. It finally chipped a decent hole in the wood and siding and opened up a space to the outside world and the waiting crowd.

An "ooh" went up from the gathered masses.

"Oh, darn," he heard Sarah say, and he immediately turned her attention to her. She was staring down at her hand. "I think I let my hand rest on the blade when I lowered the ax."

Blood was dripping from her fingertips.

Luke swore and rushed over to her.

"Luke?" he heard Madeline call out. "What's going on in there?"

He looked at Sarah and saw that her face had gone pale as she stared at the blood. "I never did like blood," she said. "I guess I saw too much of it in my nightmares."

He caught her as she collapsed, gathered her into his arms and carried her outside.

"She's hurt," he said to Madeline as the fresh air rushed up to meet him. "I let her get hurt."

The crowd was so thick he thought he was going to have to beat a path through them. Wayland got up in his face almost as soon as he exited the shop.

"Can you tell us what this is about, Luke?"

"No." Luke continued to walk.

Wayland raised a brow but hung on like a bulldog who had just uncovered a bone. "Maybe you want to explain what your interest in all of this is, then."

"No, I don't." Luke pulled Sarah closer into his arms.

"Hmm," Wayland said, and scribbled something. "What town did you say you used to live in?"

"I didn't. At least not to you."

"You're a public figure. The town wants to know about the lives of those who run the show. What exactly is your relationship to Sarah?"

"Look, Sarah's hurt. Go home, Wayland. Go home, everyone. The show is over," Luke snarled as Wayland whipped out a camera and snapped a picture.

But Luke knew that the show wasn't over for him. Sarah had gotten injured on his watch, and that just wasn't acceptable.

CHAPTER SEVENTEEN

SARAH AWOKE TO FIND Luke's arms around her as he carried her in the door of her mother's house. It had been a long time since she had been close to a man, but she knew it wasn't just the fact that she was in the arms of a man that was causing the disturbing, dizzying sensations. It was the fact that it was *this* man.

"Don't move. You're hurt." His voice echoed through her body, creating a pleasant thrumming in her skin. She had touched him earlier and had been pleased to discover that she still hadn't opened a window into his soul. Not that she had expected to. Her powers were long gone, but with Luke, she was always so physically aware of him that she had just been a tiny bit afraid that some small strand of psychic awareness might be the cause of the awareness. It hadn't been, but even the briefest contact of her fingertips on his hand had resulted in a stronger, more powerful awareness than she had ever known, a greater desire than she had been capable of imagining.

She shifted in his arms, feeling her body tingle wherever they touched.

"Sarah, are you all right?" He sounded worried.

She looked up into his eyes. He had stopped walking. He *was* worried.

She glanced down at her hand. Someone had wrapped a clean cloth around it. "There was blood," she said.

His frown deepened. "Yes."

"But it wasn't a deep cut. I pulled away before I could do much damage. I'm sure of it. You don't have to carry me. I can walk now."

He grunted. She took that as a no. "You fainted."

"Yes. It was just a psychological reaction, not a pain reaction or a loss-of-blood reaction."

She shifted again. She was altogether too aware of Luke as a man. She was dreadfully afraid that he was going to start to notice her reaction to his nearness soon. Her move was so sudden that she nearly made him lurch.

"You want me to put you down?" he asked.

No. "Yes, please."

He stepped to the blue-and-rose couch and gently deposited her there. "Madeline is sending for Dr. Hoskins. Amazingly enough, he still makes house calls. He says he needs to walk for his own health's sake."

She unwound the cloth around her hand and looked at the long shallow gash. "I doubt it needs stitches or anything drastic. I'm really fine."

"I shouldn't have given you an ax." Luke's voice was practically a growl.

She laughed. "You couldn't have stopped me, Luke. I spent too much time as a girl being under a man's thumb. It's not going to happen again. I don't want to be ordered around or manhandled."

His skin suddenly looked pale beneath his tan. "You're right. You're an adult. Your life is your own, and you have a right not to expect interference or…heavy-handedness. I'm not fond of men who practice such tactics."

"But in your job you have to play the heavy sometimes."

He shrugged. "Yes, but that's different. When a law has been broken, all bets are off. I'll be as pushy as I need to under such circumstances, but you don't have to worry, Sarah. I won't push you."

She smiled. "It's a fine line, isn't it?"

"Razor thin," he agreed. "A lot of things in life are like that. The choices life gives us are not always nice or easy, but I do my best to play by the rules."

As he bade her goodbye and left the house, Sarah knew that Luke meant what he said. He was an honorable man. And as a man who didn't want marriage, he would be careful not to lead her on. She owed him as much. He had a child, and she was proving to be notorious. No child should have to constantly be followed by whispers and gossips and weird requests. He shouldn't have to put up with the name-calling and cruelty of other children. Plus, she wasn't a woman who could stay here, and she could tell that Luke had already put down roots. He was making a good home for his child. She would only make things difficult for the two of them.

She blew out her breath in a long sigh. Well, she had never been good with men and had never used good judgment. Maybe she should start doing that now and try to stop being attracted to Luke.

Sarah wondered if that was even possible. Her musings were interrupted, however, by the sound of the door opening. Danny was napping, and her mother entered with the doctor, who proceeded to examine her, pour burning fluids on the cut and then bandage her hand, giving her strict instructions about avoiding infection.

When Dr. Hoskins had gone, the room grew terribly silent. Sarah looked up to find her mother wringing her hands together.

"I'm fine, Mother," Sarah said.

"That damned shop. If your father hadn't left it to you, you wouldn't have been in there chopping around with an ax and you wouldn't have gotten hurt. It's my fault he left it to you. I knew he was going to do it. I should have argued against it."

"You didn't want me to have it?"

Madeline shook her head. "It's not that. I knew he did it for some strange twisted reason I didn't understand and that I still don't understand. That alone should have told me it was a bad idea, but…I thought…"

Sarah waited.

Madeline sank down on the couch. "I thought it would bring you home, but it didn't. At least not right away."

"It *did* bring me home, in a way. I have to pay the taxes. That made me realize that I had to make some decision about the shop," Sarah said. Why had she said that? Her mother looked distressed at that statement about taxes. And Sarah had known saying it would upset Madeline. Had she said it on purpose? That was so wrong. Her mother was clearly distressed. She had hoped that owning the shop would bring Sarah home? That implied that she had missed her daughter.

Sarah's throat felt tight, but she didn't follow through on that thought. Her mother was undoubtedly a kind person, but she had never ever stood up for Sarah when she was so young and needed a champion.

"I didn't even think about the taxes. Of course. We'll find a way to do that, then," Madeline said, her chin jutting out. "I'll help you."

Sarah blinked. "You'll help me?"

"Yes. I'm your mother. I should help you. I'll…I'll organize something, a fund-raiser or something. I'm good at organizing things and talking people into things. I just didn't know it until recently when I started working at the diner after your father died."

Sarah thought about what her mother's words meant and wondered what her parents' marriage had been like. She knew her father as an angry, demanding man, but she had only ever thought of the way he treated *her*. At home her mother had been quiet. She had been like…wallpaper, always there in the background but never asking for anything, never standing out. The possibility of what that might have meant punched at Sarah.

"It's okay, Mother. I'm an adult. I can handle this."

Madeline's lips firmed. She looked as if she might cry. "I know that. I just…I want to help. I'm going to help this time. I need to help you," Madeline said again.

"We'll see. I'm not even sure what I'm doing yet or how long I'll be here."

The clicking of the door opening interrupted the awkward conversation. Both of them turned in time to see Cass slipping in the door.

They both stared.

"It's no big deal," Cass said, her voice sullen. "I just needed clean clothes. I didn't really want to come back."

Sarah tried to read her sister's mind and failed. Cass's words and expression were angry, but she was swaying on her feet. She had left because her mother was going to have Sarah talk to her about the lifestyle she was following. Now Cass was like a wild creature, ready to run at the wrong word or a sudden movement or noise. What was the right response? Sarah wondered.

"Clean clothes are important," Sarah said, knowing her words sounded lame.

Her mother took the lead. "Oh, yes, I hate it when my things are wrinkled."

Cass looked at them as if they were slightly insane. "I just couldn't keep using Penny's stuff. When I get my act together, I'll be gone again. I have a job, you know, at the grocery store."

"And you're old enough to do what you want," Sarah agreed, hoping desperately that she was heading down the right path.

Cass frowned. Uh, oh.

"Yes, I am. At eighteen you can do almost anything you like. You don't have to do anything you don't want to."

There was a message here. If only Sarah knew what it was.

She stopped trying to be clever and read minds and followed her heart. So much of her adult life had been spent avoiding thinking about the people she had left behind. Now here was her little sister, all grown up, and she had missed her childhood. If Cass bolted again, this might be the complete end of any relationship between them.

Her sister was still looking tense, even scared, still swaying on her feet.

"Cass, are you feeling all right?" Sarah asked, concern in her voice.

"I'm perfectly fine. I'm always fine," her sister answered. "Which you would know if you knew me."

Which was the absolute truth, Sarah had to agree.

She opened her mouth to say so, but at that moment Cass looked at the bloody pile of rags Dr. Hoskins had left behind. "I'm fine," she insisted again, and then she bolted from the room, heading for the bathroom.

LUKE ONLY HESITATED A moment the next morning before heading over to ring the Tuckers' doorbell. He had Danny with him, but Danny was merely an excuse.

"Sorry to use you, buddy," he told his son, giving him a kiss, "but it doesn't hurt that women fall all over you. You could get me past a lot of doors, if I was that kind of man." But he wasn't, and he only wanted entry through one door today. He didn't really need an excuse, but he knew he was starting to get far too involved with Sarah.

He needed to back off, for both their sakes, but he still had to know that she was all right. Danny would give him that opportunity without him having to look like some sort of overeager fool. The local police officer wasn't in the habit of checking up on every injury on his beat. People might notice. That couldn't be good for Sarah's reputation, and she was already having enough trouble with that.

Madeline opened the door. She smiled at Luke and Danny and took the baby from him. "Come in," she said. "Sarah's right in the next room."

"Standard procedure," he said, knowing that he sounded like an idiot.

"You're a good man, Luke. I know you feel a bit responsible for Sarah's accident, but don't. We Tucker women have a tendency to do foolhardy things from time to time. I'm trying to convince myself that it's one of our charms, but usually it's not. It's just a nuisance." She sounded a bit angry.

Luke raised his eyebrows.

"I'm sorry. I'm a bit overwrought today."

He had rarely seen Madeline overwrought other than the day she had sprained her ankle and was worried that Sarah might appear while she was getting patched up.

Still, he let her comment pass and wandered into the living room where Sarah was sitting on a chair with a pad of paper on her lap. She was trying to scribble with her left hand. Her right one was heavily bandaged.

He frowned.

She shook her head at him. "Don't worry. It's overkill. Dr. Hoskins needed to fuss, probably because he felt silly being called out for a mere flesh wound. I'll have this off by the end of the day."

He wanted to tell her that she would leave it on until Dr. Hoskins gave the all-clear, but she gave him "the look," the one that challenged him to argue with her. Besides, he had promised not to be overbearing.

"All right, I get it. You're fine," he said, shoving his hands in his pockets.

"Yes, but it was nice of you to check up on me," she said softly. "I do appreciate it."

He remained silent.

"Now this is the part where you say, 'I'm just doing my job, ma'am,'" she teased, but Luke didn't take the bait. His concern hadn't had a thing to do with his job, and she knew it.

"I'll see you later," he said, starting to leave. "Don't push it, Sarah, all right? I know you feel you have something to prove to this town, but you don't. I'll help you with whatever else needs doing. I'm a decent carpenter."

He turned to go.

"Luke?"

He looked back over his shoulder. "I *do* appreciate your concern. For so much of my life here I had no control over anything. Now I need to have control and prove that I'm just a normal person conducting business and leading a normal life like anyone else."

"I understand that."

"I don't think you could."

He thought of how his formative years had been the antithesis of normal, of how out of control he had felt. "Yes. I could. I respect your choices, although…"

"What?"

"I'm not sure if anyone else here will ever fully understand what you're going through. Frankly, I think they like the mystique of being able to say they have a psychic in their midst."

"I know. Even when I was young it was like that. People were in awe of me and yet they were afraid to get close. Do you think they'll hold it against me once they finally accept the fact that I can no longer pull rabbits out of hats?"

"They're mostly good people, Sarah."

She didn't respond to that. That told him a lot about what it had been like for her when she was growing up.

"I could never stay here," she said quietly.

A small sliver of pain slipped through him. Stupid. He had known all along that there was never a chance for her to be more than the daughter of his neighbor.

"Well then, it doesn't much matter what people here think, does it?" he asked.

"I guess that's so."

"Take care of yourself," he said. "You don't have to do everything alone, you know. Being in control doesn't mean never asking for help when you need it."

But by the stubborn set of her chin he knew she wasn't used to asking for help. No surprise since she had been living on her own thousands of miles from home for years.

"Cass is home," she said. "Did you know?"

"No. I'm glad she came back."

She stood and came closer to him. "This guy, this Zach, he wouldn't make a good father, would he?"

"You know the answer to that. Does that mean Cass is pregnant?"

"I think so."

He swore. "She's so young."

"Yes."

"It can't be easy being pregnant at eighteen."

"It's not."

Luke breathed in deeply. "Tell me what happened."

She told him about losing the baby.

"You don't blame yourself for that?"

She blinked. "I didn't want the baby at first, and I wasn't living in anything resembling normal circumstances those first few weeks, so there were days when I did blame myself. A doctor assured me that the miscarriage probably had nothing to do with my circumstances. But Cass…I don't know if she's told the father. I don't want to let him near her if I can help it."

"And if Cass wants him to be a part of her life?"

Sarah sucked in a deep breath. "I know I can't really

make those decisions for her, but I would hate to have a child be under the thumb of a man who would be cruel."

Luke would hate that, too. More than she knew. "You'll talk to Cass?" he asked.

"I'll try. She hates me."

"I'll try talking to her if you like," Luke offered. "I know something of Zach's rap sheet, but I'm afraid I won't have any more influence on Cass than you do. She views me as an unwelcome authority figure, but I *have* spoken to her friend, Penny. She's argumentative and sometimes on the wrong side of the law, but her heart is mostly good. She might be of some help. I'll talk to her."

"Thank you. That might help. I wish I could do more. By the time the baby gets here, I'm sure I'll be long gone. I don't want a child to grow up listening to tales about his or her crazy aunt. I wonder if Cass had to listen to that kind of thing growing up. I never thought about it."

And Luke could tell that now that she had, it was going to bother her.

"There *are* things you can't control and never will be able to control," he told her. But the words were as much for himself as they were for Sarah, because he was having a very hard time controlling his reactions to the woman.

He was going to have to do something about that. He was also going to have to find out more about Zach Claxton. Now that Cass was back home, he didn't want the guy showing up and causing trouble.

CHAPTER EIGHTEEN

A SHORT WHILE LATER, Sarah went looking for Cass, but she couldn't find her. Since Madeline had taken Danny out shopping, Sarah couldn't ask her mother if she knew where Cass was. Finally, an unusual whimpering from Smooch caught her attention, and she went outside.

"What's the matter, boy?" She bent down and stared into his expressive eyes that looked so sad and joyful all at the same time.

He cocked his head and barked, ran a short distance toward the old shed at the side of the house and then ran back, looking toward Sarah.

For dog speak, it was pretty clear. She marched toward the shed and met Cass coming out, her face so pale that her eyes looked like bright blue marbles against her skin. She was clearly frightened and stopped dead still when she saw Sarah.

"Cass, something's wrong." Which was such a stupid thing to say. Of course something was wrong. If everything had been right, Cass wouldn't have run away in the first place.

"No." Cass crossed her arms. "I'm fine. Everything's fine." For a second Sarah thought she heard a noise in the shed, and Smooch was still agitated, but when Sarah glanced up, Cass opened her mouth to speak.

"You come back here like the great savior when for twelve years you never even came home once."

"I wanted to. I would have if I could."

"Right."

Sarah wanted to explain, but something stopped her. The something was a vision of Cass as a dark-haired innocent little girl running in the door, calling "Daddy!" and hugging R.J.'s knees. That little girl had loved her father. Maybe the older Cass had loved him as well, and he was dead now. What good would explaining that *she* had not loved him do? It wouldn't help Cass.

"I came when I could," Sarah said, but she knew that wasn't the complete truth. She could have been here six months earlier. Cass hadn't been pregnant then.

"And now you're going to wave your arms and turn the world into a perfect place. Well, don't bother on my account. I like my life just as it is."

"Do you? You were sick last night."

"It's the flu."

Was that right? Maybe it was.

"All right, I'm sorry I asked." Sarah walked away. Forty-five minutes later, she passed by the bathroom and found Cass inside, down on her knees.

"Oh, baby," Sarah said, sinking down beside her and brushing her hair back. Cass looked up at her with anguish in her eyes.

Later, when the episode had run its course, Sarah looked her sister in the eye. "Have you been to the doctor?"

"I told you, it's just the flu."

"Well, then you should go."

"It will pass."

"But if it doesn't, and if it's not the flu but a baby, you need to see a doctor. At least do it for the sake of the child."

Cass laughed weakly. "Oh, that's rich, you giving me advice on being pregnant. You got rid of your baby and now you want to tell me how to take care of mine."

Sarah sucked in a deep breath. She felt as if someone had hit her very hard. Her lips felt frozen, her body refused to answer her bidding. Eventually, she escaped to her room leaving Cass standing alone in the middle of the living room.

Coming home had been a very bad idea…on many levels. She needed to get out of here soon. If only she could do it with a clear conscience.

CASS STOOD THERE STARING at the carpeting beneath her feet. She felt hateful and unlovable and awful.

Sarah had deserted her years ago and had left her to grow up without the sister she had idolized, but Cass also knew that Sarah had miscarried. She had no idea whether Sarah had wanted the child or had been like herself, wanting the baby one minute, but scared to have it and wishing it would go away the next.

What had made Cass say such a terrible thing? Resentment and hurt could only account for a small part of the cruel words that had spilled out of her.

"Zach," she whispered. He had been there in the shed. He'd thrown pebbles at her window and she had gone to meet him to prevent anyone from seeing him.

Inside the shed, he'd told her that he'd been at the shop yesterday. Watching, just as she had been. He'd told her he would be watching all the time, showing up when she least expected him. He'd wanted her to get in good with her sister.

She had done just the opposite. She'd tried to drive Sarah away. What would Zach say to that? He had left already, but what would he do if he knew she was doing anything but what he wanted her to?

Cass closed her eyes and took deep breaths.

Zach had cupped her abdomen with his hand. He'd made a clenching fist, grabbing lightly and twisting. "This is mine," he'd said. "If I want it, it's mine. If you don't do what I ask, it's mine."

She had not done as he asked.

Cass ran both hands over her abdomen. There was a baby inside her, a helpless being, someone who had no one but her.

She'd often felt that she had no one. The thought that someone as tiny and innocent as a newborn should be so abandoned clawed at her.

"I don't want to do what Zach is asking, but...I don't want you to be hurt, either, and you have to come first." What was she going to do?

LUKE DROPPED DANNY AT Madeline's the next morning, too early for Sarah to be up and about it seemed. That was good. He didn't want to talk to Sarah, to have to do any explaining about his plans. Today was, technically, his day off, and Madeline would know that.

"I appreciate you taking him on such short notice," he said.

Madeline wrinkled his nose. "You know I'd take him anytime. What time do you need him back?"

"I'm not sure yet."

She nodded. "That's not a problem."

Luke kissed his son goodbye, packed some gear in his truck and headed to the far side of town. With a little luck it was early enough that he wouldn't run into anyone yet. That was his goal, at any rate.

The gravel spit out from beneath the tires of his old white pickup truck as he pulled up in front of the Lost & Found Emporium. His headlights hit one of the dirty old windows.

A bad feeling crept under his skin. Probably just misgivings. By coming here, he was linking himself more closely with Sarah when they had agreed that wouldn't be good.

But she had plans that had to be carried out in order to give her peace of mind. Her father had abused her, and if he could have, Luke would have dragged R. J. Tucker back from the grave and beat the spit out of him. As it was, he would do what he could to make sure Sarah achieved her objectives safely. She had had her symbolic empowering moment.

What Sarah needed now was a support crew. Everyone else seemed to view her as an oddity or a celebrity, so he couldn't count on them to help her. He would do this himself and then he would free her. Maybe if he did that, she would lose the vulnerable look in her eyes and he would stop wanting to fold her into his arms.

Luke pulled a crowbar and a clawhammer from the truck and strode toward the shop. He pushed open the unlocked door.

A shuffling sounded to his right. Something clipped him on the temple and he staggered sideways, fighting blackness.

Somehow he shoved his leg out, catching whoever it was in midstride. The guy tripped, stumbled, crawled to his feet and shoved past Luke, clearing the doorway.

Luke shook his head, clearing the stars from his vision in time to see a man wearing a brown shirt and ragged blue jeans crashing into the forested area at the edge of the street.

Scrambling to keep his footing, Luke began to run full tilt. Branches caught at his arms and legs, but he could hear the sound of limbs cracking in front of him, so he pushed on. The woods would open up soon. This was just a small undeveloped area before the land sloped into county roads and scattered farm fields.

The sound of a car door opening and then slamming shut not twenty feet in front of Luke spurred him to greater speed.

"Get in. Get in, now," a male voice bellowed. Luke heard a car roar to life, followed by the sound of gravel hitting the underbelly of the vehicle.

"Damn," Luke muttered, sprinting forward to the edge of the road. In the distance a black SUV tore down the road, dust billowing behind it. He couldn't make out the plates for the dust, but for sure there were three people in the car. He was pretty sure that the guy in the brown shirt had looked like Zach Claxton.

He was equally sure he and Zach weren't done with each other yet. But for now, they were. He would go after the man later, ask some questions and demand some answers. For now he had a job to do, and he wanted it to be done by the time Sarah made her way to the shop.

SARAH APPROACHED THE SHOP, and for the first time that she could remember there was no sense of dread, no awful feeling of entrapment. She had only made a small hole in the shed but it was a hole that let in the sunlight, allowing some of her fear and bad memories to escape.

She rounded the corner, and the Lost & Found Emporium came into sight, its squat little frame body sitting all alone in the center of the block. It didn't look like the frightening place of her memories.

That didn't mean she was going to let the shed stand. It just meant that she could handle the demolition without hyperventilating.

She smiled at that. *Thank you, Luke,* she thought. He had made this possible, made it easier for her. And without demanding a thing of her.

The sudden sound of buzzing erupted in the air, loud and nasal and unremitting. It was coming from the back of the shop.

Sarah scanned the scene in front of her and noticed the tail end of an SUV sticking out from behind the building. There were lots of white SUVs in this town. Luke had one.

Something hopeful flitted through her. She frowned. She didn't believe in being hopeful. She believed in living her life day to day. That was the only way to do things. Being hopeful would only earn her disappointment or pain or betrayal or worse.

She edged around the corner of the building. Luke stood there legs spread, sleeves rolled up, wielding a chain saw as he cut what was left of the shed into pieces. He had already boarded up the gaping hole where the doorway had been.

Stepping closer, her movements must have snagged his attention. He cut the power on the saw and pushed his hat back on his head, staring into her eyes.

"Why?" she asked.

He set down the saw and rubbed one hand down his jaw as if giving himself more time to phrase his answer. "You started things here, took control, took back the power that had been stolen from you years ago, but there ought to be some acknowledgment from someone that what happened here was wrong in the first place. Someone other than you, that is."

Luke's voice was clipped, as if he was angry. Sarah shaded her eyes with one hand in order to see him better. Luke's jaw was set in a hard line, his mouth thinned out. She had felt empowered yesterday when she had been chopping at the wall, but obviously Luke hadn't experienced that same sense of empowerment. He'd gotten mad, for her sake.

She blinked, fighting the mist that threatened her vision. "I don't think anyone knew what took place here. I don't even think my father thought he was doing anything wrong. He was the kind of man who had always wanted to go places, do things. He needed money to do that, but he was good at dreaming and planning, not making money. When I balked at what he thought of as a job, it meant less money. I'm sure he felt justified in trying to goad me into doing his bidding in whatever way he wished. I think…a part of me felt he was right, that I was the one who was bad. We didn't have much, and my mother had to scrimp and save and make the best of what was there. I hated my father, but I wanted his approval at the same time. A part of me wanted to be the golden goose, but…"

She swallowed.

Luke shook his head. "A child shouldn't be forced

to face misery and the possibility of viewing death over and over." His voice was low and gravelly. His gaze, as it swept over her, was filled with heat.

But there was something she needed to know. "I know you don't believe in…what everyone else believes about me, so…" She held her hands out, unsure how to go on.

"I don't believe you have powers or visions." The words were vehement, forceful, final. "But I believe that you did actually end up facing some pretty ugly stuff. The situations you were put in were sometimes bound to end badly, no matter what road you took to get there. Whether you located Pattie Dubeaux or that box in the cemetery by logic or otherwise, the fact is that your father had to know that he was exposing you to horrors most parents would kill to protect their children from. And no matter what people believed, someone should have stepped forward to protect you. You shouldn't have been left there alone."

"Are you talking about my mother?" Sarah asked.

"I'm talking about everyone. You know how I feel about Madeline. I don't know what her circumstances were back then, but I know that what happened here wasn't right. You were left to deal with things alone. That's why I came today. You shouldn't have to deal with all of this alone as well." He reached for the chain saw again.

Gratitude and warmth and desire flowed through Sarah. She reached out and touched his arm, breaking her cardinal rule about touching people, a rule she had probably broken too many times with Luke. "I don't know exactly what you believe or why it makes you so angry, but I'll tell you what my truth is. My *real* truth, not the one where I lie to protect myself. When I was young, I *did* see things. I *did* find Pattie by means I can't explain. I found other things by touch, too. It's called clairsentience, and like it or not, I fit the definition. But I wasn't lying when I said that part of my life was over. I've closed my mind to it, I've fought it, I've turned away from it every time it threatened to overcome me and I've won. I don't have the ability anymore. My mind and my soul took new paths, and it's gone now. I thought that would change things here, but I realize now that people in Gold Tree will always see me the way I was. But no matter what they think, my clairsentience is a thing of the past."

She took a step closer to Luke as if to prove that he posed no danger to her senses, which was a complete lie. She might not see visions when she looked at Luke, but she felt desire, incredible, compelling, hard-to-ignore desire. Something more as well, something dangerous, something she refused to name.

Still, she touched him.

He stepped away from the work he had been doing, and waltzed her backward, away from the building. He took her hand and moved with her into the trees. "I know you believe that what you say about your ability was true, but I can't. You were a child, easily led, and I can't allow myself to believe such things. It would be like trying to believe in the bogeyman your child claims to see in his closet. If you allow that to be true for yourself, then it's also true for him, and you lose your power to protect him from the scary stuff. Besides, stuff like that…using things like that can be dangerous."

"You've heard things?"

His eyes were haunted. "I've lived things." His voice

was a deep, harsh whisper as he told her about his wife. "She was fragile," he said. "She was susceptible. I should have seen that and somehow protected her."

"How could you? She was an adult. Forbidding her to see her friend would have been despicable," Sarah said.

"Yes." The word was harsh, almost a cry. "I could have forced her to the hospital. It's what I should have done."

"The doctors had given her a clean bill of health. How could you know something was wrong?"

He turned. "Don't absolve me of guilt."

Sarah sucked in a deep breath. "I don't think I *can* do that. Only you can. Luke, your wife's friend was wrong. Maybe she was psychic and maybe she was a phony, but none of that matters. She had no business practicing medicine."

"I know that. I knew it then."

And this man of action would never forgive himself for not acting. He would never forget that someone like her, Sarah realized, had rendered him temporarily helpless and cost his wife moments that might have saved her life.

"Why did you tell me this?" she asked suddenly.

"I wish I knew. Maybe because you would probably have found out soon. People have told me that Wayland has been asking lots of questions about me. It won't take him long to hunt down someone from my old life who will tell him the story, and then he'll print it. Or maybe I told you so that you would understand why I am the way I am with you."

She knew what he meant. She wanted him but fought against it, too.

"Because I remind you of your wife's friend." The

knowledge was like a painful lump lodged in her chest, forcing her to be aware of the fact that her clairsentience was still cursing her even though it no longer existed.

"No. Because you remind me of my wife. You've been hurt. You could be hurt again, and I don't want to be the one to hurt you. I can't let myself be that person, no matter how badly I want you."

She could hurt him, too. No matter what he said, she would always be a reminder of his painful past, and she would prevent any possibility of his child having a normal future.

"I'm never going to get married, Luke," she said. "I'll never have that normal white-picket-fence existence. And while I'm here, I *am* alone. I'm always alone. And I want you, too. Even though neither of us could ever want a future together, I want a now. A today. For once I want to touch someone without them believing that I'm stealing their soul."

Her voice broke a little, and she held her hands out helplessly, knowing she had revealed too much, uncertain what to do.

But in the next moment, she didn't need to know. Luke reached out and set his hands to her waist. He pulled her against his body. Slanting his head, he leaned down and touched his lips to hers.

"Here and now," he whispered. "Today with no possibility of a tomorrow?"

She leaned into him. "Yes," she said on a breath, and then she didn't say anything more, because Luke's hands were in her hair, his mouth was on hers, and her body was turning to bright fire.

"Let's go," he said, breaking away.

"Where?"

"Any place where no one will find us for a few hours."

She gazed up at him and then she smiled. "I might know a place, if it's still there," she said. "If it is, I'll find it."

As they came out of the woods, Wayland Gartner called out a greeting. There would be no way to slip away without him following.

"Has anyone ever told you that you're an annoying bastard?" Luke asked.

Wayland grinned and winked. "Practically every adult in town. Now tell me, Sarah, what's going on with your baby sister?"

CHAPTER NINETEEN

SARAH'S BLOOD FELT AS if it was sizzling...in more ways than one. Her frustrated desire for Luke made her edgy, but Wayland's words, his implication, that smug look on his face...

She crossed her arms as if to hold her anger in and moved toward the reporter. "You know what, Wayland? My sister is off-limits. I don't know what you've heard, but she's not news. She's a kid going through a tough time in her life. Weren't you ever a kid?"

Wayland shrugged, so close that his coat brushed her shoulder.

An arrow of pain shot up to Sarah's temple. Nothing else. Just pain. Not awareness, not knowledge of his thoughts or feelings. And even though the pain of such encounters had been growing progressively worse in recent weeks, she still hadn't expected anything this severe.

"Doesn't matter," Wayland said. "I'm just doing my job. And Cass might not be news in California, but here she's hanging with a bad crowd. There are questions about how your mother got injured. Cass is looking haunted and has been looking more so since her psychic sister came home...could be a story in there somewhere."

Anger rushed through Sarah, but she didn't know how to stop the man.

"Cass isn't a public figure. She's barely past childhood," Luke said, placing himself between Sarah and Wayland. "I would think long and hard about harassing her. There are limits, Wayland. Don't make me hurt you." Luke gave Wayland a long, slow smile. "Figuratively, that is."

Wayland's brows grew together. He visibly bristled. "Are you threatening me, Luke?"

Luke held out his hands palm up and shrugged. "Just doing my job, Wayland. Leave Cass alone. She's a vulnerable girl trying to grow into adulthood, and she's struggling with it. That's not news. That's a story that's being repeated in thousands of households across the country. It's depressing. Worse, it's boring, don't you think?"

"But if there's more…" The reporter looked hopeful but slightly uncertain.

"Cass came back home yesterday," Sarah said. "She's working at the grocery store. Maybe you could do a piece on how people survive on minimum wages."

Wayland growled. "That's pretty much everyone in town. All right, I'll leave her alone. For now. I've got several more interesting pieces in the hopper," he said, looking meaningfully at Luke. "But if Cass starts acting up again or does anything weird, I'm on her like butter on bread."

He strode away. Sarah waited until he had gone. "You could have saved yourself. Writing about Cass and her friends would have distracted him from your own story."

"Yes, but my news is old news. There are those in

town who probably know much of it, and I'll survive anything Wayland writes about me. Cass is fragile."

And so are you. Luke didn't say the words, but Sarah knew that was what he was thinking. Once again, she owed Luke a debt of gratitude. That was worrisome. Her ties to this man were growing stronger. She needed to have no ties when she left here. And she had to leave.

Wayland was gone, but the pain in her temple throbbed on.

CASS AWOKE THE NEXT day to find the shades in her room had been drawn. There was a small plate next to her bed containing a bagel cut into small pieces, some grapes and a cup of something aromatic.

"Raspberry tea." Sarah's voice came from the doorway.

"How long have you been here?" Cass asked.

"Just now. I probably woke you bringing in the food," Sarah said. "That was probably not smart."

"I can't eat. I'll be sick."

"Just nibbles. If you eat nothing, you'll be sick all day," her sister said. "At least…that's how it was for me."

Cass covered her eyes. "I don't want you to be here, Sarah, but that comment I made about your baby…"

"What comment? I don't remember any comment. But just for the record, I *didn't* want to have a baby. I was scared at first. I was pregnant by a boy who took advantage of my ignorance and I hated him. But in the end I did want the baby. A lot. I was sorry to lose it, but I can understand why you said what you did. I was angry at the world and everyone in it during that time. If our positions had been reversed, I would have said

the same thing. Try to eat a little," she said, and she
gently closed the door as she left the room.

Cass lay there, feeling like hell, both mentally and
physically. Rebellion warred with guilt and fear. In the
end, she reached over and nibbled a tiny bit of the
bagel. She swung her legs over the bed and began to
rise. It was the last thing she wanted, but what she
wanted was beginning to matter less every day. She had
a life other than her own to worry about.

Was that how Sarah had felt when she had been across
the country and far away from anyone familiar to her?

Ugh! She did not want to start feeling sympathy for
her sister. Sarah had never acted like a sister before.

But now she was.

And Zach wanted to use Sarah. If Cass tried to stop
him…she looked down at her stomach.

"I won't sacrifice you." She whispered the words,
her voice fierce as a tear trickled down her cheek.

Stupid Sarah. Why did she have to come home?

IT WAS TIME TO GO. Probably past time to go, Sarah
admitted two days later as she took Smooch for a walk.
Cass was back home, her mother was mending and
while relationships between the three of them were
awkward and tense, that was probably something that
couldn't be changed. The only thing still to be taken
care of was the shop.

And Luke, a piece of her heart whispered.

But that wasn't true. Luke couldn't be unfinished
business. She didn't want him to be, and he didn't want
to be. They had shared that moment of desire…but the
opportunity for anything more had passed. That was
probably a good thing.

"So get going. Make some decisions about the blasted shop," Sarah muttered.

"Woof," Smooch barked, tugging on his leash as Sarah's thoughts slowed her pace down.

"Well, you didn't have to agree so readily," she told him. "I'm thinking, I'm thinking."

Two people passed her, looking at her strangely. She ignored them. Hey, she had spent most of her life having people look at her strangely, hadn't she? Lately, with Luke's support and her mother's quiet but eager attempts to make her life easier, ignoring the stares had become almost routine. Even Cass in a strange, inexplicable way had helped her deal with things. What were a few stares, after all, compared to being pregnant by a possible drug addict like Zach? Sarah thought.

And Cass, though she had complained about the little plates of food Sarah and Madeline left in her room, had started eating the stuff. Cass had highlighted some of the article on easing morning sickness that Sarah had given her. She had made an appointment with a doctor. And she'd stopped snarling at Sarah, although not talking to her wasn't much better. In some ways it was worse.

Sarah sighed. "I don't think I can just tear the shop down, Smooch," she said. "I have very little money, Mom has almost no money, Cass doesn't have much money. There's a baby on the way. The shop could help."

But the thought of resuming her old role filled her with dread, almost a physical illness.

Not that, she thought. But something…

The shop was filled with junk. Maybe some of that junk could be turned into something better. Maybe she could use her old skills of logic to locate some worth-while antiques. And since Cass was only working part-time, maybe she could become a part of things, too, help out somehow. She could take over the shop once Sarah got things up and running and left.

Cass is barely even speaking to me.

Sarah shook her head. "Let's go see what we can do. There's a lot of work ahead. I can start things on my own. Once I see if any of this is feasible, then I'll try to ask Mom and Cass if they want to help."

She moved toward the shop, let herself in, took Smooch's leash off so he could roam, opened all the curtains and windows and surveyed the situation.

The shop was loaded with dust and dirt and lots of things that looked totally worthless. Things looked grim.

Sarah blew out a deep breath, ignored the headache that had become an almost constant companion lately and put her hands on her hips. "I've dealt with grim before. I might as well wade in and see if there's any possibility that I'm not totally out of my mind for trying to do this."

LUKE HAD SOME VACATION time coming, and it had been a long while since he had taken time off or even wanted to. But lately his mind had been messed up. Thoughts of Sarah filled his senses constantly. He wanted her every minute of every day and that just wasn't a good way to be when a man had the job he did. Even in a town where crime was on the light side.

It was obvious he still had issues from his past hanging over his head. He needed time to sort things out, to do whatever he needed to in order to get Sarah out of his thoughts, and he needed some quality time with his son.

"So a few days digging out, buddy," he told Danny, "and then just some you-and-me time." His son was all he was going to allow himself in the way of deep personal relationships. If he had had any thoughts about changing that, the incident with Sarah the other day had set him straight. After Wayland had intruded, Luke had been no good for anyone or anything for most of that day and the next. He had caught himself brooding. He'd been totally frustrated, even becoming grumpy with Danny, and he had caught himself daydreaming about peeling off Sarah's clothing until he had wanted to bellow with rage at the impossibility of it all.

He needed to get the woman out of his head. If that meant helping her finish up here with whatever she needed to finish, so be it.

After confirming what he had already set up with Dugan and Jemma and the other officers in terms of covering his workload, Luke picked up his son and headed over to the Tucker house. When Madeline opened the door she was looking a bit more flustered than normal.

"Are you all right, Madeline?"

"Yes. No. I'm not sure. Sarah went out for a walk with Smooch and she's been gone longer than I thought she would be. Cass seems to think there might be some problem."

"Not a problem exactly," Cass said, coming into the room with a frown. "It's just that she said she was walking the dog and I didn't think it would take that long. Things could happen."

"Sarah's an adult," he reasoned. "Maybe she just needed to be alone."

"Or maybe she's found another ax," Madeline said, her frown growing. She and Luke exchanged a glance.

"I think I'll just take a walk over to the shop," he said.

"I'll come with you," Madeline said. She joined him and they headed toward the shop. Almost a block later, he heard the sound of footsteps and turned to see Cass heading their way.

"It's on my way," she said, her expression revealing nothing. But she kept turning around and looking behind her as they walked. Luke was sure she was looking for Zach. He really did need to find that guy just to keep tabs on where he was.

He was mentally ticking off a list of places a guy like Zach might choose to hide when they rounded the corner and came upon the shop. A pile of junk lay outside the front door, and as they watched, an old pizza pan with a hole in the middle came flying out and landed on the top of the pile. Metal met metal with a clash.

Two seconds later, he heard Sarah's voice. "Damn it," she said. "Not again."

He picked up speed. "Sarah, are you all right?" he yelled as he entered the door of the shop.

She looked up while he was still framed in the doorway. She froze in place.

"Luke, what are you doing here?"

He realized she was holding one hand in the other. A thin trickle of blood dripped down onto the old gray linoleum. A broken band saw lay on the ground next to her.

"How stupid of me. I was just moving it and it slipped," she said, staring at her fingers as if she couldn't believe her eyes.

Luke wanted to growl. "Have you had a tetanus shot lately?" he asked.

"Yes, Dr. Hoskins gave me one just the other day. Just in case."

He grunted. "Let me see that." He shifted Danny in his arms and held out his hand, indicating that she should put her hand in his.

"No. It doesn't hurt." He blinked, and then he understood. She didn't want to touch him.

His eyes met hers and while they stood there staring at each other, Madeline rushed forward. "I came prepared this time," she said, pulling a first aid kit out of her purse. "Cass, don't come in here. Sarah is bleeding again. Just give me a few minutes. Or if you do come in, just sit down inside the door and don't look."

Cass shook her head. "If I get sick, I get sick, but I don't want to be treated like a child." She stared straight at her mother. "I'm going to be a mother."

For a second, Madeline stopped working on Sarah's hand and looked at her younger daughter. "Yes, all right then. You'll need to know how to deal with blood and cuts." She made room, and Cass slid in beside her.

"Cass, you don't have to do this," Sarah said. "I'm sure you'll be a fine mother, but right now you're pregnant. It's different."

Cass gritted her teeth and shook her head. She took up the roll of gauze that her mother handed her and, somewhat clumsily, finished bandaging her sister's hand.

"That's good," Madeline said.

"Thank you," Sarah told her mother and sister. She looked up at Luke, who had been watching the interaction between the three women. "All right, I'm good to go. Back to work."

"No," he said.

She blinked and frowned. "No?"

"No. You're hurt. I'll work."

"But—"

"Luke's right. No," said Madeline.

"I'm perfectly fine."

Cass blew out a breath. "Do you always have to be center stage, Sarah? Even when we were little you were the one who was always right in the middle of everything."

Uh, oh. Luke didn't know what this was about, but it sounded private. "I'll just go start on things outside." He shifted Danny in his arms and gave Sarah another glance.

She was biting her lip and shifting from one foot to the other.

"No, you're right, Cass. I'm just not used to asking for help. I'll do something less physical. But you…"

"I won't do anything that will harm the baby," Cass agreed. "But today I can do more than you can. What are we doing, anyway?"

Sarah explained about trying to open the shop. Madeline looked worried. Cass looked ticked off.

"It's for the baby," Sarah said.

"Oh. Yes," Madeline agreed. Cass gave her sister an unexplainable look, but the two women moved over to where Sarah had started sorting things.

Sarah stood there for a minute. Then, she scanned the

perimeter of the room as if trying to find something to do that wouldn't create a problem. Luke looked at his son, but he knew Sarah wasn't completely comfortable with children. If she had lost a child, then even being around a baby might bring back painful memories. He knew she had her reasons for never wanting another baby....

"You can direct us," he told her. "You're the one who knows what your master plan for this place is."

Sarah looked uncertain. "I'm not much good at supervision."

"Nonsense, Sarah," her mother said. "You just don't like to sit on your hands. You watch Danny. He might get hurt, otherwise."

For a minute Sarah looked scared, stricken.

"He's only a baby," Cass said. "Are you going to look that scared when my baby arrives?"

Sarah exchanged a look with Luke. He had a good idea what she was thinking. She planned to leave before Cass's baby arrived.

But she held out her arms, and Luke handed his son over.

"Sar," Danny said.

Sarah looked startled at Danny's attempt at her name. She took him into her arms and held on to him as if he were a fragile bit of blown glass. She sat stiffly on the chair, looking completely uncomfortable.

Danny squirmed. "Pway," he moaned sadly. "Pway, Sar."

Her stricken eyes met Luke's.

His heart broke for both his son and for this normally strong, proud woman who was so afraid of hurting a child that she wanted to protect him from herself.

"Here, Sarah," Cass said, walking over and handing her a pink-and-blue-polka-dotted ball about the size of Danny's head. "I washed it in the bathroom sink."

Immediately Danny clapped his hands together and reached for it, letting out a little squeal.

Sarah looked to Luke as if asking permission.

"I trust you," he said simply.

She didn't look convinced, but she got up and let Danny slide down to the floor, taking his hand and leading him outside. "I feel like I'm being lazy, not doing my part," she said just before she stepped through the door.

Luke exchanged a look with Madeline and Cass. "Go," they all said in unison.

"And don't come back until you've made Danny laugh," Cass ordered. "Heavens, even I know how to play with a baby."

Sarah stopped. She raised one brow and lifted her chin. "I never wanted to be center stage," she told her sister. "I just wanted to be a normal person. Like you."

Cass looked as if someone had hit her with a frying pan. Her eyes blinked wide. She stopped sorting the pile of junk she was going through. For a minute she didn't say anything.

"Well, then, I guess playing with Danny will be a start. Playing with a baby is a pretty normal thing to do."

"Not for me," Sarah said.

Luke clenched his fists. He had no idea what Sarah had gone through, but if he could have he would have gone back in time and changed her life for her. As it was, there was pretty much nothing he could do, except tell her the truth.

"Danny likes you," he said, gazing into her eyes. "Just…like him back."

She gave a shaky nod and smiled down at Danny. "I do. Let's go play some ball, sweetheart."

Danny gave her his best, melting smile. Together they walked out into the sunshine. Luke looked beyond them and saw that a few curiosity-seekers had stopped on the sidewalk to see what was the cause of the sudden activity at the shop.

He gritted his teeth. If anyone dared to intrude on this fragile moment between Sarah and his son, he was just going to have to go bust some heads together.

He really hoped they could just have one normal day with no incidents.

CHAPTER TWENTY

SARAH LOOKED DOWN AT the child sitting on the grass behind the shop. He was smiling, but somewhat tentatively, as if he knew that she wasn't really in charge. As if he knew that she didn't really know what to do. Danny stared at the ball longingly.

She sat down on the grass, too, and looked at the ball she was holding. She had never been good at sports in school. Coordination wasn't her strong point.

Still, a child was waiting.

She rolled the ball gently across the grass toward Danny.

He squealed with delight and reached out for it, giving her a joyous grin. "Ball," he said adoringly.

She chuckled. "Looks like you don't really care if I'm totally inept, do you, sweetie?"

"Ball, Sar," he said, pushing it from him toward her with as much force as he could muster.

It rolled about two feet, angling away from her and stopped.

Danny clapped his hands and climbed up on his sturdy, chubby little legs. He ran toward the ball, sat down and pushed it again. It rolled a little farther this time, though not any straighter.

Sarah laughed and clapped her hands together. "Way to go, Danny. Way to keep trying."

He flashed her an amazing smile.

Her heart filled. She let him roll and chase the ball until he had finally gotten it to her.

"Now I'll send it to you," she said, pointing. "Go sit down."

He dropped his butt right where he was, eighteen inches away from her, gazing up at her expectantly and with something akin to adoration in his eyes.

Sarah felt moisture at the backs of her own eyes. How dear and accepting this little boy was. Without thinking, she leaned forward and dropped a kiss on his forehead, his fine hair silky beneath her lips. He smelled like…baby. She breathed in the intoxicating scent and tried not to think of what she would never have.

"Ah, but we have today, don't we, Danny, my man? Again?" she asked, holding out the ball.

"Gen," he agreed, holding out his little arms as if he would capture the world.

Sarah prepared to roll the ball to him, aiming carefully so that he could experience the success of catching it this time. A whispering sound came to her, and she looked up to see a woman pointing toward her and then turning toward her companion.

The woman's companion, Geralind, waggled her fingers at Sarah. "Looks like there's big doings at the shop," she said.

Sarah shrugged. "Not so big. I just thought I'd see if we could keep it open a bit longer."

Geralind gave a nod. "Sounds good." She glanced down at Danny. "Getting to know little Danny? He's a treasure, isn't he?" the woman said.

Perfectly normal conversation. Nothing at all strange about it, but she heard one of the women standing behind Geralind. "She touched the baby," the woman whispered.

Sarah almost dropped the ball. She *had* touched Danny and she hadn't thought anything of it. No, that wasn't true. She had thought *everything* of it. It had been a rare moment. Her head hadn't even hurt…or rather, it was hurting so constantly these days that she hadn't really noticed it. Her headache wasn't any worse than it had been.

What was worse was the fact that Danny had suddenly become the object of the crowd's attention. People were associating her with him. At least one person was speaking in that awful, hushed tone Sarah had become used to as a child.

She glanced back over her shoulder, and saw that Luke was working at the open window. He had to have heard the conversation, but he hadn't come out and jerked his child away from her. She didn't make the mistake of thinking that he wouldn't do so, however, if he thought Danny was at risk. She wouldn't blame him.

"Danny *is* a treasure," she told Geralind. "And he's an innocent little boy."

Then, unable to subject him to any more of this scrutiny, Sarah got up and called to Danny. "Let's go see what your daddy is up to." She would have preferred not to give the whisperers any more ammo, but Danny was used to having his hand held, so she reached out and took his, walking him back toward the shop.

When she moved into the dimmer light of the shop, she felt Luke rather than saw him clearly.

"You did just fine, Sarah. They didn't best you. They didn't hurt him."

"Only because he isn't old enough to understand

what's going on," she said, and she knew there was nothing he could say to that.

He reached out and tucked a strand of hair behind her ear, then leaned down close. "If anyone tries to hurt you, I will tear them limb from limb."

She wanted to laugh, to cry. "I don't think your job would allow you to punch someone for insulting me or hurting my feelings, but I really do appreciate the thought. Anyway, it's not me I'm worried about. It's Danny. How can you protect him?"

"It goes without saying that if anyone dares to try to hurt him, I'll protect him in any way I can," Luke said.

But she knew that Luke was referring to the people doing the whispering and gossiping. She also knew that none of that whispering and gossiping would be taking place if she weren't around to incite it.

Her time here was limited. For now Danny was safe, but now wouldn't last forever. If she stayed too long, even someone as young as Danny might begin to realize that something was wrong.

Besides, her headaches were getting stronger. She normally never touched anyone, but since she had been here, there had been a lot of touching. The throbbing was becoming too intense.

She needed to get away, to slip back into her anonymity, but as she stared up at Luke, a sense of longing so strong it nearly bent her over with pain shot through her.

She had dreamed about Luke again last night, the dream about Luke walking away from her. She wondered if, when she left here, she could ever live a reasonably calm and untroubled life again or would Luke forever haunt her dreams?

THE NEXT COUPLE OF DAYS had moved along at an awkward, halting gait, Sarah thought. She and her mother and Cass and Luke all worked side by side, getting the shop back in some kind of shape, and Danny moved freely from one adult to another.

It had been the most relaxed Sarah could ever remember being in her life. She and her mother and Cass didn't speak of the difficulties that lay at the heart of their relationship. They never mentioned the past, but they each made an effort to reach out and communicate. Without the specter of R.J. there, there was at least room to breathe and talk.

With Luke, it was a different story. He watched her when she wasn't looking. She could feel his attention on her, and she did the same to him. The need to reach out and touch him, the ache to have him hold her, was like a constant thrumming inside of her.

Her fingers itched, her body hurt, the longing was so great. It was too great, this thing between them. Far too powerful for a relationship that was going to end just as soon as the shop was back up and running. Cass and her mother had agreed to take turns at the helm. Sarah insisted that any profits should be split. Cass's baby's needs must be met, and her mother must be free to stay in her home. Sarah was the only one who had no true responsibilities. Knowing her father had meant his gift as a punishment, she was determined to thwart him and make it profitable, something he had never been able to do.

So she pushed herself and tried not to think of Luke. For two days and nights she devoted herself completely to getting this job done. She barely ate or slept.

It was a perfect solution. By the third day she was

so exhausted that she nearly fell asleep over her morning coffee.

"Sarah?"

Her mother's voice seemed to come from far away. She glanced up.

Madeline was looking worried. "I have to work at the diner today, and Cass has gone to the doctor. Maybe you should sleep in."

Sarah sat up straighter. "I'll be fine. I just haven't had my coffee yet."

"Yes, you did."

Looking down, Sarah realized that yes, her cup was empty, a teaspoon of coffee all that remained at the bottom of the cup.

She tried to shrug. "It'll kick in in just a moment. You know how I am in the morning. Or at least how I used to be."

Her mother looked unconvinced. "No sharp objects."

Tired as she was, Sarah couldn't keep from smiling. "Yes, Mom."

To her surprise, her mother ran one hand over Sarah's hair. "I should have been a better mother. I was too cowed by R.J. He told me that he never hit you, and I...I believed him."

Sarah woke up a bit. "He didn't."

"But he told me that he would if I didn't let him ask you to help him at the shop. He threatened to steal you and to take you from me if I balked. Maybe people would have thought I was silly for believing him, but...I think he would have done it, scooped you up and relocated somewhere else. I should have fought, but I thought that if I could just be here, if I could somehow stay with you and show you that I loved you, everything would be all right."

For a second, Sarah closed her eyes. *I wish you had fought,* she thought, but she remembered what it had been like with her father. Her mother had been no match for a man like R.J. "He was a very convincing man when he made threats."

A lone tear rolled down Madeline's cheek. "I do love you. Don't get hurt today," she said, and she swiped at the tear and rushed out the door.

Sarah knew then that she would not tell her mother about what had happened in the closet at the shop. Maybe someday, maybe never, but definitely not now.

She slumped over her empty cup. The sound of the doorbell ringing came from what seemed like very far away. She shoved her chair back and forced herself to her feet and to the door.

When she opened it, Luke was standing there before her looking like an ad for the perfect male body. His crisp white shirt was open at the throat, his jeans fit his thighs snugly. His hair was slightly damp from the shower. Sarah breathed in and smelled lime and man.

"I ran into Madeline on her way out. You're home alone?" he asked.

"Yes."

He smiled and tapped her nose with his finger.

"Ask me in," he said.

"Excuse me?"

He chuckled. "We're standing here on your doorstep, and you appear to be wearing your pajamas." He allowed his gaze to travel from the top of her head, down over her pink-and-white-heart pajamas to her bare toes.

She raised her hand to her throat, even though the pajamas covered her fully. "Come in," she said, even though she knew it was a bad idea. They were alone, and when she was alone with Luke she wanted too much.

She stepped aside to let him in, then closed the door behind him.

As soon as the door was closed, he bent and touched his lips to hers. He licked at her lips, kissed her throat, placed his palms against her back, then brought his hands up and forward, resting them beneath her breasts. He kissed her again. And again.

"One more," he said, against her lips.

She rose on her toes and wrapped her arms around his neck. She leaned against him, and he groaned. For one second, his thumbs rested against her nipples.

A moan escaped her, and he placed his hands on her arms and stepped back, steadying her.

"Sorry," he said. "I've been wanting to touch you for days, but it's probably not smart. I'm sure there were at least a few people who saw me enter your house. When they see Madeline at the diner and realize Cass isn't home, either, there will be talk."

"That's not good," she agreed. She was pretty sure he didn't care much what people said about him and that he was holding back for her sake. She was glad that he was holding back. Not because of the talk, but because she was afraid she couldn't touch him and then leave town.

She had to leave. No looking back. No regrets. That meant keeping things light.

"Can't let the ladies of Gold Tree find out that you went into a woman's house and felt her up," she said.

"The line outside the station would prevent the other officers from getting to their crime scenes quickly. All those women wanting their turn…"

"Don't push it, Tucker," he said, grinning.

"Push what?" she asked, keeping her expression innocent.

He reached for her, and she scurried away. "I'll be dressed and ready for work in a minute. Where's Danny?"

"He's at Geralind's." At Sarah's startled look, he chuckled. "I know. She's nosy, but she likes Danny and—"

"She's honest nosy," Sarah supplied. "Yes, I'm beginning to like her, too. At least, if she has something to say, she says it and doesn't whisper behind your back. Were you worried that he might get hurt with only the two of us to watch him while we worked today?"

"We're not working today."

"Excuse me? Luke, I have things I have to get done. The taxes are due on the shop, and I have to earn at least enough money to pay those."

"You will. You're moving at the speed of light, and like it or not, when you open the doors, the curiosity seekers and souvenir hunters will descend. You'll earn enough money. But Madeline tells me you're not sleeping. You're worrying, you're planning and you're driving yourself. I see it every day."

He was concerned. How could she tell him, a man who had set himself up as a protector of women, that he was the main reason she was driving herself so hard? Taking that path could only lead to trouble.

"But Luke…"

"Just one day. Let me do something good for you just for one day."

"You help me every day."

"But that's also for Cass and Madeline. Let me do this thing."

The urge to be pampered and cared for just once in her life was almost overwhelming. And when the man offering to pamper her was Luke, well…

"Where are we going?"

"The lake."

"Just you and me? To do what?" she asked, staring at his lips.

"I'd love to do that, as you well know," he said, "but that's not the main purpose. Today is just for you."

Sarah quickly found out that Luke meant just what he said about pampering her. Once they arrived at the lake, he set out a blanket and a picnic basket. "For later," he told her.

"All right. What's for now?"

"This." He took a box out of his truck and started setting up a stand. Then he pulled a length of rope and hooks and canvas from the box.

"A hammock? We're going to…um…lie in a hammock?" she asked.

He smiled, his eyes lighting up. "Much as I'd like that, no. This is a one-person hammock. It's for you."

"I don't understand."

"Nothing to understand. Madeline says that you're driving yourself so hard that you aren't sleeping. I can see that's true," he said, brushing his thumb against the delicate skin beneath her eye. "You're tired."

"*Haggard* is the word you're looking for, but it's not true."

"No, haggard implies something unattractive. That's not you, and yes, it's true that you need rest. It's obvious that you can't get it back at the house, but here with the sound of the wind in the trees and the sun and the breeze against your skin, maybe you'll sleep. Might as well. There's no work to be done today."

"I can't do that. What will you do?" The thought that he might watch her sleeping filled her with heat.

"I need rest, too. A different type. You sleep. I'll fish. We'll both go back home energized."

"Luke…"

"Sarah, do this one thing, please. I want to touch you. I want to hold you, to make love with you, to fall asleep with you, but I can't do any of those things without starting something we might not be able to stop. Let me do this one thing for you…and if you allow this, you'll be doing something for me, too."

"I don't believe you."

"Believe me." His voice was low, hoarse. He leaned forward and kissed the top of her head, his palms gently clasping her elbows. "Please."

Well, what was a woman supposed to say to that? Especially with the warm sun beating down on her and making her drowsy, anyway.

"I'll be self-conscious if you look at me."

"All right, I'll go far enough away that you won't notice me," he said, moving to his truck and picking up a fishing pole. "Rest," he ordered.

She climbed into the hammock, even though she was certain she could never sleep under such circumstances. But the breeze was wonderful, the fresh air was intoxicating, and the sound of Luke whistling low in the distance as he baited his hook lulled her. Her eyes drifted shut. She would just relax for a while. After all, what could happen in the space of a few moments?

CHAPTER TWENTY-ONE

LUKE HAD SAID HE WAS going fishing, and he hadn't meant it to be a lie, but in the end it turned out to be just that. No matter how hard he tried, he couldn't keep his mind off Sarah sleeping just a short distance away.

He could see her from here, her pretty brown hair sliding over the edge of the hammock, her lashes brushing her cheeks. She wasn't really sleeping. He could tell that much. It was probably because his presence was making her self-conscious, but at least she was resting a little. She wasn't in the shop, running herself ragged.

It had been a good idea to bring her here, even if staying away from her and keeping his hands on this darned fishing pole was proving more difficult than he had anticipated.

The sound of ringing dragged him from his thoughts, and he scowled. He had considered turning his telephone off, but he was a police officer and a father. Disappearing completely wasn't an option.

He put the phone to his ear. "Yes?"

"You have to come, Luke. Right now. He's lost. I let him get lost." Geralind's normally confident voice sounded hoarse and out of breath.

"What do you mean?" Fear clenched his heart and he could barely get the words out.

"He was here one minute, gone the next. I don't know what happened. I've been looking and looking, calling and calling, but I just don't know where he is. Luke, please come."

"I'll be there. Keep looking." He clicked off the phone, threw down his fishing pole and headed toward the hammock. Sarah was already up.

"What's wrong? I heard your phone ring, the worried sound of your voice."

"Danny's lost. I have to go."

She didn't argue or start to gather things. She just took off toward the car. He'd left it unlocked and by the time he got inside, she was already there. Luke spared her a glance and saw that her face was parchment-white, her lips pinched. No doubt his own face looked the same.

And then he didn't notice anything else. He just drove.

SARAH'S HANDS WERE FOLDED tightly in her lap, her fingers twisting together. A child was lost. Danny was lost. And she was useless. She didn't know what to do.

She glanced at Luke. His jaw was hard and set. What must he be thinking, feeling? She didn't know. She'd never lost a child, at least not in this way. Not a child she had known and nurtured and loved.

Danny's joyful, trusting little face swam in her memory. She wanted to cry out with the pain of knowing that he was lost, maybe alone and frightened with none of the adults who loved him near him.

But she couldn't do that. She had to be strong for Luke.

"Where are we going?"

"I'm dropping you at home, then going on to Geralind's."

"I'll go with you."

He glanced to the side, a frown on his face.

"I wasn't suggesting that I use my ability," she whispered. "I know you don't believe in it. I'm no longer capable, and I would never get your hopes up that way by promising you something like that. That would be cruel."

He gave a curt nod. "You should go home."

"Probably, but at the very least, I can help you with Geralind. She'll be distraught."

He didn't argue, but drove straight to Geralind's. The woman ran out the door to meet them. "I've got the neighbors out looking. I've called and I've called for Danny. He's so little. He can't have gone far."

Her voice was hopeful, scared. Sarah felt for her but, seeing the fear and despair in Luke's eyes, she felt for him more.

"What was he doing when you last saw him?" he asked.

"He was playing with his trucks out in the yard. I was talking with Lorena on the phone. She was saying things I didn't like, and I got a little angry and distracted, I guess." Guilt filled the woman's voice. From the way Geralind looked from her to Luke, Sarah assumed the conversation might have had something to do with herself and Luke.

"When I got off the phone, Danny was just…gone. I've looked everywhere. I've combed the neighborhood."

A car drove by, and Sarah's heart stuck in her throat. There wasn't a ton of traffic in Gold Tree, but it would be so easy for a little boy who didn't know any better to run out in front of a car or truck. Danny obviously hadn't done that yet or they would have heard about it, but where could he be? He wasn't big enough to get very far on those chubby little legs.

"You're sure he's not in the house?"

Geralind shook her head. "I looked."

Luke's lips thinned out. The expression in his eyes was bleak. He went into the house anyway, Sarah and Geralind following. "Danny?" he called. "Danny, don't hide, big guy. Daddy's here."

"He might think it's a game and not come out when you call," Sarah told Geralind.

"I know, but…"

But Geralind *had* searched thoroughly. Danny wasn't here.

When they had covered every nook and cranny, Luke swore. He punched his fist into Geralind's wall. "I'm sorry. It's not your fault," he said. "I've had plenty of times I thought he was lost, too, but—"

But this time he really was lost.

Luke pulled out his phone. He talked to Jemma, but she hadn't heard anything about Danny being lost. "I'm going to search the area around the house again," he told her. "The creek—the creek is too damned close to here," he said, his voice breaking. He looked at Sarah, and she knew he was thinking about Pattie Dubeaux. "While I'm doing that, put out an APB." He told her what Danny was wearing. Then he started walking briskly toward the creek, calling Danny's name all the way.

Sarah wanted to run after him, to help him. Her throat was closing up. The creek *was* very close. Her heart was pounding, pounding. She felt so horribly useless.

But running after Luke wouldn't help. She needed to think. Luke was a police officer, but police officers needed evidence, clues. He was a father, but right now fear was his driving force, and fear was seldom careful.

Sarah closed her eyes, feeling tears threatening.

"Did he take the truck with him?" Sarah suddenly asked Geralind.

"No, it's still in the yard."

Sarah rushed to where Geralind was pointing. Her heart was thundering in her chest. The little red-and-yellow truck lay in the grass. She reached out.

Her head didn't hurt, not at all. She picked up the truck and felt cold metal, the sticky rubber of the tires. Nothing else.

She squeezed the truck hard, tried to concentrate, to stop breathing, to stop thinking, to just feel.

Nothing, nothing, nothing.

A cry escaped her.

"Do you see something?" Geralind's voice was hopeful, anxious.

Sarah shook her head slowly, sadly. "Nothing. I don't see anything anymore." Not even a headache. For once in her life, she longed for a headache. The only thing that was slightly gratifying was that she didn't feel the dark, cold dread she had felt with Pattie. But then she wouldn't, would she? Even if something had happened to Danny, she wouldn't feel it.

In the distance, she could hear Luke calling for Danny, his voice more and more frantic and desperate. Her heart broke for him.

She lowered her head. All right, she no longer had

her clairsentience. She had gotten rid of it, but…she had been locating things all her life, and not just through feel. Logic had been a part of it, too. Think, think, she ordered herself.

Sarah dropped to the ground, closed her eyes. She tried to remember everything she knew about Danny, which wasn't much. He liked cookies, he loved her mother and his father. He laughed a lot, he had a rubber duck. He called her Sar…

Hot tears formed behind her lids at the thought that she might never get to know more than this about the child, and Sarah got up. Thinking wasn't doing any good.

She slowly walked the perimeter of the yard, still clutching the useless truck. In one direction lay the creek where Luke had gone, opposite that was the road that led to the town. That might be the most logical direction. Maybe Danny had tried to go home, to find his father. Sarah trudged on. There was nothing much at the next corner of the house. Geralind's house was on the edge of things, and only open fields lay beyond her property. A frumpy little park that had never been kept up was there, but the playground equipment had been torn out years ago and never replaced. No enticement for a child there.

Turning to retrace her steps, something at the far corner of her vision registered. She strained to make out what it was. It was low to the ground, red, small.

She leaned down farther, hoping for a child's eye view. The object was at the far edge of the park, tangled in weeds. It was round. Nothing.

The truck felt warm. No doubt because she had been clutching it so tightly, but her heart jumped, and Sarah began running toward the object.

"Danny! Danny, love," she called, running faster and faster.

Suddenly her foot caught in something and she pitched forward, the now-hot truck flying from her fingertips.

"Oomph!" She hit the ground hard and lay there, stunned. Her ankle burned, but she didn't care. She was lying half in a small trench, grown over with weeds. It must have been built for drainage from the park, but the park had not been kept up, and the trench was no longer visible beneath the vegetation.

She'd lost the truck. For some reason that fact seemed very important. But she had no time to wonder why. The trench was long, not very deep, but then a two-year-old child wasn't very large.

Crawling forward, Sarah searched beneath the foliage.

"Danny!" she called. "Danny, please, please answer me. Answer Sarah."

A very small sound came to her. Maybe just the breeze in the tall grass.

"Danny, say something. Say anything, sweetie," she begged, hoping she wasn't speaking to the wind.

She listened long and hard. Nothing. Nothing.

Sarah bit down on her lip. A whimper came to her. "Sar." The tiniest whisper carried on the breeze.

"Luke!" she screamed. "Luke! Luke! Geralind! Over here, over here! He's here!"

She crawled forward on her hands and knees in the direction of the small voice. Danny was crying. Her heart was breaking, with sadness, with joy.

A small patch of blue-and-white caught her eye. Danny had been wearing a blue-and-white shirt, Luke said. She reached out and parted the weeds and stared down into Danny's big blue eyes.

"Ow, Sar," he said, and she saw that his left leg and arm were caught beneath a tangle of thick weeds and exposed tree roots. He must have fallen backward and then been caught up in the undergrowth when he tried to wiggle out. Still, he was alive.

"Danny, love," she said with a smile, her voice filled with tears. "You'll be fine, Danny. I'm so glad to see you. Luke!" she called again, but then she felt him beside her. He reached down and disentangled his son, lifting him up high. He held him close to his chest, raining kisses on the top of Danny's hair.

"Thank God, thank God," he whispered. "Thank you, Sarah. Thank you."

Their eyes met. Sarah knew there would be hell to pay for this moment. She knew people would think that she really was psychic, even though it wasn't true, but for now she didn't care. For this moment, she and Luke and Danny were alone in the world and that was all that mattered.

LUKE PACED THE FLOOR of his kitchen, waiting for the crowd to thin out, wishing they would all go home but reluctant to ask them to. These were the people who had come running when the word had gone out that his son was missing. They had scoured the town. He couldn't refuse them their questions or deny them his hospitality, but he wanted nothing more than to shut his doors on all of them.

He had not been alone with Sarah since the ordeal had ended. Geralind had asked to come home with them.

"I feel so guilty," she had said. "At least let me make you something to eat, put up some coffee for the searchers who are bound to stop by."

He couldn't refuse. "You're a good woman, Geralind. I don't want you to beat yourself up about this. Children move quickly."

"It was the ball," Sarah had told her gently. "In the field. I could barely see it, but from Danny's height, it was more visible. He probably saw it and just took off ·after it. Danny likes balls."

Luke remembered her and Danny playing together at the shop.

"So you didn't find him…you know, that way?" Geralind had asked.

"No, it wasn't that," Sarah said emphatically, her hands clenching. Luke knew that she would be asked the same question over and over, and she had been. Even Madeline and Cass had looked askance at her when they arrived at Luke's house, though neither of them had asked the question.

Word was already circulating in the town that Sarah had "found" another child. That child was in his bed, sleeping now, and Luke was like a caged bear. He sent a look Dugan's way. ·

"All right, now, Luke has had a scare, and you all know what that's like. Once it wears off, exhaustion sets in. I think we'd all better go home. It's getting late," Dugan said.

"It's only seven o'clock," Lorena Branford said.

Madeline looked at her daughter and Luke. "Obviously, you've never lost a child," she said. "I'm going home. So should you." She crossed her arms and stared Lorena down.

Luke thought he detected a twitching of Dugan's lips, but his friend and employer didn't say a word.

"You're getting huffy in your old age, Madeline," Lorena said.

That got Dugan's attention. "Maddie old? I don't think so. Old is when you start getting whiskers on your chin. I don't see any on Madeline."

And Lorena had plenty. Luke felt a chuckle move through him for the first time in hours. He rubbed one hand across his jaw to disguise his turned up lips.

Fire flashed from Lorena's eyes, but she sailed out of the kitchen and everyone else followed her. "Thank you," Luke said to Madeline and Dugan.

"Well, the woman has no sense of common decency," Madeline said. "And I do, too, have a few whiskers," she told Dugan.

"Really? They must look good on you, then," Dugan said. "I hadn't noticed." He took Madeline's arm as they left he house.

Sarah, the last person remaining, got up to follow them. Luke snagged her by the arm and gently pulled her back.

"Don't go yet," he whispered.

"But I thought—"

"We need to talk."

She raised alarmed eyes to his.

"I'm not going to badger you and ask you lots of questions," he told her. "You found my son. I don't care how you did it. He was tangled up pretty good and far enough away from the house that he might not have been heard if he cried. If you hadn't found him…"

"It was luck," she said, "and a little logic. That was all. Anyone could have done it."

"But you were the one who did."

"I was never so happy to see anyone as I was to see him. I was just so glad that he was unhurt and alive," she said.

And he knew then that she had been worried about the same things he had worried about, that they would find a tragedy instead of a happy ending. It was natural for him, because he was Danny's father, and it was natural for her, because she had once gone on a child hunt that hadn't ended well. What must have been going through her head? What nightmares still haunted her? He didn't know, but he wanted no nightmares to linger in her mind from this day.

He knew how tenacious nightmares were. He had a few of his own. They couldn't always be banished forever, but sometimes they could be banished for a while.

He wanted to banish her nightmares tonight. He wanted to banish his own, and he wanted…what he'd wanted since the first day he'd seen her.

Luke tucked his finger beneath Sarah's chin and tipped her head up. "I need to kiss you, Sarah, so very much."

CHAPTER TWENTY-TWO

"I WANT TO KISS YOU, too. I have to," Sarah said, and she rose on her toes to meet Luke's touch. She wrapped her arms around his waist.

He bent her back, raining kisses down her cheeks, stopping at her lips for a taste, nipping her chin and savoring the hollow of her throat.

"You're so warm, so alive," he whispered as he grazed his lips across the sensitive skin just beneath her ear.

She shivered in his arms. Yes, that was what this was. They had both feared death this day and had managed to evade it. There was a sort of desperation in that. Life needed to be reaffirmed. That was all this was.

She didn't care. Right now, she needed to be close to someone. Those moments when Luke had gone looking for Danny and she had searched alone, when she had for the first time in years tried to call up a power she had once run from, were still vivid in her mind. She needed to forget them.

She especially needed to forget that she had not been able to claim her clairsentience, and then it—or something—had rushed at her when she had been least prepared. That heat from the truck…what had it been?

She didn't want to know, didn't want to think. In

Luke's arms she could feel without thought. She needed that, and apparently, so did he. Just for this night.

Luke ran one palm down her back, clutching at her buttocks. Pressed tight against him, she could feel his arousal. An ache began within her. She shivered.

"If you want me to stop, tell me now, Sarah," he urged, his lips near her earlobe.

"Don't stop. I need you. I need to feel you." As if to show him, she slid her hands up his chest and cupped his face. She rose on her toes and pressed her lips to his. "I want to give in tonight. And you don't have to worry, Luke. I can't…I can't read your thoughts."

He smiled against her lips. "You think I'm worried about that?"

"I don't know. All the things people said tonight…I thought you might be."

"I'm not, but I don't really believe that you can't read my thoughts."

Alarm rushed through her. She started to pull back.

Luke kissed her again, his tongue sweeping her mouth. He nibbled at the corners of her lips. He brought his hand to her breast, gently kneading, his thumb brushing the tip.

She gasped as the peak hardened, and he groaned into her mouth. "Sarah," he said on a groan. "Tell me what I'm thinking. You know what I'm thinking. I'm not doing a very good job of hiding it."

Now she understood. Sarah smiled and licked his lips. She swayed, her breast brushing against his hand. She could barely keep from wriggling herself, so deep was the ache inside her, so great the need.

"You're thinking that you want me, that you wish I'd unbutton my blouse."

He chuckled. "Oh, you're very close, Sarah. Actually, I was thinking that *I* wanted to unbutton your blouse."

Luke slid his hands to the placket on her blouse, slowly, slowly undoing each button. He peeled the cloth back from her shoulders and dropped it on the table. Then he reached for the catch on her lacy bra and flicked it open.

Her breasts sprang free and she wiggled her shoulders, her breasts swaying as the bra fell away. Luke's eyes were filled with admiration and desire.

Sarah swallowed. "I—I'll bet you can read my mind, too. What—" She swallowed again as Luke gazed at her nipples and the peaks turned even harder. Painfully hard. "What am *I* thinking?" she whispered.

He reached out with one fingertip and just barely touched the tip of one nipple.

Sarah's breath left her body in a whoosh. The ache between her legs grew.

"You're thinking that you wish I would touch you, that I would taste you," Luke said.

"Yes, yes, please taste me," Sarah answered on a strangled gasp.

Luke lowered his head and took her nipple into his mouth. Sarah couldn't control the moan that escaped her.

"Luke, please. Please don't wait," she begged. "I want you so much."

Before the words were out of her mouth he had swept her into his arms and carried her to the bedroom. She clawed at his shirt, sending buttons flying. She rested her hands on the muscles in his chest, nothing between the warmth of his skin and hers now.

When she touched him, passion vibrated beneath her fingers. Desire such as she had never known pulsed. Dark need vibrated between them.

She wanted to be closer, to feel more, and apparently Luke felt the same way. "I have to see all of you," he said, and he deftly opened the catch on her shorts, skimmed them down her legs, her lace panties following.

Now she was naked, and he was not. "You are amazing," he whispered. He kissed the curve of her shoulder, and she tipped her head as he worked his way up her neck, sending shivers of delight throughout her body.

Heat engulfed her. "I want—I want…" She could barely voice the words, so great was her need.

Luke was breathing hard, the evidence of his desire clearly outlined against the dark cloth of his pants. "What do you want, Sarah? Tell me. You control things this time."

She opened her eyes at that and saw that he had stopped movement. His jaw was clenched.

"I want you so much I can barely stand it," he said through gritted teeth, "but I don't want you to feel coerced in any way."

She understood then. She'd told him of how other men had treated her. They had had all the power. Now he was returning some of it to her.

"Free will," she said, reaching out and loosening his belt, lowering the zipper on his pants and pushing down the dark cloth. She gently cupped him in her hands, and his head fell back with a gasp. "I'm doing this of my own free will," she whispered. "Touch me, Luke. Make me ready." Even though she was already on the edge.

He kicked free of his pants, slid one hand behind her

back and carried her down to the mattress. With an expertise that took her breath away, he slipped his fingers between her legs and brushed his thumb over the sensitive nub that lay hidden there.

She cried out, arching off the bed as she began to come apart.

"Come with me. Inside," she pleaded, and he entered her in one fluid move. He filled her, his gasps reaching her ears as she climaxed around him.

Slowly, rhythmically he moved in her, teasing her, daring her.

"Again, Sarah," he urged. "Will you let me please you again?"

"Again. Yes." As he stroked within her, over and over, the tension built again. This time when she called out his name, she brought him with her.

Long moments passed. Sarah stirred. She turned into Luke's hand, and he stroked her face. "What am I feeling?" he asked.

She smiled like a lazy cat as she stared into his eyes. "Satisfied?"

He chuckled. "Oh, yeah."

They lay there tangled together, just breathing, smiling, cuddling.

Sarah was kissing Luke again when she heard a clatter and then a crash.

She and Luke froze. They sat up.

"It wasn't here," she said.

"No, it wasn't. You stay here. I'll check."

She wanted to argue, and if someone didn't need to stay with Danny she would have. Because while the crash hadn't been here, it had been close. And the closest thing to Luke's house was her own.

LUKE LOOKED AT THE rock that Cass held up to him. "This came through the window," she said. "That was what the noise was." Cass glanced from him to Sarah, curiosity in her expression, but she didn't question her sister's disheveled appearance or the fact that Sarah had shown up carrying a sleeping Danny who was now safely snoozing in the next room.

Sarah's face had paled at Cass's statement. Luke was pretty sure he knew what she was thinking. If she had been called a witch when she was younger, there might still be someone in town who believed it was so and didn't like her.

"Was there any indication of who it came from? Did you see anyone, Cass?" he asked gently.

She hesitated, looking at her sister. Then, as if she had made up her mind about something important, she whispered, "It was Zach."

Luke heard Madeline gasp behind him. "He threw a rock through your window?" Sarah asked, anger in her pretty gray eyes. She clutched Danny's baby monitor in one hand, so tightly that her knuckles were white. "What if he'd hit you? What kind of a man would do that to the mother of his child? He knows you're pregnant."

"Cass," Luke said. "Do you have any idea why Zach used this means of getting in touch with you? He could have just rung the doorbell."

Cass's hands were visibly trembling. She wrapped her arms around herself. "Zach's not been himself lately. I think he has a lot on his mind."

Sarah studied her sister. "Are you sure it was Zach?"

"I saw him. He spoke to me."

"Can you tell me what he said?" Luke asked. He saw

immediately that she didn't want to answer. She kept glancing at her sister. Was Cass one of those who thought that Sarah could read her mind?

"He didn't say much. We argued the last time we saw each other. I think…he wants me to meet him."

Luke watched Cass carefully. She was hiding something, but calling her on it was unlikely to reveal what it was. No doubt it was something that didn't concern him, anyway.

"Don't meet him," Sarah said. "At least, don't meet him if you don't want to. You don't have to. I'll stand behind you on this. I could talk to him if you like."

"No. No, I can handle things," Cass said. "I don't think—he won't be back."

"I'm sure you can handle things," Sarah said. "You've proved yourself more than capable at the shop. You'll be a fine mother."

Her sister didn't answer, and Sarah didn't look at all happy.

When Luke said his good-night to Sarah on the porch, he cupped his palm around Sarah's jaw and kissed her on the lips.

"Do you think she's telling the whole truth? Do you think he'll be back or that he might hurt her?" Sarah asked.

"I don't know," Luke said truthfully. He didn't add that he was wild with worry that if Zach did come back, Sarah might get hurt as well. "I'm going to look for him," he promised Sarah. "I swear to you that if he's in the area, and I'm sure that he is, then I'll find him."

He only hoped that he would find him before Zach did something worse than throwing a rock through a window.

LONG AFTER EVERYONE ELSE had gone to sleep, Cass
lay in bed wishing that she could find the answers to
her dilemma. Beneath her bed lay the crunched-up
note that had been attached to the rock that had sailed
through her window.

Three days and your time is up, the note had said.

Zach hadn't actually spoken to her. He hadn't
needed to. When she had looked out the window, he had
been standing there. He looked down at his stomach,
gave her an evil grin and then he had turned and jogged
away.

"Why didn't you tell Sarah the whole truth, that he
wanted her help?" she asked herself.

Because if she told anyone, then the story might
get out. Zach would find out. He'd come for her and
take her baby. He might even hurt her so much that
she lost the baby.

She covered her mouth to keep from crying out. She
knew that her mother and Sarah and Luke would want
her to tell, so that Luke could look for Zach.

But Zach was devious and he was desperate. He had
friends who would hide him. And if Luke didn't find him
first, then Zach would come for her, and he would get
her.

Maybe she should just tell Sarah. Maybe Sarah
would do what Zach wanted and then he would go
away.

Cass rolled over, trying not to think about that. Sarah
was fixing up the shop so that there would be money
for the baby. Besides, she had heard Sarah tell people
that she couldn't find things anymore. If she failed to
help Zach, he would lash out, maybe hurt her.

Sarah wasn't the answer, and it was partly her own

fault that Zach was doing this, Cass thought. He wouldn't have taken as much of an interest if it hadn't been for the connection between her and Sarah.

She had to do something, but what?

"Three days," she whispered to the walls. What would Zach do in three days?

LUKE NEARLY FELL ASLEEP at his desk the next day. He had left Danny with Madeline and Sarah and then he had gone out all night, interviewing people, asking them if they had seen any trace of Zach, if they had seen him coming into town or approaching the Tucker house. He'd interviewed Penny Mickerson again, but she hadn't been any more cooperative than she had before.

"Zach hasn't been here since Cass left," she said, barely cracking the door. "Frankly, that's a good thing, Officer. He isn't all that nice a guy, and I'd rather he not find out that you've been talking to me."

Alarms went off in Luke's head. "You think he might be violent?"

"I think he's capable of anything. Crystal meth isn't as expensive as cocaine, but it's ugly stuff and if you use it enough, you can run low pretty fast. Now that it's more difficult to get the supplies to make the stuff, dealers can charge more. Zach needs money. That makes him desperate. I don't want to get on his bad side."

She started to close the door. Luke put a hand out to stop it. "Do you know anyone who might tell me where he is?"

"No, I don't," she said.

But Luke knew Penny was lying so he had staked

out her house. Sooner or later someone might show up
who could help him.

A voice drifted in, and Luke blinked awake. His
desk was a hard pillow.

"Go home," Dugan said, shaking Luke. "You're not
any good to me this way. I'll take your shift."

Luke shook his head. "I'm fine."

Dugan's mouth was a thin line. "I might have you
lined up to take my job when I retire, but for now I'm
still in charge. I say you go home and get some sleep."

Luke frowned, but he rose to his feet.

"Did you find him?" Dugan asked.

"Not yet. But I will."

"And when you do?"

Dugan and Luke exchanged a look. "I'll keep it
legal," Luke said. But he would also make sure that
Zach left town. The man had become a threat to the
Tuckers, and anyone who threatened them didn't
belong in Gold Tree. He tried not to think about the fact
that Zach might have been in Sarah's shop the other
day. Luke had already asked Dugan to have officers pa-
trolling that area more regularly.

But he and Dugan knew that an officer couldn't be
at the right spot every hour of every day. A crafty
intruder could still find his way inside.

"And already the crowds have heard what happened
with Danny," Luke muttered as he detoured past
Sarah's shop on his way home. People were already
starting to flood the place even though she wasn't of-
ficially open. A crowd could be a good thing. There
was safety in numbers. But a crowd was also a good
place to hide, a good decoy so that someone who didn't
want to be seen could sneak in on the side.

Luke pushed through the door. There was quite a hum going on inside. He frowned with anger. Couldn't everyone just leave Sarah alone? She'd be gone soon enough.

As the door clicked shut behind him, a group of women turned to stare at him. He was, he realized, the only male in the place.

"Evening, ladies," he said, nodding to them.

"Have you come to help out?" Geralind asked.

He blinked. Yes, he had come to help out, but he wasn't quite sure that he and Geralind were referring to the same thing at the moment. There didn't appear to be any crimes going on, and none of the women was wielding a hammer or tool of any kind.

Sarah gave him one of her best smiles. "Mother invited all the ladies over to help us decide the new direction that the shop should take. We've got the space and a lot of junk, but I wasn't sure I wanted to go back into the junk business. It was never very satisfying."

"I thought our friends might like to give us some feedback on what they think this town needs," Madeline said with a flustered shrug, and Luke knew without a doubt that Madeline had planned this moment as a decoy to keep anyone from pestering Sarah about how she had found Danny. Madeline's eyes were, for once, not tinged with sadness. "We've come up with so many ideas that this might have to be a multipurpose shop. Maybe one of those mini-exercise facilities, and Cass might add a juice bar. She's got some good ideas about nutrition, and heaven knows all women, but especially women of my age, need to think about how to keep fit and healthy. Don't you think so, Luke?"

At least ten pairs of eyes turned to him. Talk about a loaded question. Luke automatically glanced to Sarah and saw that she had her hand over her mouth, trying to stifle a laugh. Like her mother, this was one of the few times he'd seen Sarah without shadows in her eyes. She was glorious, amazing, luscious. He remembered her naked and sated in his bed, and all he wanted to say right then was that he wanted her again. He stared at her for so long that he heard someone clearing her throat and he blinked and turned to the women.

"Excuse me, you ladies have a tendency to distract me," he said.

Geralind chuckled. "I'd say that it's Sarah that distracts you."

She was so right. "You're all lovely," he answered, and he meant every word. Sarah was laughing. These women who had joined with her on this venture had to be partly responsible for the joy in her eyes, Luke realized. "But I also think those are very good ideas. This town needs new businesses and new life."

"I thought we might provide child care as well," Sarah said. She didn't look at her sister, but Luke saw that Cass turned toward Sarah. "What could be more natural? A lot of women working together and supporting each other, getting healthy and caring for babies together? It would be a little taste of friendship and home."

"I think that's a much better idea than a junk shop," Luke agreed. "If a man's opinion counts." He tipped his hat. "Guess I'd better be getting home." He looked askance at Madeline.

"He's sleeping in the back room," she said. "I'll bring him home when I leave here, if that's okay."

"That's fine, Madeline. May I speak with you outside, Sarah?" he asked. "Sorry. Business," he told the other women.

Sarah nodded, Cass rolled her eyes, Madeline looked a bit worried and Geralind snorted. Except for Sarah, Luke ignored them all and held the door open for her.

They walked around to the windowless side of the building, away from prying eyes. Only Smooch served as an audience, and he seemed more interested in an old tennis ball he was pushing around with his nose.

"Your mother played interference?" he asked.

"Yes, and it worked."

"I was worried." He touched her hair. "I'm glad no one gave you a hard time."

A bit of her smile left her eyes.

"Sarah?"

She shook her head. "It's been mostly good, and frankly, I didn't want to even show you this, but after that incident with Cass and the rock, I thought you should just take a look at it."

She held out a piece of paper. "It says, *I know what you are. I know where you are.*" Her hand trembled a bit.

Luke took the paper…and her hand. "Where did you get this?"

"It was in the shop this morning, shoved beneath the door. I don't think Cass saw it yet. I don't want her to."

"You think it's Zach?"

"I…maybe. I'm not sure. When I first came home I had a phone call that seemed a bit threatening."

"You didn't tell me."

"I had a lot of phone calls those first few days. At first I even thought it might be you."

Something rough and terrible slid through Luke. Someone had threatened her, and he hadn't known about it. "We need to talk. Come with me," he said.

CHAPTER TWENTY-THREE

SARAH FOLLOWED LUKE INTO the woods behind the shop. It occurred to her that with any other man she might be afraid. The woods were dark here. But this was Luke, and although he was clearly upset, she didn't fear him.

He motioned to a fallen tree trunk, then joined her there when she had sat. He crooked one knee over a place where there had once been a branch and faced her.

"Sarah, why didn't you tell me? Why did you think I might have been the one making the threatening call?"

She shook her head. "I didn't. Not really. At least not for more than a second. I could tell that you had a problem with the clairsentience thing."

"You weren't the woman who led my wife down the wrong path."

"No, but I was of her ilk."

He shook his head. "No, she played with fire. That's not you."

Sarah thought about the heat from the truck the other day. She should share that with him, be totally honest, but she didn't really even know what it meant. Maybe she had imagined it.

"There are things I haven't told you, either," he said, "and I should have."

Dread started to build up inside her. This was going to be something bad.

"Someone was in your shop when I came by one morning. I chased him, but I lost him. I think it may have been Zach."

"You didn't say."

"You had so many worries, and right after that, we secured the shop. At the time, I thought Zach was probably just finding a place to crash. He's a druggie, frequently not welcome. An abandoned building might have been enticing. Now I'm not so sure that's what it was about. I'm also not totally sure it was him, but you need to know. I should have told you. There are times when I tend to play at being more than I am. I'm a bit controlling."

Sarah studied his face. He knew that was just the sort of thing she didn't want in her life. Was he telling her that for a reason? Because he knew she had had enough of controlling men? Was he worried that she would make too much of their lovemaking last night?

Honesty compelled her to accept the fact that both of them had been overcome by the emotion of losing Danny and then finding them. Lovemaking was a reaffirmation of life.

"Thank you for telling me," she said, and she wasn't sure if she was referring to the information about the intruder or about Luke's controlling nature.

"I've asked Dugan to have the men make extra rounds close to here and your house. But if you see anything or hear anything at all…"

"I'll call." She laid the note in his hand. Her fingertips brushed his palm. She grasped his hands. "Luke?"

He raised their joined hands and kissed the tip of her thumb. "Yes?"

"Before Mom took charge this morning, there *were* some nosy people asking questions and demanding answers, Wayland among them, and Danny was in the store, wide awake and taking everything in. You understand what I'm saying?"

"I know what you're trying to say, darlin'," he told her. "And I'd like to tell you it doesn't matter a bit. That's what I want to tell you more than anything." He leaned down and kissed her lips. "But it's something I've got to think about."

Her eyes burned, but she admired him for his honesty and for being a good father. Good fathers were so important. "That's as it should be, Luke."

And if he was truly a good father, the kind of man she would admire most, he would choose Danny and ignore his own wants every time.

She closed her eyes, hoping that if she blinked once or twice the tears wouldn't come. "I have to get back inside," she whispered. "Cass has been looking haunted all day."

WHEN SARAH RETURNED TO the store, the women had gone home to make dinner, Madeline had taken Danny home, and only Cass remained. Considering the emptiness of the place and Cass's own feelings about herself, she was surprised to find her younger sister still there. She wished that she knew how to break through the awkwardness and discomfort that seemed to surround them.

"You came back. Why?" Cass asked, as if she hadn't been expecting Sarah.

"Do you want me to leave?"

"I didn't mean now. I meant the other. I know what you said, but why did you really come back after staying away for so long? What's in it for you?"

Sarah shrugged. "I suppose this is where I'm supposed to try to appear noble and say that there's nothing in it for me."

"I wouldn't believe you."

"No, I didn't think you would. And you'd be right. I did have selfish reasons, although I didn't really know that when I came here."

Cass waited.

"I hated this place," Sarah said, "but there were parts of it that I loved."

"Don't say I was one of them."

Sarah pursed her lips. "All right, I won't, since you've asked me not to. But I did have good memories of parts of my childhood, Cass, and you were a part of that. A big part for a while."

"You left and didn't come back or come see me. Mom and Dad…you were all they thought about. I was nothing. He left you this." Cass held out her hands to the walls.

"He did it because he hated me."

"He didn't hate you. He was angry, but he talked of nothing else but you. He chided me for not being like you."

"Thank heavens you aren't. Oh, Cass, I don't want you to be like me. Be yourself. That's so much better."

Cass shook her head. "Oh, right. Even Zach…he's obsessed with you."

Sarah looked up in alarm. "Cass, I've never even spoken to him."

"I don't mean that way. He's obsessed with what he thinks you can do. Like everyone. And I know you say that you don't do that anymore, but you have done it. You can never change that. Everyone says it's a gift. I don't have a gift," Cass said, her voice anguished. "Not a talent, not a skill, not anything that sets me apart."

"You have a baby growing inside you. You're young and pretty and bright," Sarah said. "You can have a normal life with no interference from anyone. That's such a gift. I envy you."

Cass frowned. "I don't believe you. You're just trying to snow me."

A muffled cry erupted from Sarah. "No, Cass. It isn't like that at all. And Dad…" She stopped.

"Go on."

"No. You loved him. I won't say anything bad about him."

"I'm not a child."

"No, but you're a human being, a daughter, a woman with feelings. I won't besmirch those feelings. My arguments with Dad were mine alone."

Cass pressed Sarah several times for an explanation, insulted her, argued with her. Sarah refused to say more.

"This shop…" Cass said.

"Will be yours and Mom's. I don't want it. You'll do a fine job of running it with her."

Cass stared, silent for several moments. "How do you know?"

Sarah stared at her sister, long and hard. She reached out and touched Cass's hand. "You have a baby on the way. You care about your child. You'll be a good mother. I feel it."

And she walked out of the shop.

ZACH LOOKED AT THE information he had printed from the Internet. It was about the thousandth time he'd gone over it in the past few days.

"Hidden treasure, and nobody's managed to find it after all these years. It's still lying there, waiting for someone to come dig it up. But to dig it up you have to know where it is, don't you?" He chuckled and fingered the piece of paper.

People had been looking for Dillinger's stash all this time, and he was going to be the one to claim it. He had it all planned out. Get Cass to deliver up her sister, take Sarah someplace where she could be in the same room with some of Dillinger's historical pieces, maybe touch one if he was lucky, then have her lead him directly to the money.

What happened afterward wasn't so clear. Zach twisted at his collar. His clothes didn't even feel right anymore. He was getting so thin, and these damn crank craters, these open sores on his face, were driving him nuts. Maybe if he took more…yeah, if he could only get more, he would probably be fine.

He needed more. Lots more. Sarah would be the means, but he couldn't let her lead anyone to him.

Zach started to sweat. Yeah, if Sarah could lead him to the treasure, she could lead the cops to him when he was through with her. He couldn't let that happen.

Closing his eyes, he tried to remember what it was like in those first few moments when the crank took effect. He reached for that feeling, fought for it, but it just wouldn't come. He needed the stuff. Now.

Maybe he wouldn't wait the two more days he had promised Cass. Maybe he would try to get Sarah now.

But if he did that and she didn't come willingly,

there might be screaming and fighting before he got the money. If he had the money he could get all the drugs he needed.

"Have to wait, have to wait, have to wait." He squeezed the paper so hard that it ripped beneath his fingers.

He swore. He needed relief now. He glanced at the few parked cars on the dark street. People kept change, CD players, stuff he could trade in their cars. Which one looked like the best bet?

The big white van? Yeah. Maybe.

Zach picked up a rock and began to march toward the car, sizing up the window.

In two days, he'd never have to do this stuff again. He hoped Sarah Tucker wasn't a screamer.

IT HAD BEEN A HELL of a long day, Luke thought. He'd made his usual rounds and then started tracking Zach. For a guy who was a jerk, he had a lot of friends who were willing to lie for him. Or maybe they were just afraid of him. Maybe he knew all their darkest secrets and had things he was holding over their heads.

Still, Luke had made progress. He had some ideas where to look for Zach. Right now, however, his main idea was to go talk to Sarah. Since their conversation the other day, he had been feeling a little desperate, more than a little desperate.

She was slipping away. Somehow he had to figure out how to let her go. It was what she wanted, and so it was what he had to want, too.

But not yet. Not just yet.

It was about the time of day she would be going home from the shop. He turned his steps in that direction, picking up the pace.

"Shouldn't be looking forward to seeing her so much," he told himself. But he was, and when he saw her moving toward him, he couldn't help the grin that lifted his lips.

"Sarah," he said, smiling.

She smiled back at him.

"You've been working hard," he told her.

Tilting her head, her brow wrinkled with confusion. "How can you tell?"

Gently he traced a line from her forehead down to her jawline, the skin soft beneath his fingertip. She shivered beneath his touch, and he knew he shouldn't touch her. He also knew that he'd done lots of things he shouldn't have done with Sarah. "Dust smudge," he explained.

"Yes, I'm a mess," she agreed.

"Okay by me. Gives me an excuse to touch."

"Luke," she drawled.

"I know. I shouldn't."

She lifted her face. "Touch me again."

He chuckled, and she joined him. He'd never felt so miserable and so alive all at the same time.

"Sarah, Luke, I've been waiting to see both of you," a female voice said. They both turned. Luke recognized the woman immediately. He could see that Sarah did not.

"Sarah, this is Rhonda Levens." What he did not add was that Rhonda's husband was a notorious philanderer who had run off and left her three weeks ago, but he figured that Rhonda was getting to that part.

"Luke, you know my husband is missing. I gave my information to the police three weeks ago, and they haven't told me a thing other than the fact that they do not suspect criminal activity."

He knew that. He also knew that Rhonda was distressed. He'd seen her walking the streets all hours of the night. He'd taken one or two of her calls and had tried to console her without hitting her with the truth. Rhonda knew the truth. She just didn't want to acknowledge it. He didn't really blame her. Losing someone you loved, even if that person wasn't deserving of that love, was hard. To not know the whole story must be more so.

The woman twisted her hands together. "I heard how Sarah found Danny…."

Damn! Damn! He'd known it was going to come to this, and already he could see the fear in Sarah's eyes. She wouldn't want to help, but Rhonda was nothing if not persistent.

"Sarah didn't find Danny through the means you suspect, Rhonda."

"Yes, but she might be able to—would you…" She turned desperate eyes on Sarah.

Luke could practically feel the fear rolling off of Sarah. He had to help her.

"I'm so sorry," Sarah said, "but I can't find your husband."

"Please try," Rhonda begged. "Luke, please ask her…. I see you two together. She'll listen to you. Ask her to try." She grabbed Sarah's arm. He saw how Sarah flinched and her eyes grew wide, shocked. She gasped, but she didn't pull her arm away. What she did was stand very still.

"I can't," she told the woman, and there was pain and sympathy in her voice. "I'm touching you, but I don't feel the kind of things I should feel to do what you're asking of me."

Rhonda started to cry, long silent tears that tracked down her cheeks.

Gently, Luke reached forward and loosened Rhonda's grip on Sarah. He wanted to tell both of these women that things were going to be okay, but he couldn't do that. By rights, he should just excuse himself and Sarah and walk away, but Sarah was looking almost as anguished as Rhonda. Both of them were breaking his heart.

"I know a private detective in Sawtown," he told Rhonda. "He's pretty good. I'll put you in touch with him, and I'll stay on top of the progress of the case. This is not official police business, you understand."

Rhonda looked up at him gratefully, the tears streaming down.

"You're a good man," she told him.

"No, that's not me. I'm just a friend. And Rhonda?"

She looked at him.

"You know this may not turn out the way you want it to?"

Rhonda nodded. She looked at Luke and then at Sarah. "I know it won't. My husband liked to cheat," she told Sarah. "But I just want to know that he's alive, you know?"

"Yes, I know," Sarah said. "I really do." Luke was pretty sure that Sarah had a good handle on what it was like to hope and pray that someone turned out to be alive.

Rhonda walked away.

"Thank you," Sarah said.

"You were handling it pretty well yourself."

She shook her head. "I don't mean thank you for helping me out. Difficult as it is, I know how to say no, but you didn't have to go the extra mile for her. As you said, this isn't really police business."

It wasn't, and much as he pitied Rhonda, this wasn't the kind of thing he was wont to do. He'd done it for Sarah, because even though she had been handling things just fine, he knew she would feel better if this wasn't hanging over her head.

"Have people been approaching you a lot since you found Danny?"

She smiled at him. "You're frowning. But you don't need to. Actually, no, people haven't been approaching me. A few have given me funny looks, a number of them have asked for the details, but once I've explained that I found him using the kind of blind dumb luck that anyone could have used, most of them have lost interest. I think…in the short time I've been here, I've had more curiosity than requests. I'm beginning to think that my father actively went searching for desperate people and he probably made up some lies about me and embellished the truth. Gradually, most people are beginning to accept the fact that I can't come up with miracles anymore, I guess."

Sarah looked more relaxed than he could remember her since they had met. He reached out and cupped her jaw, smiling at her. "It must be a relief to have people realize the truth."

"Yes," she said. "It is." She tilted her head and rubbed her cheek against his hand. "But, Luke…"

He waited.

"It doesn't change anything. What I am now doesn't change what I once was. I will always be an oddity around here. You can't change that. You can't make things perfect for me the way you do for Danny. You can't protect me from the Rhonda Levenses of the world. As long as I'm here I'll always run into one or two people like that now and then. And you can't keep rescuing me."

"My job is to rescue."

She rose on her toes and kissed his cheek. "That's different. This community is your responsibility, but I'm not, and Luke, I thank you, but I can take care of myself. I have to do that. Otherwise I can't function. I can't live my life waiting to be rescued."

Turning, Sarah walked away. Luke watched her. He'd been trying to protect women all his life, and here was one who didn't want his help.

He remembered how she had dug her way out of that shed years ago. Sarah Tucker didn't need him.

What was a man supposed to do when the woman he wanted to protect didn't want his protection?

CHAPTER TWENTY-FOUR

SARAH DROPPED A HAMMER, just missing her toe as she jumped aside. "Damn it," she said.

"Please. The baby will hear you," Cass said.

Sarah looked at her sister and blinked. Suddenly Cass smiled, just a bit, and Sarah realized that her sister had been joking. It was the first time they had ever shared a joke as adults.

Sarah smiled.

"You didn't get much sleep last night, did you?" Cass asked.

She hadn't. All night long she had been thinking about Luke. It had taken all the guts she could muster to hand him that line about not needing him—it was so very important that she leave him as happy and contented and worry-free as she had found him—but her words had been a lie. Walking away from that man was going to be the hardest thing she could imagine.

"I was thinking about the shop," she lied.

Cass raised a brow. "Okay. I knew you were awake because I was up with leg cramps, and don't tell me to eat bananas for the potassium. I hate bananas."

"You always did," Sarah said with a chuckle. "Mom tried so hard to get you to like them."

As if she'd heard her name, Madeline came through

the door at that moment. "Well, everything's finalized. Harvey gave me the loan for the start-up costs. We can start ordering what we need. I think this is really going to be something, Sarah. It's going to make a difference to us and to the town. Already women are stopping me on the street to ask questions."

Sarah realized that that was true for her as well. Lately more people had been asking her about the business than her so-called gift.

"It was Cass's idea," she said, remembering the day when her baby sister had noted that Jemma had bemoaned the fact that she had to drive fifty miles to find a place to exercise with other women.

Cass blushed slightly. "Selfish," she said. "Someday I'll need to lose a lot of weight fast."

Sarah shrugged. "Just a little selfish. I've certainly been selfish in my time." She and Cass exchanged a look, and Sarah knew that if she was going to mend any fences with her sister, it would have to be today, while all of them were happy about the shop, and before she left town and sought the anonymity of the city once again.

"I never thought about what my leaving would do to you, Cass," she said. "I guess I was too scared about what Dad would make me do if I came back. I'm sorry I didn't pay more attention, that I didn't consider what it might be like to be so young and have your only sister desert you."

She looked at her sister, and saw that Cass was looking distressed.

"What did he do to you?" It wasn't Cass who asked. It was Madeline. "I should know. I should have known then."

Sarah hesitated. "He didn't hurt me, Mom. He never touched me. It was more the thought of what I might have to do someday that scared me so."

Madeline's jaw was set and hard. "I could beat that man to death if he were alive. I wish I could dig him up and do it, too. But I didn't protect you when you were here, did I?"

Fighting tears, Sarah knew her mother had done all she was capable of. "You gave me soup when I was sick, you sang me lullabies, you sewed me new dresses."

She knew that her mother was on the verge of saying that it wasn't enough, and Sarah didn't know how to tell her that it had been…because strangely enough, in this moment, she realized her memories of her gentle, retiring mother and her little sister's sunny disposition had been the bright spots in her life. They were the things that had given her the courage to believe that if she ran, she might find comfort somewhere else.

The bell clanging over the door at that moment kept Sarah from saying anything further. Wayland was there with his camera.

Unfortunately, the man didn't know what he had walked into. "Get out of our store, Wayland," Madeline began, advancing toward him. "We don't want you here."

"Now, Madeline, your door was open and this is a store," he said.

She picked up her purse. "I know what you're here for. You want to ask a bunch of nosy questions about my daughter Sarah, maybe about both of them, and I'm fed up with that kind of thing. I haven't always been a good mother, but even someone my age can learn."

"I'm not here to question your abilities as a mother."

"I don't really care what you're here for. You're mean and vindictive and nosy, and I don't like you." She wadded up the strap on her purse. "Are you going to get out?"

He opened his mouth to protest.

"I don't know what all I've got in here," she admitted, "but I'm sure there's enough to hurt if I swing hard enough."

"That would be assault."

"Yes, it would. Maybe you'd like to call Dugan or Luke to arrest me."

The unlikely possibility that Dugan would lead Madeline away in cuffs made Wayland sniff. "I'll be back."

"I wouldn't advise it. It's taken me a long time to find my nerve, and now that I have it, I'm not letting go."

"You better listen to her," Cass said.

"Yes, I've seen what's in that purse, and it's not pretty," Sarah agreed. "It might mess up that smug expression you wear all the time."

Wayland gave her a look of distaste. He turned to the door and shook his head at Madeline. "I see that no one in the Tucker family has any concept of the power of the media. I was just going to do a write-up about the new shop."

The door clanged shut behind him. For several seconds no one said or did anything. Then Madeline dropped her purse. "What did I just do?"

Sarah couldn't keep from smiling. "I'd say you just told Wayland off, Mom."

Cass giggled. "Pretty good, too."

"I did, didn't I?" For a minute, Madeline stood taller, pride in her eyes. "Oh my, he was going to write about the shop."

"Don't worry, Mom. Geralind is your best friend, and no one can get the word out like she can. She can scoop Wayland any day," Cass said.

Sarah couldn't help laughing then. Cass joined in, and then Madeline did, too. They were still laughing when Dugan and Luke came through the door. It was time for Luke to pick up Danny, who was sleeping in a crib in the back room, and Dugan...well, Sarah was beginning to realize just how many excuses Dugan made to stop by and check on her mother.

"Luke. Dugan," Sarah said, another chuckle slipping out.

Dugan raised his brows. "I just saw Wayland coming from here. Was he telling jokes?"

Sarah shook her head. "Mom kicked him out of the store. She threatened him with her purse. I think he was scared of her."

"Mad, you did that?" Dugan asked, looking at Madeline, who was blushing.

"I was angry."

Sarah noted a look in Dugan's eyes that seemed to indicate he liked her mother angry. She glanced at Luke, whose handsome smile was in evidence.

"Remind me not to get you angry, Mad," Luke teased.

"You're not the one threatening my daughters," she reminded him.

Instantly Luke's smile faded. "Sarah?"

She shook her head. "No one was threatening me this time. Mom was talking about stories Wayland has written in the past."

His dark gaze stayed on her, as if trying to decide if she was telling him the truth. "So…do you think he'll leave you alone?"

She knew what he was asking. Earlier in the week, Wayland had run his story about Luke, complete with the account of his wife's death. Almost everyone had been appalled at Wayland's bad taste, but they had still read the story, herself included. Now Luke was asking her if she needed an ally, but he was also trying to give her the independence she had told him she needed.

If he only knew that she wasn't afraid of Wayland anymore. Her secrets were out now. Her life was public, which meant she would be subjected to rude questions and outrageous requests for help as long as she stayed here. But knowing that, she was able to handle it. What she couldn't handle was the fact that she wanted nothing more than to walk right into Luke's protective embrace and stay there.

She didn't need his help, but she loved the fact that he offered it. She loved *him,* she realized, nearly gasping as the truth hit her. She loved a man who could be hurt by her love. If his child had to grow up with questions about her, how much would that hurt Danny and Luke? If Luke felt that people were attacking her and he was helpless to stop it, how would that make a man like him feel? And if he got angry enough to overstep the law when he *was* the law, it would tear him apart inside.

"Sarah?" he asked again.

"I don't think I have to worry about Wayland anymore," she told him, and it was the truth. Her mother had the loan, together they would scrape up enough to pay the taxes on the shop; and Cass was back home and becoming a strong woman. Sarah had to leave now. If she didn't, the temptation to stay would be too great.

And staying wasn't an option.

"Oh," she heard Cass say. She turned to her, and saw that her sister's face was pale. She was looking toward the window.

"What did you see, Cass?" Luke asked.

Cass shook her head. "Nothing. It was nothing. I thought a car nearly hit someone, but everything is okay."

CASS WAS LYING. LUKE was sure of it, but he wasn't certain what her lies meant. For a minute there she had looked as if she had seen an ax murderer. She looked a lot like she had the night the rock had been thrown through the window, but it was clear that she wasn't going to tell him anything.

It was also pretty clear that she and Sarah had built a few shaky bridges. He couldn't ask Sarah to violate her sister's trust and question her. At best, those shaky bridges might crash and burn. Then he still wouldn't know what was happening.

He was afraid that whatever was going on meant possible heartache for the Tucker women.

It's not your business, he told himself. *You're not even related and you never will be.*

A curse came to his lips. He held it back and did his best to smile at his child, who was playing with wooden blocks on the floor. Luke didn't want his son to have to suffer for his own bad attitude.

He knew what that bad attitude meant. He cared about Madeline and Cass. He felt a responsibility for them, but Sarah...what he felt for Sarah was more. She was strong and beautiful. She had come back to this town where she had known nothing but hurt in hopes of helping her mother and sister. Wounded from the loss of her own child, she had nonetheless opened her heart to his child. She had gone against her cardinal rule of searching for missing persons in order to save Danny. That made her more. It made her...

He didn't want to think the words, because it was pointless. Sarah didn't want a man. She didn't want to love a child.

That didn't make it any easier to stop thinking about her. Or to accept the fact that someone—it was Zach, damn it—was threatening her family's happiness, threatening Sarah's happiness.

Sarah wanted to deal with her problems alone, but Luke remembered the chill white of Cass's face when she looked out the shop's window—probably seeing Zach outside.

"Come on, Danny, let's go see Mrs. Stoddard. Dad's got to go on a hunt tonight."

Danny laughed. "Hunt," he repeated.

"I'm glad you approve," Luke said. "I'm not sure anyone else will."

THE NEXT MORNING, CASS went into the kitchen. She looked around to see if anyone was in the room and then she picked up the telephone and dialed.

"Penny, it's Cass. I need your help."

"What kind?" Automatically, Penny sounded suspicious. Cass didn't blame her. The misfits who had been staying with Penny were mostly an untrustworthy group. Users and losers. The word "help" usually conjured up thoughts of illegal acts.

"I need to know where Zach is." The clock had run out. Her three days were up, and she had not come up with one solution. She couldn't hand over Sarah to Zach and she couldn't let Zach harm her child. Her only hope was to try to talk to him. If she got him at the right moment, maybe she could convince him that there was another way to get some money. At least trying to talk to him was better than ticking him off by forcing him to wait any longer for her to ask Sarah to help Zach. This way at least the danger would be in front of her, and she wouldn't have to worry about Zach jumping out from some dark alley to nab her and Sarah.

"Why do you need to see him?"

"Penny, you know Zach and I have issues we need to work out. We've argued, but maybe I can fix things up with him." Okay, that was a lie, but she couldn't completely trust Penny not to repeat every word she said.

"Are you working with that cop?"

Cass stared at the floor, trying to choose her next words carefully. "Penny, you know how I feel about my sister. Do you really think I'd willingly have anything to do with a man she hangs around with?"

Penny didn't answer right away. In fact, the line was silent for so long that Cass was beginning to be afraid that she had hung up the phone. "Penny?"

"Why do you need him?"

"It's about our baby," she lied. She hadn't told Penny about the baby, but it was the most convincing argument she could think of.

"You're having a baby? With Zach?"

"Who else? Penny, I really need to find him."

Penny's sigh was audible. "All right, I don't actually

know where he is, but I can think of a few places he might be. Rob told me that Zach has sneaked in and crashed in his basement once or twice, but I doubt he could stay there during the day with Rob's mother there. He's been known to sleep in his car pretty much wherever he can find a place to park."

Panic began to spread through Cass. Neither of those suggestions was likely to help her find Zach.

"Of course, he stops by here almost every day. When he doesn't have any money, it's the only place he can find food. Not that food seems all that important to him anymore."

Cass knew. The drugs were all that was important to Zach. Still, Penny's place was the best bet on meeting up with him. She really needed to be the one to initiate the contact. She didn't want Zach catching her off-guard.

Telling her mother that she had another doctor's appointment, Cass set off to Penny's house. Maybe things would work out right. Maybe just once she would be lucky.

CHAPTER TWENTY-FIVE

SARAH GATHERED UP THE rolls of wallpaper she had
picked up at the hardware store and struggled to escape
the feeling that something wasn't right. She had a
headache, a terrible one, and she hadn't had one since
the day she had located Danny.

"Everyone gets headaches," she muttered to herself
as she moved down the street, but she knew that not
everyone got headaches like this. Combined with the
dull throbbing was a sense of doom, of anticipation, a
feeling that she needed to be doing something she
wasn't doing.

She tried to block it. *No, no, no,* she begged. *I
thought I was past all that.* She pushed open the door
of the shop. Her mother was humming, hanging
curtains.

"Where's Cass?" she asked.

Madeline stopped what she was doing. "She said she
had another doctor's appointment."

"So soon? She just had one."

"That was what I thought, but then everything has
changed medically since I had you girls. Cass told me
that it was just routine and that I shouldn't be concerned."

"I suppose that's true, and I never really saw a doctor

when I was pregnant." She'd lost the baby too soon for that. "She took your car?" The doctor's office was only a few blocks away.

"She said she had some errands to run afterward."

A sharp pain shot to Sarah's temple. Probably just irritation at Cass for taking her mother's vehicle. Her fingertips felt warm, but then she had been clenching her hands into fists. She forced herself to breathe deeply, to relax her hands.

Madeline was standing on a stepladder. She climbed down now. "You don't think she's run away again, do you?"

"No. I don't. She's been happier lately."

Madeline breathed out a sigh. "She'll be back soon then."

"Yes, I'm sure she will." But Sarah was no more sure of her words than she was that a painkiller would get rid of her headache.

The thing to do, she told herself, was to simply stay calm. The thing to do was to wait.

"Here's the wallpaper," she told her mother, dumping her package on a table. "I'm going over to see Jemma. She's thinking of having a shower for Cass, and I want to see if she needs any help. Before I return to California, I want to make sure that Cass is set up with everything she needs."

Madeline smiled at her daughter. "You're a good sister, Sarah."

"Thanks, Mom. I'll be back soon, and I have my phone with me if you need me." She headed for the door. Her story about Jemma had not been entirely honest. Jemma *was* thinking of having a shower for Cass, but Sarah was sure the young woman was perfectly in control of things.

What Sarah really needed was some time to be alone, to lie down and get rid of this darned headache, but if she had told her mother that, Madeline would have worried needlessly. Surely Sarah had caused her mother enough concern in this lifetime.

The thing to do right now was to lie down and relax, stop wondering why her hands were warm. The one thing she couldn't do right now was panic and go running off to find Luke.

CASS DIDN'T GO INTO Penny's house. She waited outside, not wanting to have a discussion with anyone but Zach. She had seen him out the window of the shop yesterday, and the look he had given her had been threatening. He had held up one finger and motioned toward Sarah.

He wanted her sister to help him, possibly to do something illegal, and Cass knew Sarah wouldn't do something like that.

She tried not to think how Zach had reacted when she had thwarted his plans, how he'd slapped her. If Sarah didn't do as Zach wanted… Well, she wasn't sure how Zach was going to react.

"Well, well, well, look who's here." Zach's voice sounded behind her. She hadn't heard his car drive up, and when she turned around, she didn't see any trace of it.

"Where's your car?"

He chuckled. "Got me a new one. A utility van." He hooked his thumb, gesturing toward the woods. In the distance, between some trees, she saw a patch of white.

She needed to humor him, to cajole him. "It's very nice." Even though she couldn't really see much of the vehicle.

"Yeah. Got those panel doors, no windows on the side. Nice for hiding stuff."

Cass felt a trickle of fear slide through her. Zach's eyes looked wilder than usual.

"Where's your sister?" he asked.

She bit her lips. "She's gone back to California."

He narrowed his eyes. "You're lying."

"No, she gave the shop to Mom, so she headed home. But it's okay, Zach. Mom and I are going to run the shop. I can give you a little money now and then."

"A little money? How much?"

She tried to keep breathing normally, to hide her fear. "I don't know exactly. We haven't opened the shop yet, but…some."

"When?" He reached out and grabbed her arm.

"Soon. Soon."

"Soon isn't good enough. I need money now." He pulled on her, roughly, and she stumbled. "Get up and walk," he ordered.

"No!"

Zach slapped her hard, dragging her toward the woods. "Walk, or you and that baby are dead."

He pulled her toward the van.

"Penny!" she called out, hoping her friend was around and could hear her.

But there was no answer. Zach hustled Cass all the way to the van, pushed her in and closed the door, locking her in. He circled the car and in a minute she heard the sound of the door opening and closing and then the car starting up. He began to drive.

Fear gripped her. She pounded on the compartment that separated them. "Zach, let me out."

"Not going to happen, but I'll stop soon."

"Then what?" She didn't want to ask but she had to know what he had in mind.

"Then you find some way to get your sister out here or that baby of yours will never be born."

LUKE RETURNED TO THE station and tried not to yawn. He'd been working late for the past couple of nights, following Zach Claxton's trail, and the extra hours were starting to show. Right now he wanted nothing better than to finish up here at the office, go home and sleep for a couple of hours, but Jemma was looking at him expectantly.

"There's a message here from Sarah. Two actually."

Instantly he was awake, alert. Sarah wasn't the kind to leave messages. She definitely wasn't the kind to leave another message if someone didn't call her back right away.

"Is she at the shop?"

"No. Home."

He picked up the phone and dialed. The phone rang four times, five times, six. He was just about to hang up when Sarah's voice came over the line, tense and broken.

"Sarah, what's wrong?"

"I don't know. I don't know, but…something. Can you come here?"

He was there in five minutes flat. When she opened the door, she practically stumbled. He caught her and moved her inside, shutting the door behind him.

"What's wrong?"

She looked up at him through pain-filled eyes. "I don't know. Something's wrong. Cass, I think."

"Did something happen to her?"

"No. Yes. I don't know. She told my mother she was

going to the doctor, but…I have this headache, this feeling that something bad is happening. It's… like Pattie, only different. I know you don't believe, but…"

He didn't believe, but Sarah was clearly in pain. "Did you take something to ease your headache?"

"Yes. It doesn't work."

"I'll go and check on Cass."

"She's not back. I called the shop and Mom was alone. I told her not to come home, because I needed a nap." She lifted her pain-filled, fear-filled gaze to him. "Something's wrong with Cass, Luke. Really wrong. I can't tell you how I know, but I do."

He looked to the side. "Have you tried—" He didn't even want to say the words. Saying it would make it too real.

"I tried…but I can't. I can feel something. Some heat, but not…what I need. I think I'm too afraid. And a part of me is sure I'm just flat out wrong. It seems unrealistic to be worrying this way, doesn't it? Except for that rock Zach threw."

And that expression of fear Cass had worn looking out the shop window, Luke thought.

He dropped to his knees beside Sarah. "We're going to find her, Sarah. If she's just at the doctor's, then we'll feel a little silly, but that's okay. No matter what, we'll find her. I've been trailing Zach lately. I have a few ideas where to look for him."

Sarah clutched at his hands. Tears filled her eyes and she threw her arms around him. "Thank you. I know I sound like I'm being ridiculous and ominous and completely unrealistic."

He gathered her close and kissed her just beneath the ear. "You're being a loving sister. Now come on."

"Okay. Let me get my phone. I left it in my purse, but I don't want Mom to call and not be able to reach me."

She went into the other room. When she came back, her face was ashen. "I missed two calls."

Luke knew without asking that they had been from Cass. Sarah was frantically punching buttons to call her sister back.

He watched her expression as the phone was answered on the other end. He heard her give one strangled "Cass," and then watched her listen. "Wait, don't go!" she cried, but the connection had obviously been cut.

Sarah looked up at him, terror in her eyes. "Zach has her."

"Where?"

She shook her head. "I don't know. He wants me to come find them, to use my powers to find some buried treasure or something. He says that if I'm the real deal, I'll be able to find them and quickly."

"And if you're not?"

"Then he's taking Cass hostage and leaving the area. Maybe worse. We've got ninety minutes."

Luke reached for his radio. Sarah's hand on his wrist stopped him. "He says if there are any police officers nearby, he'll kill her and then himself. I have to do this alone."

"That's not going to happen. I can't let you go into danger."

"How do you know I'm not in danger here? Zach knows where I live and work. There aren't many places in town where I could hide. Besides, despite the fact that my clairsentience isn't what it was, I think...no, I know I have access to information you could never have." She hesitated, then added, "I had it with Danny. I never said, and I didn't want to believe that was how I found him, but it was…at least partly."

Luke took her by the arms and held her so that she had to stare up at him. "It's too dangerous. Sarah, I've spent some time checking Zach out. This guy is a meth addict. If he has some wild scheme for you to get money for him, that means he doesn't have enough to support his habit, and as meth isn't a particularly expensive drug, he must be truly broke and desperate. A meth addict will do anything to get the next fix. It's an extremely powerful addiction. He's not going to let Cass go, and if he gets you, a woman he feels might help him keep up a steady flow of money to buy drugs, he'll never let you get away."

"But if he sees a police officer and he's truly desperate…"

"I'll do my best not to let him see me. I won't call in reinforcements unless I think we can do so safely. The boys on my squad are good, but they're not known for stealth. That said, I'm coming with you, Sarah. There's no stopping me. Don't even try. Like it or not, you have to give up some control this time."

"ALL RIGHT, LET'S GO. I just have to get one thing." She ran into the next room. Earlier she had picked up one of Cass's sweaters. The heat from it had suffused her fingers but had yielded no results. Now that she knew the danger was real, she had to do better. Much better. With the clock on the bedside table ticking away the minutes and her heart pounding out a frantic accompaniment, she quickly searched the room.

There were lots of things. She picked them up and put them down. Not hot enough. Not nearly good enough.

Dropping to her knees, she searched beneath the bed. In her childhood, Cass had been wont to hide her treasures under the bed in a box. Feeling around, Sarah's fingers lit on a cloth bag. She pulled it out. Inside were two knitting needles, a clump of tangled yarn, one finished pale yellow baby bootie and half of another. The minute Sarah's fingers closed around the bootie, overwhelming heat nearly had her jerking away. She grabbed the small bit of fluff and ran outside to her car, where Luke waited for her.

"It's a baby bootie," she told him. "Because Cass has stronger feelings about this object, I'm hoping that it will help us."

"I've spent some time talking to all of Zach's friends. They weren't particularly cooperative, but I did find out that Zach doesn't appear to have a permanent home right now. Other than a few stays at Penny's or at her friend Rob's place, he's been sleeping in his car or in the woods. A few days ago a utility van went missing. No one has seen it, but I've found tracks in the woods, places where the undergrowth has been disturbed. He'd want to be near water most likely, and those tracks have born that out."

"But he might not care about that today."

"No, but habit is a strong motivator. If he's found a place where no one has called him on the theft for the past two nights, he might go back there."

"Do you have a specific spot in mind?" Sarah asked.

"No, just a general area. It's bigger than I'd like."

"Then we'll have to narrow it down," Sarah said. She gripped the baby bootie more tightly and closed her eyes.

CHAPTER TWENTY-SIX

IT WASN'T WORKING. It wasn't working. Sarah tried not to think the words, but it was true. Luke was driving toward the area where he thought Zach might be, and the yarn beneath her fingers felt hot to the touch, but there were no pictures in her mind, not even vague ideas about which direction to go.

Traveling over the rough ground, the car hit a rut. The vehicle lurched slightly, and Sarah gasped.

"I'm sorry," Luke said, and his voice was so hoarse that she knew he was talking about more than driving over the rut. "Sarah, I'm going to have to call for backup. We're going to have to flood this area with officers. We can't be subtle about this any longer, not with the clock running down."

"But if Zach feels cornered in any way—"

"We'll do our best not to make him feel that way."

But he knew, as well as she, that approaching a dangerous man in the woods wasn't an ideal situation for a standoff, especially when a hostage was involved. Every movement in the trees could spook Zach, and if he knew there were police officers surrounding them, he might panic.

"I'm sorry, Sarah," Luke said again, and he reached over and took her hand.

Immediately, his touch had a calming affect on her. His hand was big and strong and warm. She knew that he was a caring man and that he was a man who had devoted his life to protecting women. He would move heaven and earth to protect Cass.

She took a deep breath and stopped fighting as much as she could. After all, she wasn't really being a help, anyway, and Luke was right. They needed help. Luke would do what was right. She trusted him. If anyone could help Cass, it would be him.

Having admitted that, Sarah relaxed slightly.

The image hit her like a cannonball. A white van, a pump, an old crumbling bit of building.

Sarah gasped.

Immediately Luke released his grip. "Did I hurt you?"

"No. No. Give me your hand again. I need your help, Luke. And I need you to stop the car."

Without question he did as she asked. He turned to her and folded his hand around hers.

She leaned into his touch and relied on his strength. "I trust you to protect us as best you can," she said. "Trust me, too."

She raised her eyes to his and Luke nodded. "I trust you. Tell me," he said.

"I don't know exactly." She told him what she had seen.

She could see him digesting the information, studying the possibilities. "I've only lived here in Gold Tree a year," he told her, "but when I first came here I used to put Danny in a pack on my back and hike the woods. It's been a while, but…I think, just a little farther." He gestured toward the steering wheel, and she gave him her trust.

"All right," she said as he silently and slowly rolled the car through the trees. One hundred feet, two hundred feet, three hundred. Sarah held on to Luke with one hand and her sister's knitting with the other. The vision stayed clear and true. It strengthened. "A small tombstone," she said suddenly.

Luke stopped the car. "I know the place. Someone buried a favorite pet there. It was a turning-around spot on our hikes." He opened the door. "Don't shut it," he said, lowering his voice. "We're close. He'll hear."

She slid out the door and stood up. The minute her feet hit the ground and Luke grabbed her hand again, the heat and the vision grew stronger.

"This way," they both whispered at the same time.

Stealthily they crept in the direction where they both knew the van lay, not talking, careful where they stepped. Coming out into a clearing, the van suddenly appeared only fifty yards ahead of them.

"I want you to stay here," Luke whispered against Sarah's ear.

She didn't want to agree, but she nodded. Her part here was done. Now she needed Luke to free Cass.

Luke gave her a reassuring smile, then slowly began to circle the clearing in order to get closer to the van without being seen.

Suddenly Sarah felt a hand clamp over her mouth. She tried to scream, tried to bite down but only managed a muffled yelp before the hand covered her nose as well, smothering her.

Luke whirled and pulled his gun.

"Oh, no, that would be such a terrible mistake, Luke," Zach said, taking his hand from Sarah's mouth and wrapping it around her neck. "Because if you look on the far side of the clearing, you'll see that I have a gun trained on Cass."

Sarah's heart went stone cold. With Zach holding her still, her peripheral vision was limited. She couldn't see much, but she could see enough. Cass was tied up, hands and feet, the end of the rope staked to the ground in front of the small tombstone Cass had seen in her vision.

"If you shoot me, I shoot Cass," Zach explained. "But if you let me take Sarah, everyone wins."

"If you think I'm letting you put Sarah in that van and drive away with her, you're wrong," Luke said.

"Oh, really? Watch." Keeping the gun trained on Cass, Zach kept Sarah between himself and Luke's gun and shuffled closer to the van.

Sarah knew that if she got in that van, she might never get out alive again. She looked straight into Luke's eyes and saw the agony written there. This was a man who felt responsible for his mother's beatings, who felt responsible for his wife's death, who cared about what happened to her. If things went wrong here, not only would she and her sister lose their lives, Luke would never be able to live with the results.

Think, Sarah, think, she told herself, and she knew Luke was telling himself the same thing.

Zach was still moving her along toward the van. Time was running out.

"Luke, I think—no, I *know* I'm having a vision," she said suddenly. "It's like this thing I can't control. It's making me do things I don't want to do."

"What are you saying?" Zach demanded. "What do you see? What are you talking about?"

He squeezed tighter as he grew more agitated, and Sarah fought to keep breathing.

"I—" She stared straight into Luke's eyes. Desperate. Desperate.

"Sarah, don't," Luke begged, and she knew he was frightened for her. He was only one man, there were two women here, and Zach was growing wild. She could barely catch a breath now as Zach's hand began to wave wildly and he tightened his hold yet again.

She stared into Luke's eyes and prayed that he would understand what she was about to do.

Sarah took a deep breath. "I see—the knitting needles I used to locate Cass." She gasped out the words, hoping that Zach's attention was on her and that he would do nothing as long as she was talking. "I'm holding them in my left hand…. I don't want to stab Zach. I hate hurting people, but—I can't stop."

She gave an anguished cry, lifted her hand slightly and stabbed downward with her hand with all the force she could muster.

Zach screamed, loosening his hold as he tried to move back and stop her from plunging the needle into his thigh. She dropped as he swung his gun toward her.

The sound of a shot rang out as Luke fired, knocking the gun from Zach's hand.

Sarah hit the ground and rolled, then crawled toward her sister, throwing her body over Cass.

She turned to see Zach running toward the van with Luke behind him calling for backup on his radio.

"Freeze," Luke shouted. His gun was still trained on Zach, but she knew he would never shoot a fleeing man in the back.

Zach must have known it, too, because he climbed in the van, put it in gear and started to drive away. Through the open window he called out, "You and me aren't done, Sarah Tucker." Then he floored the van and roared out through the trees, dirt and rocks and twigs flying as the vehicle accelerated wildly.

"Not done? Oh, I think you are," Luke muttered, his voice grim, and then he calmly shot out the tires on Zach's van.

The vehicle jerked wildly. Sarah heard Zach's scream just as the van slammed into a tree full force. The crash was deafening, the silence afterward more so.

Automatically she looked at Luke, who was running toward her, anguish in his eyes. She knew what he was thinking. She might have died.

Kneeling next to her, he reached out and touched her face, his fingers brushing her lips. "Are you all right?" he asked.

"Yes." Her voice came out broken and raspy, but she reached up and touched his hand. "Yes," she said again.

He then looked at Cass.

"I'm okay, too," she said, nodding, her body shaking.

Tears filled Sarah's eyes. "Thank you," she said to Luke. "For trusting me. For everything."

A grim smile lifted his lips. "You're the best kind of woman, Sarah. A man would be nuts to doubt your word…or your vision."

He looked down at the hand where she had been holding the baby bootie…and no knitting needle. "That was some vision," he said.

"The most useful I've ever had," she admitted, "but the man who was quick enough and trusting enough to follow it was more important." Her voice broke as tears of relief clogged her throat. Luke wrapped his arms around her and hugged her close. Then he seemed to realize that Cass was watching.

He quickly set Sarah from him and began to untie her sister.

"I'd better get someone over here to take you home," he said. "I still have work to do here." He didn't motion toward the van, but Sarah knew that he believed the crash might have been fatal.

Cass said nothing. She looked as if the world had beaten her up.

"I'll see you at home," Luke promised.

Overcome, Sarah nodded. Love filled her soul, more love than her heart could hold, more love than she should be feeling for a man like Luke. This situation today could have cost him dearly, both professionally and emotionally.

He had trusted her and used questionable methods to resolve the frightening situation. And if something had gone wrong, as it so easily might have, he would have never forgiven himself.

And if she hadn't come home three weeks ago, Zach wouldn't have had any reason to kidnap Cass.

"I'll see you," Sarah finally managed to say, but she knew now that coming home might not have been the right thing for her to do. And for sure, she had already stayed too long.

It was time to do the decent thing and leave so that everyone could get their lives back to normal. With her here, it was obvious that nothing would ever be normal.

WHEN LUKE FINALLY MADE it home that night, he found Sarah sitting in his living room. His tired expression lit up at the sight of her.

"Is it over?" she asked. He didn't have to ask what she meant. Word that Zach had died in a car crash was all over the town.

"It's done. How is Cass bearing up?"

"As well as any woman could who has been through as much as she has lately."

"And you?" Luke studied Sarah closely.

She looked up at him with sad, dark eyes. "I'm good."

A harsh laugh escaped him. "You're not a very good liar, Sarah."

She rose then and walked toward him. "No, I'm not, but I *am* all right, Luke. Cass is alive and she's safe now. *You're* alive."

He couldn't help looking taken aback. "You were worried about me?"

Slowly, she nodded. "If something had happened to me or Cass, I knew you would risk everything for us, including putting your own life at stake. And Zach wasn't a guy who would care whether you lived or died."

But she cared. She cared so much that her eyes were haunted. The thought nearly broke his heart. He reached out and folded her into his arms.

"It worked out," he whispered, "thanks to you."

"And you," she said. "Luke, did you mind...I mean...the whole clairsentience thing...I know how you feel about that...."

He leaned down and caught her lips in a kiss that scorched her soul and made her toes curl. "Sarah, you saved your sister's life today. However you did it, I'm grateful."

Something that looked very much like relief filled

her eyes. She rose on her toes and returned his kiss, her soft lips tasting of the sweetness that was Sarah.

Desire slid through him, and he tugged her closer. "Your mother just offered to keep Danny tonight. He was already sleeping, and she thought I might be too tired to see to things."

Instantly, she froze in his arms. "Oh…well, I should go."

He tugged her close, kissed her again and smiled against her lips. "I'm never too tired for you."

She slid her arms around his waist, pressing her body against his. "You're sure?"

He pulled her closer, molding her body against his and showing her just how sure he was.

"Then, yes," she said on a breath. "I'm…I'm leaving in the morning, going back to California, and I wanted to…I wanted *you*. I wanted to say goodbye. I forgot you would be tired."

His heart had stopped. Tired was the least of the things he was suddenly feeling. Denial, resistance, heartbreak, all warred to be first in line. He wanted to fold her up against his heart and beg her to change her mind and stay.

But this town had been beating on her all her life, robbing her of her right to a normal, peaceful, happy life. If he asked her to stay, she would feel guilt and regret. And there was no way he could ever hurt Sarah that way.

"I can't think of anything I need to do more right now than make love with you," he whispered against her hair.

She snuggled closer against him. "I feel the same way."

He ordered his mind and all the protests to stop then and there. This night was theirs and he would give his whole heart to this time with her. If there was to be no more, then he didn't want to waste a second on regrets. His every move and thought and feeling would be dedicated to making this night good, to ending things right.

"Come with me," he whispered. He took her hand and led her to the screened-in sleeping porch on the back of his house. It looked out onto the woods that ran up to the west side of town. Moonlight spilled into the room.

"It's beautiful," she said.

He smiled at her. "It's why I bought the house. I don't sleep back here often. The other room is closer to Danny, but tonight…"

"I know," she said. She reached for the buttons on his shirt. "I want to see you in moonlight."

Her slender fingers slowly undid his shirt, peeling it back from him. Then she laid her cheek against his chest and breathed in.

Luke nearly came undone. He had never felt anything so erotic. He brought his hands up, sliding them beneath her plain white blouse. "You're magic beneath my fingers," he told her.

She smiled in the moonlight. "I never liked the word *magic* very much," she conceded. "Now I do. Love me tonight, Luke. Let me love you, too."

He knew she was referring to the physical act of love, and he knew the smartest thing he could do would be to give her body pleasure and try his hardest to keep his heart out of things. He also knew damned well that he wasn't going to.

"Come into my bed, sweet Sarah," he said. He carefully undressed her, kissing every inch he unclothed. Her skin was hot beneath his lips, her mouth sweet as raspberries, her cheeks and throat and the valley beneath her generous breasts scented with her own unique perfume that drove him mad.

When he took her nipple into his mouth, she mewed softly, and his arousal grew harder.

Shucking the remainder of his own clothes, he lay back on the feather mattress of the bed and drew her down on top of him. "I want you, Sarah," he said.

"Yes, oh, yes," she said as she slid onto the length of him.

Sometime in the night, hot kisses were exchanged.

Sometime in the night, Luke went over the edge, and Sarah came with him.

At some point, when he was sure he had exhausted her, she reached for him. "Again, please," she begged, and they traveled to the brink of passion and beyond one more time.

But in the morning when Luke awoke with the scent of Sarah on his skin and a feeling of satisfaction such as he had never known, he looked to the side and found an empty bed.

Sarah had gone, and an honorable man would consider her wishes and leave her alone.

He had always considered himself a most honorable man, and yet…he couldn't help himself. He threw on his clothes and went outside, walking toward her house.

He saw her sitting on her mother's front steps, staring at him.

He started to take another step toward her, but then he saw the sadness in her eyes. He saw goodbye. A final goodbye this time. He knew if he pushed things, he would only end up hurting her. If he tried to make her stay here in Gold Tree, he would just break her.

He would be another one of those men who had tried to control her.

Turning around, Luke walked away from Sarah. It was only a few steps back to his house, but it was the longest walk he had ever taken.

CHAPTER TWENTY-SEVEN

"I WANT YOU TWO TO have the shop free and clear," Sarah said, facing her mother and sister. Her bags were packed. "There are still a couple of weeks before the taxes have to be paid. I'm sure I can find enough work to manage that, and then I'll have all the paperwork transferred to your names."

Madeline opened her mouth, to protest that Sarah didn't have to do that, Sarah supposed.

"That will ensure that the baby is cared for," Sarah explained, effectively shutting off any arguments.

Her mother nodded, but then she looked up, and Sarah saw that her eyes were misting, that she was blinking rapidly.

Oh, please. Oh, please, let me do this right, Sarah thought as her own eyes started to fill with tears.

"I love you, Sarah," her mother said suddenly. "And oh, I just can't let you go without telling you how sorry I am that I wasn't the kind of mother you should have had. I married your father for all the wrong reasons, I let him tell me how you and Cass were to be raised and I let him bully you. All of that was so wrong, Sarah. I can't help thinking that if I had done things differently, you could be happy here."

Cass crossed her arms and frowned. "Mom, it isn't

you. No matter how much you let Dad run the show, I think Sarah and I always knew that you loved us. If Sarah is leaving this time, it's my fault. I've been mean to her since the minute she got here. I was so jealous of you," she told her sister. "You always got the attention I craved, and even though I knew it wasn't your fault that I wasn't you, I blamed you for every bad thing that happened to me. But Sarah," she said, her voice suddenly breaking, "I was wrong. I was stupid. Can't you see how stupid I was? With all the mistakes I've made these past few weeks, I would think it was obvious. You can't decide to go just because your sister is a jerk."

Tears spilled over Sarah's lashes. "I love both of you so much," she told her mother and sister. "You know I didn't leave the first time because of you, don't you? And you know that the reason I stayed away was because of Dad, not because of you, don't you?"

"Yes, but—" Madeline began.

Sarah shook her head. "No buts. I'll admit the things that were said and done, or not done, hurt me, but I'm pretty sure all people who care about each other make some pretty bad mistakes and hurt each other. I obviously hurt both of you by not trying harder to come home and by not staying in touch more often. I know that you love me," she said to her mother.

She turned to her sister. "I should have been there for you when you were younger. And…even if you can't say it, I know that you love me, too. If you hadn't cared, then you would have turned me over to Zach the minute he asked you to."

Cass nodded tearfully. "Yes, of course I love you. You're my sister. You saved my life."

"And I'm not leaving because of anything either of you have done," Sarah said. "I just have to. There are other reasons, other complications, things I can't explain."

"Wayland," Madeline said, her voice hard.

"No, not even Wayland. Don't ask me to explain. Just please accept the fact that I can't stay here anymore."

Cass took a long, shaky breath. "Will you write? Will you call? Will you visit?"

Sarah smiled and took her sister's hand. "I'll write. I'll call. You'll visit me. We won't ever be separated completely again. And I want to see your baby when it's born. I intend to be a doting aunt who spoils him or her rotten."

Cass managed a shaky laugh. She hugged her sister.

Sarah turned to Madeline. "Mom, I know you worry. I know you think you did things wrong, but you did so many things right, too. I want you to be happy."

Madeline tried to nod through her tears.

"I'll do that," she said. "I'll do it for you."

Sarah managed a shaky smile. "You might begin by admitting that Dugan Hayes would make a good husband."

Madeline blinked. "I don't think—"

"Mom, the guy's crazy about you, and you know it," Cass said, laughing.

"We were in love before I married your father," Madeline admitted.

Her daughters raised their brows.

"But I wronged him by marrying your father. I made so many mistakes with those men and with the two of you, I don't even trust my judgment anymore."

"Do you love him?" Sarah asked.

Madeline stared at her daughter. "I'm not sure. I might, but marriage is such a big step. My last one—"

"Was to the wrong man. Maybe you should at least give Dugan a chance to see if he's the right one."

"Sure, Mom, give the man a chance," Cass added.

Madeline looked flustered. "I can't believe my own daughters are giving me advice on men."

"We work well together," Sarah said, smiling at her sister. "And we want what's best for you. Think about it."

"I'll do that," Madeline promised. "I definitely will." For a few seconds, Sarah thought she saw her mother's eyes grow soft and dreamy. She wondered if it was because she loved Dugan. She hoped it was.

But that was between her mother and Dugan Hayes. And Sarah had to leave. Smooch and San Francisco were waiting.

"Come on, sweetie," she told her dog as she led him to the car.

"Madeline, is that daughter of yours still talking to animals?" a passerby called to one of the woman standing in the doorway.

"My daughter has a gift," Madeline called out. "Just because you don't know how to talk to animals, doesn't mean that everyone is as limited as you are." Her voice broke a little.

"You tell 'em, Mom," Cass said fiercely, tears dripping down her cheeks, as the two of them stood there with their arms around each other.

"Goodbye, Sarah," Madeline and Cass called.

"Goodbye." Sarah barely got the word out.

"Aren't you going to say goodbye to Luke?" Cass suddenly asked.

Sarah turned anguished eyes to her sister. "I already did. Last night." Then she got in her car and headed for the road out of town.

LUKE WAS IN THE squad car, making his rounds when he got a call from Jemma. "It's Cass Tucker. She says it's urgent."

Luke's heart started pounding so loud that he could barely concentrate on what Jemma was saying, but finally he determined that Cass was at the station. He turned the car around and headed back into town.

Cass was waiting outside the station and ran to the car when he pulled up. "Can I get in?" she asked.

He reached across the car and opened the passenger door.

"Drive," she said. "Toward the west end of town."

"What's wrong?"

"It's Sarah."

He gripped the wheel so tightly he feared that it might break. "Is she hurt? In trouble?"

"She's leaving."

He put on the brakes. He turned and looked at Cass. "I knew that."

She gave him an exasperated look. "Don't you even care?"

He pushed one hand back through his hair. "Of course I care."

"How much?"

"What?"

"I said, how much? How much do you care?"

Luke let out a long sigh. "Cass, this is between your sister and me."

"I know that, but…aren't you supposed to be a man of action? A lawman?"

"Yes, I'm a man of action, and in this case I'm taking action. I'm leaving her alone."

"How can you do that when you care about her?"

The pain in Luke's heart grew greater. He hadn't thought that it could, but knowing that she was on her way out of town right this minute—

"I'm letting her go *because* I care. She's been hurt, Cass. By men. She doesn't want to get involved again."

"But you wouldn't hurt her."

He wished he could be so confident. "I would try not to, but I might still end up hurting her," he said.

"And she would know how hard you had tried to avoid that. That's the difference, if you ask me. No one else ever even cared enough to try. And believe me, I know what I'm talking about."

Longing welled up in Luke, but he knew the issues. He knew how she felt about Danny, about men, about this town. She felt she could never be a normal woman with a normal life.

"Why are you doing this?" he asked Cass.

"I want her to stay."

"For her?"

Cass didn't answer right away. "Not completely. She's my sister, and I'm just beginning to know her. We're just starting to build bridges, and I want to keep doing that. I want her to be here for my baby's birth. But I also don't want her to be alone. I don't want her to spend her life having to hide from who and what she is. That's what will happen if she goes back to California. She'll blend in again, work hard at being anonymous. Because of that, she'll never let anyone get truly close. That can't be good."

Luke closed his eyes. He thought of Sarah somewhere alone, always worried that someone would find out her secrets. She would be alone when there were people here in Gold Tree who loved her.

He turned to Cass. "You're only eighteen. How did you get to be so wise?"

She laughed. "You know my record. Wisdom isn't something I'm known for, but lately I've been following my heart. When your sister throws her body over you to protect you from danger, it certainly makes a girl examine what's truly important and what isn't. Sarah's happiness is important, and you're important to Sarah. So…are you going to do anything about that or are you going to be like everyone has always been around here and just let her go her own way with no real support system?"

"Ouch," Luke said. "So…you think it would be a crime to let her leave."

"Of the worst kind."

"I'll drop you at home."

Cass raised a brow. "So you're going somewhere?"

Luke took a shaky breath. "Cass, a crime is being committed and I'm a man of the law." Minutes later, he was driving down the road, lights flashing and sirens blaring.

This is probably a fool's errand, he thought. Sarah wanted to leave. She wanted to leave *him.* He couldn't deny that, and while he had been many less-than-admirable things in his life, a fool wasn't one of them.

"So, take a chance," he whispered. "What's the worst that can happen?" But he knew the answer to that, and he didn't want to think about it.

Sarah was ten miles out of town, but her heart was back in Gold Tree. Tears clogged her throat.

"To think that I didn't want to come here, Smooch," she said to her companion, "and now I can't bear to leave."

Smooch gave her his best sad look.

"I know, I know. I could have stayed, but Luke…I could never justify what my staying would do to Luke. He'd have to spend all his time defending me or worrying about me, and then there's Danny. A child deserves to grow up with normal adults. I know I did the right thing. It was just friendship between Luke and me, or at least friendship and lust."

Her voice broke, and Smooch whimpered.

"Sorry, buddy," she said. "This isn't your problem. I'll be better soon. When we get home, we'll find a good place to live where they like dogs, I'll find work and then everything will be fine. Just you and me." She reached out and patted his fur.

Then she did her best to stanch the tears that threatened.

Behind her, somewhere in the distance, she heard a siren and, instinctively she let up on the gas even though she wasn't speeding. She glanced in her rearview mirror and pulled slightly to the side to allow the squad car to pass.

But when the car got closer, she looked in the rear view mirror and saw Luke behind the wheel. Her heart skidded. Something was wrong.

She pulled over and fumbled with her seat belt. Her nervousness made her fingers clumsy and at first she didn't realize that she had locked the door.

Then Luke was standing next to her car. He reached

in and pulled up the lock, opened the door and took her hand as she stood to meet him.

Instantly, heat, awareness, longing meshed with her fear.

"Your mother and sister are fine," he said quickly. "I didn't mean to frighten you."

"Nothing's wrong?" Her heart didn't believe it.

He shook his head and brought her hand closer, holding it against his chest so she could feel the thud of his heartbeat and the heat of his skin beneath his shirt. "Not in the way you mean. No one you know or love is in danger."

"You had your sirens on."

"I know. That was wrong. I knew that, but I had to talk to you."

Sarah looked up into Luke's eyes and felt as if she wanted to look at him forever. Having her hand in his felt so right, but…

"Why did you need to talk to me?" she asked.

"You're going back to California. You're leaving me. I know the reasons you're going. You've told me often enough. I convinced myself that the noble thing would be to let you go without complaint, but Cass came to see me and…"

"What did she say?"

"Let's just say your sister has a gift for getting to the heart of the matter. I love you, Sarah."

"No, you can't." Tears threatened again. It was so hard to go. Her reasons were good, but it was so very difficult.

"Maybe I can't, but I do. Feel." He pressed his hand gently over hers, molding her palm to his chest. His heart was thundering wildly. "That's you, Sarah. That's how I feel when I'm with you and it's also my fear of losing you."

"I can't…" she began.

His eyes looked so dark and sad. "Because you don't love me."

"Because I *do* love you. Luke, look what these past few weeks have been like for you. You've had to keep saving me, you've had to keep defending me. You've worried about me."

"Yeah, pretty wonderful stuff," he said with a small smile.

A tear slipped down her cheek. "Luke…" she drawled.

"Sarah…" he drawled back. "Worrying about the woman you love is a part of life, a very necessary part in my case. Don't go, Sarah. At least not yet. Let me find a new place where you can be happy. Let me have a chance to show you that it wouldn't be so terrible being loved by a man like me."

Sarah drew her brows together. She pulled her hand away. "Terrible? You know darn well that I would consider it wonderful if you loved me, but Luke… Danny…"

"Adores you."

"Because he's a baby."

"Because you're adorable and because you adore him right back. Nothing is going to change that, Sarah."

"You say that now. You say that you love me now, but when years have gone by and people are still approaching me to find their lost belongings or loved ones, how will you feel then?"

"Sarah, it's only you I care about. I don't care what

other people say or do. And if you *do* care, if you want to move elsewhere, I'm there."

"I don't want to move elsewhere."

He raised his brows and looked at her car.

"I know," she said. "I didn't want to come back to Gold Tree, and I was scared about what would happen, how I would feel about people's reactions to me. And some of those reactions *are* nosy and critical and even mean, but most of them aren't. I'm an oddity, but not like I was when I was young. That was my father with his snake-oil routine. I realize that I spent most of my time worrying about how people would react because I knew how *you* felt about psychics."

He lifted one hand and stroked her cheek. He leaned forward and placed his lips against hers. "There are things I don't understand, sweet Sarah, but one thing I understand completely. I love you, all of you, all that you are, and nothing you can say or do or be can change that. But I don't want you to have to live your life in fear. I don't want you to ever be afraid of what I might think, because what I think is that you're wonderful."

Sarah closed her eyes. She leaned into him and pressed her lips against his chest. "I love you, Luke."

"Then stay with me, Sarah. Stay with me… somewhere. Anywhere. Don't leave me. Don't leave *us*."

He pulled her into his arms and rocked with her, holding her close. She breathed in the scent of him as hope began to trickle in and fill her heart.

"Anywhere?" she asked, her voice muffled against the hard wall of his chest.

"Absolutely. Name it."

She smiled and pulled back, gazing up into his eyes. "Alaska?"

He smiled back at her. "I've always wanted to see a grizzly."

"Japan?"

"I've heard Mount Fuji is really pretty."

Sarah smiled and wrapped her arms around his waist. "Gold Tree is nice, too. I've missed the woods and the lakes. I've missed cranberry festivals and…I've missed home. If I leave here, after knowing you, I'll miss you. More than anyone or anything I'll miss you and Danny, and I'll never stop loving you or missing you."

"Then stay with me, Sarah. You'll never find a man who loves you or wants you more."

"I'll never find a man I love more, Luke." She rose on her toes and kissed him.

"Luke?"

"Mmm…" He nuzzled his lips against her throat.

"When I touch you, I feel…I feel something so much stronger than when I touch anyone else."

Luke took her face in his hands and kissed her lips. "So do I, Sarah. I think it's called love."

Then he helped Sarah get Smooch into the squad car. "I'll send someone back for your car later," he said. "For now, let's go home and start over."

She smiled at him. "I have a feeling it's going to be a good beginning."

Luke laughed. "That's good to hear, my love, because your feelings are as good as gold."

Everything you love about romance...
and more!

Please turn the page for Signature Select™
Bonus Features.

ANGEL EYES

BONUS
FEATURES
INSIDE

Could Someone Please Find Me a Hero...Heroine?
by Myrna Mackenzie

Oh, for a magic character wand. What I wouldn't give to acquire one! I wonder if anyone is selling a used one on the Internet today....

No? Hmm....

4   All right, I'm talking total nonsense, of course, so let's talk truth instead. The point is that every romance needs a to-die-for hero and a heroine that every woman wants to be, but how does an author come up with these two essential and compelling characters? It's more than just searching through a name book and choosing appealing names and adding attractive features. Indeed, the process of coming up with two such characters is one that often mirrors the process one goes through when meeting a new acquaintance.

I usually begin my books with a conflict, and the characters are born from that conflict. In *Angel Eyes*, the heroine has been running from the evidence of her psychic abilities all her life until she is forced into coming home and facing her demons. My first question to myself, then, was who is this woman? Who was she when she was born, what happened to her and how did her circumstances affect her?

A story begins to unfold in my mind. Most of this initial story will never even make it into the book. It's all about the heroine's background, stories that involve her childhood friends and family and experiences. This part is loads of fun. I can let my imagination run wild. No one will ever read this material, yet it's essential for me to engage in this process. I really need to get to know this woman almost as well as I know myself. So I brainstorm. I treasure hunt for the heroine's past.

Now I have a heroine. I still don't know her very well (she hasn't actually made it onto the pages of my book yet), but I know her well enough to ask myself what kind of a man would be the worst kind of man for her. In other words, who is the hero? He has to be a man she will both battle against and be attracted to (in spite of the fact that she knows she can never have a happy ending with him).

The hero's background begins to emerge....

I'm ready to throw the two of them into conflict with each other, but I still don't completely know them, so I write the scene...and I rewrite it, possibly many times.

The story continues to unfold. I'm slowly getting to know these two people just the way you would get to know a new friend. Of course, I'm always keeping in mind that the heroine must be a woman I can both relate to and admire. The hero must be a man I can fall in love with.

They begin to circle each other, to interact, to pull away and then rush forward.

Now I know them better. I may go back and rewrite some of their earlier action and dialogue. Sometimes I'm amazed at my original work. Once I know these people, I know they would never act the way I had originally written the scene!

I press on, and—here is where the magic happens. I love this part. As the book develops, I stop thinking so much. I stop asking myself questions. At this point, the hero and heroine have become so alive to me that I no longer orchestrate their thoughts, their movements and their dialogue. They are now the ones running the show. They've become real.

They've morphed into a true hero and a true heroine. My job is merely to listen and watch and take dictation. That's why, if you live with a writer, you'll frequently find yourself in the embarrassing position of coming upon her with tears in her eyes. She's no longer the puppet master. She's watching a movie—she's living through her characters rather than her characters living through her!

It's a wonderful and terribly exciting and fulfilling experience that happens to me every book, and I highly recommend it.

Having said all that, what are some characteristics I aim for at the beginning (when those pesky characters still allow me to pull the strings)?

A Hero:

May not have always taken responsibility for his actions, but he does so now

Is protective of others

Is cognizant that nothing he does happens in a vacuum

Is always aware of the heroine, whether he wants to be or not

Doesn't have to be physically strong or attractive, but must be mentally tough

A Heroine:

Must be independent—she doesn't wait for others to get her out of scrapes

She doesn't have to be beautiful outside, but must be beautiful inside

She is nurturing, but that doesn't necessarily mean she is domestic

She believes in pushing herself to be the best she can be, no matter the task

She is always aware of the hero, whether she wants to be or not

8

These are, of course, just my own guidelines. They might not work for others, and, as I use them as a starting point, there is always the possibility that I will whisk them aside once the story begins to take on a life of its own.

And that is the inherent joy of writing the hero and heroine. Whether the heroine begins her book life spunky or tough or vulnerable, whether the hero starts the journey broken or militant or wary, at some point they grab the reins away from the author.

I love that moment, that fairy-dust moment. It's the very reason I have to write.

If I Could Have Any Dog I Wanted…
by Myrna Mackenzie

Writing fiction certainly has its benefits. As a person who loves choices, one who is addicted to window-shopping and things of that ilk (choosing a pretend wardrobe, decorating a pretend house), I've always adored any activity that allows me to imagine myself in situations I'll never actually live through. Catalogs are my weakness. I also love those magazines that feature hundreds of home plans, and I was hooked on travel brochures from an early age. Between the pages of such publications I can have anything I like, live anywhere I want to, travel to countries I'll never actually get to in real life.

I suppose part of the reason for this fascination is that I'm allowed to choose from literally hundreds, sometimes thousands of dresses, shoes, luxury homes and destinations when my real-life circumstances may limit me to only a small number of choices. So part of the appeal of writing is getting to choose names of characters, settings and, for the book *Angel Eyes*, a very special dog.

Sarah Tucker, the heroine, had to have a dog. She told me so herself. But I was the one who was given the chance to choose her pet, and it had to be a very special creature. What fun!

Now, mind you, although I love dogs, I don't have one of my own. This was going to require a bit of research, and I couldn't wait to get down to business.

I roamed the Internet (I love the Internet) and found a fascinating abundance of information about dog breeds there. I learned that Chinese cresteds are prized for being loving companions, as are Japanese chins. That would be good. And keeshonds are wonderful at helping those who have experienced emotional trauma.

Basenjis don't bark.

Salukis are independent and fastidious about cleaning themselves, but they need plenty of room to run.

Newfoundlands are sweet tempered, though prone to drool. They love water and are good with children.

The Bouvier des Flandres breed makes a good watchdog, and they're also very good with children. During World War I they were used for various tasks, including getting messages to the front. Several times this breed faced extinction, the most notable being when one bit Adolf Hitler, and he ordered all Bouviers to be killed on sight. Fortunately for this wonderful animal (and for dog lovers everywhere), there were those (from Belgium) who helped reestablish this fine breed.

Now I was really enjoying my research. Studying the characteristics and history of various breeds had me wanting to give my heroine more than one pet. Maybe she could have...twenty dogs. Whoa! Have I mentioned that up until recently she lived in an apartment? Definitely a one-dog woman.

Oh, well. I continued on.

An Airedale would be a protector and a good friend. Besides, one of my neighbors had two of them, and my husband and I fell in love with the pair before their owners moved away. (They took their pets with them. Imagine the nerve! We weren't even asked for our opinion.) Ah, forgive me, I'm getting silly here. But an Airedale might be a good choice.

A cairn terrier? He's adaptable. He needs room to run, but thrives as long as there are people for him to love.

Or a pug, a friendly little creature who will curl up beside you.

My, the choices were getting out of hand. And no wonder. The American Kennel Club has over

150 breeds listed on their site, and worldwide there are 400 breeds that are recognized.

I was having tons of fun, but my head was beginning to spin, and my heroine, meanwhile, really needed a heart's companion. I plunged on.

There were designer dogs: schnoodles (a schnauzer-poodle cross), puggles (a pug-beagle cross) and poochins (a poodle–Japanese chin cross), but my heroine told me that she just wasn't a designer dog kind of girl. She was losing patience with me (that's the downside of being a catalog, reference-book kind of person—the number of choices can be daunting).

Meanwhile, a little bark (okay, a somewhat large bark) kept whispering in my ear (if a bark can be called a whisper). An image began to form in my head. I think it was the torn ear that got to me at first. Smooch (the name was on his tags—I swear it was) looked a little forlorn. How could I resist? He wasn't cute, he wasn't small and cuddly. He looked as if he'd been in a few brawls, maybe more than a few. He'd been treated badly, but then so had my heroine. They would bond over that. His wounds and his sad eyes would steal her heart, as they stole mine.

Smooch was a rescued dog. Sarah found him at a shelter, and her heart went out to him. He wasn't a purebred but a cross, possibly between a golden Lab and something else, maybe even many something elses. It didn't matter. It was character that counted, and Smooch had it in abundance. He was wary of people at first, but Sarah won him over, and then he won her over many times. His loyalty was undisputed. He was meant to be her dog. How could I have missed that for so long?

Oh, yes, I know. I was looking for the perfect dog, searching the catalogs while he was there, patiently waiting his turn all along.

He was well worth the wait. Sometimes things happen that way. Look and search and explore all the possibilities, and then life hands you a possibility you never imagined. My problem was solved, and the journey had been an enjoyable and informative one.

Of course, I was looking for a fictional dog. Had my search been for a real animal, there would have been other considerations. We've all heard about the rush to buy dalmatians after Disney's *101 Dalmatians* was released, even though the breed requires lots of exercise and isn't for everyone.

If you happen to find yourself in the position of looking for a dog, chances are that you know more about the process than I do. But if you don't, consider this: dogs have needs and personalities. Some have inbred tendencies toward certain medical conditions. Consider your circumstances, the size of your home, whether you have young children, whether you have the time and space and energy to exercise a dog that needs room to run, whether there will be someone at your home available as a companion for a dog that needs lots of company.

If you don't know where to find the information you need, there are sites on the Internet that might help you—www.canismajor.com is one, as is www.wonderpuppy.net. There are others, of course, and there are also books that cover the subject, but these two sites might give you a start. If you're looking for a rescued animal, ask questions at your local shelter. The people there are devoted to matching the right owner with the right pet and making sure that the pet's needs are met.

And if you find that the creature that steals your heart isn't at all like the one you had imagined...well, I wouldn't be surprised at all.

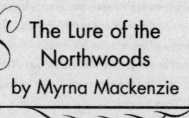

The Lure of the Northwoods
by Myrna Mackenzie

I first visited the Northwoods of Wisconsin when my oldest son was two and my youngest was on the way. My husband and I had come to the conclusion that travel would no longer be easy, and so we decided to try renting a summer cabin. We wanted a place where we could bring all the necessary baby gear and plop down for a week with no need to board a plane, move from place to place, or leave while the maid cleaned the room the way we would with a hotel. Our one-week fact-finding vacation was meant to be a whirlwind tour of Northwoods resorts that would, hopefully, end with the discovery of the perfect resort. It turned out to be all that and more. It turned into a love affair with this unique area.

Even today, several years after my last trip there, I can still close my eyes and smell the wonderful pine scent of the forest. I can hear the lonely, haunting call of the loon at dusk and see the gently lapping waves along a pristine lakeshore.

Curving county roads lead from town to town, but in between are forests and glacial lakes (more than a thousand in Vilas County alone), hiking and biking and equestrian trails, as well as the occasional house nestled in the woods. There's a lure that calls the traveler back again and again, and so it seemed only natural that when I needed a hometown area for my heroine to return to, I should choose this area that I have returned to many times.

What brings me back to the Northwoods time and time again? What is there to do there? What do I remember when I close my eyes?

This is what I remember:

- Hiking Franklin Nature Trail, an easy one-mile loop absolutely drenched with beauty. The trail leads past Avenue of the Giants, 400-year-old giant white pines and a wonderful stand of old-growth hemlock. It passes Butternut Lake, a lovely little body of water with a sandy beach and a swimming area.
- Canoeing on the lakes, listening to the sound of the paddle swishing in the quiet waters.
- Roasting marshmallows over a crackling wood fire to make s'mores.

- Driving up to the Gateway Golf Course, even though I'm not a golfer. Because, after all, even a nongolfer can't resist the appeal of a nine-hole course where you play half the game in Michigan and then cross the road and play the rest in Wisconsin.
- Taking a short drive into Michigan's Upper Peninsula to visit scenic and charming Bond Falls, one of the area's best-kept secrets.
- Watching the sunset and knowing that there is really no reason to rush away until the final hint of purple fades to black. Here time is meant for observing and experiencing the outdoors.
- Watching an eagle soar overhead.
- Waking up in the middle of the night to a dark so intense that even after hours your eyes don't adjust and you still stub your toe walking across the room.
- Seeing stars that you can never see around the city and can never begin to count.
- Taking the time to interact with nature, with your loved ones and with your own imagination.
- Reading a book while curled up on a blanket under a tree in the middle of the forest. Now, that's atmosphere.

So what is northern Wisconsin? It's all of the above. It's also the colorfully lit ice palace in Eagle River in winter. It's fishing for those who fish. It's cranberries and wild rice, wildflowers and hummingbirds. It's an area lush with history: Native Americans and fur traders, loggers and homesteaders.

In summer there are fish boils.

In the fall, the gold and orange of the trees will take your breath away, and in winter the green of the pines will still take your breath away.

In winter there is snowmobiling. Indeed, the first snowmobile was invented in the area.

And in spring, oh, yes, there is the promise that it will all begin again. Another summer in the land of lakes and trees and sky and soaring eagles.

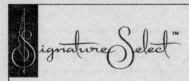
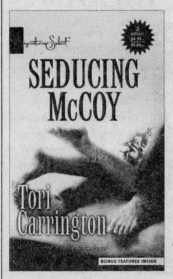

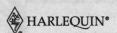

SPECIAL PRICE!

This riveting new saga begins with

In the Dark

by national bestselling author

JUDITH ARNOLD

The party at Hotel Marchand is in full swing when the lights suddenly go out. What does head of security Mac Jensen do first? He's torn between two jobs—protecting the guests at the hotel and keeping the woman he loves safe.

A woman to protect. A hotel to secure. And no idea who's determined to harm them.

On Sale June 2006

HMITD

Four sisters.
A family legacy.
And someone is out to destroy it.

A captivating new limited continuity, launching June 2006

The most beautiful hotel in New Orleans,
and someone is out to destroy it. But mystery,
danger and some surprising family revelations
and discoveries won't stop the Marchand sisters
from protecting their birthright…
and finding love along the way.

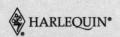

HARLEQUIN®

American ROMANCE®

IS PROUD TO PRESENT A
GUEST APPEARANCE BY

QUILL
BOOK
AWARD
WINNING
AUTHOR

NEW YORK TIMES bestselling author
DEBBIE MACOMBER

The Wyoming Kid

The story of an ex–rodeo cowboy,
a schoolteacher and their journey to the altar.

"Best-selling Macomber, with more than
100 romances and women's fiction titles
to her credit, sure has a way of pleasing readers."
—*Booklist* on *Between Friends*

**The Wyoming Kid is available from
Harlequin American Romance in July 2006.**

COMING NEXT MONTH

Signature Select Collection
A FARE TO REMEMBER by Vicki Lewis Thompson, Julie Elizabeth Leto, Kate Hoffmann
A matchmaking New York City taxi driver must convince three women he's found their life matches...but it's hardly a smooth ride.

Signature Select Saga
YOU MADE ME LOVE YOU by C.J. Carmichael
For six friends, childhood summers on a British Columbian island forged lifelong friendships that shaped their futures for the better... and the worst. Years later, death brings tragedy, mystery and love to two of them as they explore what really happened.

Signature Select Miniseries
SEDUCING McCOY by Tori Carrington
Law-enforcement brothers David and Connor McCoy find that upholding the law can get in the way of love as they try to convince two women not to settle for less than the *real* McCoy!

Signature Select Spotlight
CONFESSIONS OF A PARTY CRASHER by Holly Jacobs
Though her friends agree that it's a great way to meet men, Morgan Miller isn't comfortable crashing a posh wedding reception. Then again, it's better than not going at all...especially when wedding photographer Conner Danning enters the picture!

Signature Select Showcase
LOVE SONG FOR A RAVEN by Elizabeth Lowell
A ferocious storm plunged Janna Morgan into the icy water of the frigid sea—until untamed and enigmatic Carlson Raven saves her. Stranded together in a deserted paradise, Raven is powerless to resist his attraction to Janna. But, could he believe her feelings were love and not merely gratitude?